Before Familiar Woods

Before Familiar Woods

A NOVEL

IAN PISARCIK

CROOKED
LANE

NEW YORK

Copyright © 2020 by Ian Pisarcik

Published in the United States by Crooked Lane Books, an imprint of The Quick Brown Fox & Company LLC.

Crooked Lane Books and its logo are trademarks of The Quick Brown Fox & Company LLC.

Library of Congress Catalog-in-Publication data available upon request.

ISBN (hardcover): 978-1-64385-295-9
ISBN (ebook): 978-1-64385-316-1

Cover design by Mimi Bark

Printed in the United States.

www.crookedlanebooks.com

Crooked Lane Books
34 West 27th St., 10th Floor
New York, NY 10001

First Edition: March 2020

10 9 8 7 6 5 4 3 2 1

To Sarah. You are home to me.

Well silence is a mighty big grave,
and whatever goes down there is as cold as the clay.

—Tyler Childers

MATHEW FENN

THE BOYS WALKED ALONG THE ROAD, HARDLY MORE THAN WOVEN shadows. The air was warm, though the sun had fallen beneath the dark steeps, and the boys wore short-sleeved shirts and carpenter shorts. Mathew carried a backpack and thumbed the straps. Sweat beaded down his face. William carried the tent in a swamp-green rucksack with worn leather fastenings. He picked up a hickory husk and threw it into the woods.

"It's going to be buggy by the stream," William said.

"Not on the ridge. It won't be buggy up there."

William turned and spat. "Still. It's hot. I don't see why we couldn't go on Saturday."

The boys continued along the graveled road. There were no cars. Only the sounds of their feet. Small and quiet.

"Did you start reading *The Gunfighter*?"

Mathew shook his head.

"Come on," William said.

"I've been reading this book about black holes." Mathew slid his hands down the straps of his backpack. "You can't see them. The only way we know they exist is by watching what's pulled toward them."

"What would happen if you got pulled into one?"

"You couldn't escape. Not even if you moved at the speed of light." William picked up another husk and threw it into the woods.

"If you looked at the universe from inside the hole, everything would look different. The light that wasn't close enough to get pulled in would be bent, so everything would seem distorted." Mathew looked back at the road. The undersides of his arms were damp with sweat and his muscles felt rigid. He thought there was something else he wanted to tell William about the black holes and what scientists believed might be inside them, but his thoughts swirled inside his head like dust and smoke. "It's hard to explain," he said.

"Well, there's nothing hard about *The Gunfighter*. It's just about a guy who kills Indians." William picked up another husk and squeezed it and let it fall to the ground. "The main guy's name is Hoss, and he's always quoting from books before he kills someone. That's the part I think you'll like. He quotes a poem or something while the Indians are tied up, and they just look at him like he's crazy. That's the thing. People don't understand him. But he's just Hoss. That's just who he is, even if it don't make sense to no one else."

Mathew looked back again at the road. He caught himself shaking a little. "Let's start into the woods," he said. "We're close enough."

"How far is it?"

"It's not far. We've just got to listen for the stream."

"How do you know about this place?"

"My dad took me a couple times."

William pulled a cigarette from his pocket. "My dad doesn't like to camp no more. He was an Eagle Scout, though. That's the highest rank you can get."

"Come on," Mathew said.

The woods were dense. Mathew felt his bare skin brush against the hairy goldenrod leaves. He pulled a small flashlight from his pocket and pointed it at the ground. The light swept over packed earth and flowering shrubs.

After some time the canopy opened, and Mathew looked up into the cloudy sky. He stopped instinctively and put his hand on William's shoulder. Then he leaned in close and pointed. William took a drag from his cigarette and coughed a little and held the cigarette smoking by his side.

"Can you see it?" Mathew asked.

William shook his head.

Mathew had been trying to teach William to identify the constellations, but William couldn't find them without Mathew's help. Mathew thought maybe he was just pretending. William had told him once that he liked listening to Mathew explain things. That he liked how when Mathew got excited, he talked slower instead of faster, like he wanted everything to last.

"Hercules," Mathew said. "Between Arcturus and Vega."

William took another drag and flicked the cigarette dramatically a couple of times. A soft wind rustled the leaves. Mathew heard a noise and looked back to the road. In the distance he saw slow-moving headlights quartered by dark trunks.

He turned off the flashlight. "Quiet," he said.

RUTH FENN

Ruth Fenn sat on the porch chair with her husband's deer rifle laid across the caps of her knees and the steam from her black coffee rising up beside her and listened to the sound of studded snow tires splash the water from the bottoms of the ruts.

She watched the Ford with the broken side mirror come up the gravel drive and stop a good twenty feet from the house. She watched Della Downing get out of the truck and put her boot on a spot of gravel where the snow had stuck.

"You can stop right there," Ruth said.

Della closed the driver's side door. "How are you doing, Ruth?"

"Ain't any of your damned business how I'm doing."

Della pulled the lapels of her jacket close together and took a step toward the house. Ruth tightened her grip on the rifle just enough to let Della see her do it.

Della paused. "It's not you I'm here to see."

"Should I assume you've gone senile and forgot who's living in this house?"

"It's your husband I'm here to talk to."

Snow clouds covered the sky over the southernmost portion of the Green Mountain range. The birches that crowded the ten-acre property were tall and white and shedding their bark. A low morning fog clung to everything as though the trees had gotten themselves caught up in cobwebs. Ruth, fifty-two, her face rigid enough to unlock a keyhole, round rimless glasses and gray hair that rested on her shoulders, faced the cold and blinked against it.

"What is it you want with Elam?"

"Horace didn't come home last night. It was Elam he said he was going out with."

"Why would that be?"

"I don't know exactly."

"And you didn't wonder to ask him?"

"I didn't have a chance. He left a note." Della took another step forward. She wore ten-inch muck boots and a wool coat. Her dark hair came straight down under her snow hat. Dark as night. Not a thing like Ruth's, which had turned the color of wood ash. "Can I assume Elam didn't come home neither? Can I assume that's why there's no truck in the drive and you're sitting there with that gun in your lap?"

"Just 'cause I had it out for him don't mean I won't use it on you."

Somewhere in the distance a truck drove by on the road, and then there was silence.

"Both our husbands are missing, then," Della said.

"Your husband's missing. I got a pretty good idea about where to find mine."

"He ain't at the Whistler."

Ruth took a sip of black coffee and set the mug down on the wooden side table.

"Horace's truck is still there. Parked in front of the bar. But Elam's ain't."

"Maybe Horace went home with someone, then."

Della shook her head. "That ain't like him—that ain't like Horace."

"I don't know nothing about what Horace is like."

"You know him. He's not somebody different than the man who grew up three houses down from here. The one that used to take your boy to Little League practice when you had to work late."

Ruth took the rifle from her lap and leaned it against the clapboard. "I'm not sure why you're here."

"I came here to talk to Elam."

"He ain't here."

"I understand that now."

"And yet you're still in my drive."

"I figured you might have some thoughts on the two of them being together."

"It's Horace who said they were together."

Flurries landed on the steps. The wind blew some onto the porch, and some clung to Ruth's arms and legs.

There had been no flurries the night Ruth's boy and Della's boy went missing. It was three summers ago. The middle of a hot July. Della had shown up in the same truck. She had driven right up to the house, though. Come up the porch steps and let herself inside like she had done a million times during the fifteen years of their friendship. Ruth met her in the hall and sat her down at the kitchen table and put her hand over Della's hand and told her that it would be okay—even though it didn't turn out that way.

"You want to know what I think?" Ruth said. She shifted a little. Her bones ached. "I think you ought to check the stalls at the Whistler."

"He's two years clean," Della said. "You might know something about that if you set foot outside this house once in a while. You might know something about what's been going on in this town. But then you never made it your business to know what was going on, did you? Not even when it was going on inside your own home."

Ruth stood, but she didn't reach for the rifle. She just stood there thick in the shoulders until Della took the hint and got back into her truck and started the engine and backed down the long gravel drive.

When the sound of the engine had faded, Ruth went inside the home and hung her coat on the nail and leaned the rifle against the wall. Woodstock lay on the worn hearth rug in front of the wood-burning stove.

"Some good you did just now," Ruth said. "That woman could set fire to this house and I'm not sure you'd do nothing but wonder at your good fortune at finding heat in the middle of the winter."

The old dog looked up at Ruth with its oil-slicked eyes peering out from under its gray whiskers and then laid its head back down on the floor, its collar clinking on the wood.

Ruth bent in front of the stove. "It ain't even lit, you know. You think you're feeling something, but it's only in your mind." She opened the glass door and added some newspaper from the basket and some kindling. She struck a match and lit the newspaper and waited for the kindling to catch and then shut the door.

The border collie Ruth had named North came loping into the living room followed by the redbone coonhound named Emmylou and the Irish setter named Mud.

"Well isn't that something. You got good noses. All of you. Or at least one of you does and the others have the mind to follow." Ruth stood and laid her hand on her back where it was beginning to stiffen. She felt older than she was—tricked by her own body. As though it had for years led her through a slow-moving river only to lacerate her skin and stir up the silt.

She watched the dogs vie for position in front of the woodstove. Mud was the youngest of the four. Ruth had found him the previous fall in the pouring rain while driving home from the salvage yard in Pownal.

Her house was the last on Stub Hollow, an out-of-the-way country road bounded by thick woods, and it was there that people had taken to tying their dogs to trees when they got tired of feeding them or otherwise taking care of them. Ruth never could drive that last stretch of road without rolling down her window and listening for the howls, and as a consequence there were times her home felt more like a shelter.

The old wood creaked as Ruth crossed the living room to the kitchen. The house had been built in 1892. The wide plank floorboards slanted a little to the east and were covered with deep scratches and a sheen of patina. Dark-green wallpaper covered the walls, and some of Ruth's ceramic pots sat dusty on the wood shelves. She still threw on the wheel most mornings, and for the last ten years she had taught classes—first at the Vermont Potters Guild and then in the shed in front of her home to children referred to her by the Department for Children and Families in Bennington. She no longer put her finished pots on the shelves, though. She let the children take home the ones they wanted and she let the others stack up behind the shed collecting rainwater.

Ruth poured a cup of coffee and stirred in a small amount of butter and cold water. She carried the mug down the narrow hall to the guest room, where her mother sat upright in bed with a quilt drawn over her lap, watching the news on the television. Her face was thin and the lines that ran obliquely along the sides of her nose were dark and seemed to hold the ends of her lips like the ropes of a porch swing.

"Anything I'm missing?" Ruth asked.

"Everybody's crazier than hell."

"Well, that ain't nothing new."

Ruth studied the television propped up on the dresser in the corner of the room. A man stood in front of his home in a buffalo plaid coat gesturing violently and talking about how the salt from the road was damaging his plants.

"I heard you talking," Ruth's mother said.

"I wasn't talking."

"You were. I heard you. It's who you were talking to that I couldn't make out."

Ruth turned from the television. "Someone lost is all."

"I hope you didn't give 'em no directions. Anybody lost in North Falls is headed someplace they shouldn't be going."

Ruth set the mug on the nightstand next to a glass of water and went over to the window and pulled the curtain open even though there was hardly any light—only tall trees with smoke-colored bark that had cracked, split, and peeled. "The stove is lit," she said. "It'll be nice and warm in the living room."

"I've got the news on."

"You won't miss much. It's just gossip and weather."

"I'm fine right where I am."

Ruth studied her mother. Seventy-nine years old. Her mind more often than not scattered like grains of pollen across fields and porches and hoods of parked cars.

"Fine," Ruth said. "Suit yourself. Wait another minute on that coffee."

Ruth went to the kitchen and turned on the AM radio station out of Warren she had found a while back where callers told stories about being abducted by aliens and transported to strange planets. She poured herself another cup of black coffee and grabbed a bottle of fluorometholone from the cupboard above the refrigerator and sat down at the table and pulled a cigarette from her vest pocket. The dogs lay side by side in front of the woodstove. Putting up with the closeness of each other for the benefit of the heat.

Ruth smoked her cigarette and tried to remember the last time she had seen Della. There was the time at the grocery store when she saw her talking to Emma Perkins by the meat counter, and the time she saw her leaving the church when Ruth was driving her mother home from the hospital. But she couldn't remember which of those was the last time, and she supposed it didn't matter. There was a new last time. Standing in her own drive. Della Downing in sheep's trappings.

Ruth smoked her cigarette and played the conversation over in her head. It wasn't unusual for Elam to run off. He had done it for days at a time ever since they'd lost Mathew. It worried her at first, and she had followed him a handful of times from the Whistler to a place they used to go together. A large outcropping over the brook, where he sat and drank beers in the cab of his truck until he passed out. And so she put up with it—understanding that he wasn't seeing someone, that he only wanted to be alone. It hurt her. But she understood he was putting up with things too. She had disappeared same as him.

The only difference was she didn't leave the house.

What didn't make sense was for Elam to be with Horace. The two of them had never been close. They'd made small talk whenever Ruth and Della had gotten together and made the mistake of dragging them along, but anyone could see they were different people, and if there was something beneath the surface that connected the two, neither one seemed interested in finding out what it was. It occurred to Ruth that Della could be lying, but she couldn't see the reason. She took another drag from her cigarette and pushed the smoke upward toward the apex of the roof, which had been stuffed with a feathery white chinking. Then she rested her cigarette on the ashtray and thumbed open the bottle of fluorometholone. She tilted her head back and dropped the solution under her eyelids.

The wind picked up and whipped against the side of the house. The man on the radio was talking about a cave in the Sego Canyon where paintings of aliens covered the walls. After a moment Ruth pulled the black paisley handkerchief from the pocket of her blue jeans and dabbed at her eyes and looked out the window at the gravel drive and the bare trees and the faint shadows of the branches moving across the dead grass and thin patches of snow. The clouds were still thick over the mountains, and she told herself there wasn't enough sunlight on a cold morning to wake an old drunk passed out in his truck somewhere. She sat there at the same table she'd been sitting at for thirty years and told herself that Elam not being home was as simple as that.

MILK RAYMOND

When Milk Raymond woke on the pullout couch, he sat upright and then folded the blanket and set it on the cardboard box next to his cigarettes and the bottle of aspirin and the crinkled wrappers that contained two tablets of Zoloft and three tablets of Paxil. He put on his blue jeans and white undershirt. He lifted the metal frame and pushed the bed into the couch and then stuffed the cigarettes and aspirin and Zoloft and Paxil into his pockets. He looked around the empty living room at the muted light that played along the nicotine-streaked walls, and then he made his way down the hallway to where his boy was sleeping in the bedroom.

"It's time to get up," Milk said.

Daniel shifted under the bedsheets and then turned over and faced the window, where a little bit of sun was coming in through the blinds.

"Come on. Breakfast is ready."

Milk went to the kitchen and removed two plastic bowls from the cabinet. He turned on the burner and mixed some water from the tap in a metal pot with a couple of oatmeal packets the previous tenant had left in one of the cupboards. "Breakfast," he said again. He lowered the burner and turned from the kitchen and started down the hallway but stopped when he saw Daniel in the bedroom pulling on his sweat shirt.

The two sat down at the table and ate from their bowls. Milk watched his boy. Eight years old and skinny as a rail post. Brown wavy hair that came down over his ears and fell against his unmarked skin. He wore oversized goggles with thick yellow plastic around the eye cups and a black rubber strap that said JUNIOR RACER.

"How'd you sleep?"

Daniel shrugged. He lifted a spoonful of oatmeal to his mouth and looked around the kitchen while he chewed. "How long are we going to be here?"

"I don't know. A couple months at least." Milk continued to watch his boy. He tried to tick off the things he knew about him. But the things he thought he knew from the first five years of the boy's life, he wasn't sure he knew. He wasn't sure they were still true after three years of being overseas and hardly seeing him at all.

Daniel lifted another spoonful to his mouth. He chewed the oatmeal slowly and looked down at his bowl. "It doesn't taste good," he said.

Milk took a bite. The oatmeal didn't taste like anything. He lowered his head to the bowl and smelled the oatmeal. "Don't eat it."

"Why not?"

"It's no good."

"Is it old?"

"Yes."

"How old? One hundred years?"

"Not one hundred years."

"How old, then?"

"I don't know."

Daniel put the spoon down.

Milk studied his boy for another moment. "Put your shoes and coat on. I know where we can find something better."

The boy got up from the table and headed toward the bedroom. Milk rinsed out the plastic bowls and set them upside down on the counter to dry. He threw out the remaining oatmeal packets and then went to the closet and put on his boots and his coat and his Boston Red Sox cap, and when the two were ready they left the house.

"Where are we going?" the boy asked.

"Put your belt on."

The boy pulled the seat belt over his chest and snapped it into the buckle. Milk started the engine and turned up the heat.

"Am I coming back?"

"What?"

"Am I coming back with you?"

"Why wouldn't you be coming back with me?"

The boy shrugged. "I don't know."

"Open that vent," Milk said. "Go on. Flip it open."

The boy flipped open the vent. Milk pushed the clutch to the floor and shifted into first. He looked back at the blue one-story duplex and then pulled out onto the road.

Stub Hollow ran north and south. It was covered in braided channels and potholes, but Milk was five days removed from a three-year stint in Iraq and he was used to bad roads, most of them strapped with explosives. He put the truck in second gear and turned on the radio. A rap song blared from the speakers, and he quickly changed the station.

After following the narrow road for a couple of miles, he reached the center of North Falls. The town looked the same. A little worse for the wear, maybe. Some more cracks in the sidewalks. But the town that had seemed like it was on life support when he was growing up was somehow still not dead. He passed the general store with the large oak tree outside and the orange CLOSED sign hanging from the front door and thought back to how it had been the spot the popular girls used to work during the school year before the lifeguarding jobs opened up on the pond. He wondered who worked there now—or if there was some other place the popular girls worked.

He continued past the town hall and the library and the fish-and-tackle until the homes were spaced farther apart and the woods became more prominent and were sometimes broken up by small patches of farmland and old farmhouses set back from the road. He followed the road past the gas station, where a truck hauling two-by-fours sat parked next to one of the pumps, and then he turned west at the blinking light and pulled onto Route 7 and continued south for several miles until he saw the big red Donut Shop sign. He pulled into the lot and parked in front of the shop next to an empty newspaper holder. He sat there with the engine rattling and stared at the shop.

"Shit," he said.

"What's wrong?"

"Wait here."

Milk killed the engine and got out of the truck. He went to the window of the shop and put his hands against the glass and peered inside at the long silver counter and the shelves behind the counter lined with metal trays. He stepped back from the glass. A piece of paper taped to the window on the other side of the door said NOTICE OF CLOSURE: CLOSURE OF PREMISES ASSOCIATED WITH NUISANCE OR DISORDER. He looked around at the empty lot and the wind-torn trees that surrounded it and the chain-link fence and the yellow dumpster where somebody had spray-painted JESUS LIVES. JUST NOT HERE.

Milk returned to the truck. He lifted his hat and ran his hand over his shaved head. He felt a headache coming on. The dull pulsing behind his eyes like someone trying to dig into hard ground with a coal shovel. Daniel still wore his goggles, and after a moment he pulled them from his face and spit into one of the eye cups and rubbed the plastic with his fingers.

"What the hell was that?"

"What?"

Milk nodded toward the goggles.

"That's how I keep 'em clean."

"Well, all right," Milk said. He reached into his pocket and pulled out a cigarette. When he had the cigarette lit, he rolled down the window and started the engine.

"Are we going home?"

"We're going somewhere else."

"Where?"

"I don't know. Somewhere."

Milk headed farther out of town. He kept his eyes open for somewhere he could get the boy something to make up for the stale oatmeal and to start making up for everything else the boy had been through during the last three years, but there were only homes same as the homes in North Falls, and so he found a dirt turnaround and drove back toward town, passing again the clapboard homes and the Donut Shop. He slowed as he approached the gas station, and then he pulled into the lot and parked in front of the window next to where the truck hauling two-by-fours had been. "Wait here," he said.

A young girl with short black hair and green eyeshadow and multiple piercings lining her right earlobe stood behind the register. She wore a black sweat shirt with long sleeves that had holes for her thumbs.

"Do you have doughnuts?" Milk asked.

"They're long gone," the girl said. "You have to get in before eight if you want any."

Milk looked around the store.

"We've got Chillers. Those are popular too—even in the winter."

"What's that?"

The girl pointed toward a machine in the corner of the store.

"Soda?" Milk asked.

The girl shook her head. "You ever have a Slurpee?"

Milk nodded.

"It's just like that. It's like our version of a Slurpee."

"How much are they?"

"A dollar thirty-nine for the large one. Ninety-nine cents for the small one."

Milk reached into his pocket and pulled out a small billfold. "I'll take the large one." He handed the girl five dollars.

The girl took the money and put it in the register and gave Milk his change.

Milk stood there a moment.

"It's self-serve," the girl said.

Milk looked over at the machine.

"Here. I'll show you."

The girl came around the counter. She wore tall winter boots and tight black pants and Milk almost stumbled over his feet watching her walk. She reached the machine and grabbed a large blue cup from a stack of cups. "This here is the large one. There's raspberry and there's blueberry. You can have one of them or you can have both. I like to mix them."

"I'll do that, then," Milk said.

The girl pushed the cup against a metal prong under a spout. Milk saw that she had a small tattoo on her neck under her left ear. It looked like a crow or a black star, but he couldn't tell for certain and he didn't want to stare. The girl moved the cup in a small circle, and when it was half full with liquid, she pushed it against the prong under the second spout and moved the cup again in a small circle until it was full. Then she removed a plastic top from the cupboard and stuck it on the cup and poked a thick red straw through the opening. She handed Milk the cup. "Now you know how to do it."

Milk nodded.

The door opened and an old man in a flat cap and leather tab suspenders pulled tight over his flannel shirt walked into the store and went to the counter and pulled out his wallet.

"Thanks for the help," Milk said.

"You'll be back," the girl said, smiling. "They're addictive."

Milk nodded and left the store. He got in the truck and handed Daniel the cup.

"What is it?"

"It's like a Slurpee. Have you ever had a Slurpee?"

The boy shook his head.

"Don't drink it too fast. You'll get a headache if you do."

The boy studied the drink.

"Go on," Milk said. "It ain't gonna kill you."

The boy hesitated and then took a sip. He pulled his lips from the straw and studied the drink. "It's good," he said.

"I know it. That's why I got it for you."

RUTH FENN

Ruth watched from the uncurtained window at the front of the house as Polly Bishop came up the drive in her grandmother's station wagon with the fake-wood paneling and the plush stuffed animals lined up in the back. After a moment Polly got out of the car, followed by two little boys with shaved heads and oversized winter jackets who took to running after each other and laughing. Ruth grabbed her coat from the nail and pulled open the door and came down the creaking porch steps. "It looks like you're feeding those two coffee and sugar cubes for breakfast."

"I wish that was true. They're like this all on their own. All the time, too."

The boys ran circles around Polly and Ruth. One of the boys pulled the jacket off the other boy and the boy broke free.

"Where's Lila?" Ruth asked.

"She's in the car seat sleeping."

The boys continued to chase each other.

"Quit it," Polly said. "Quit messing around and say hello to Ms. Fenn."

The boys stopped long enough to say hello between gasps for air and then took off chasing each other around the station wagon.

21

"Elam ain't here?" Polly asked.

"No—he ain't here."

"I was gonna have him take a look at the car. I got something rattling in the back."

"Could be the exhaust is loose."

"I already checked that."

"What about the trunk?"

"What about it?"

"Maybe you got yourself a dead body in there."

Polly laughed. "I wouldn't put that past Grandma Evelyn. I ought to ask her about it."

"Maybe. It might depend on whether there's still room left in that trunk." Ruth looked back at the boys just in time to see Billy twist his foot in a rut and land hard on his face.

"Dammit, Billy," Polly said. "What did I tell you?"

Billy got to his knees. Blood covered his lower lip.

"Shit," Bobby said.

Polly turned to Bobby. "Watch your language."

"Take it easy," Ruth said. "Everybody's all right." She walked over to Billy and bent down in the gravel. "Can you open your mouth?"

Billy opened his mouth.

Ruth grabbed hold of Billy's chin. "Does this hurt?"

Billy shook his head.

Ruth reached into her pocket and pulled out her handkerchief and wiped away the blood. "Nothing's broke, then. You just split your lip is all. You ain't afraid of a little blood, are you?"

Billy shook his head again.

"I didn't think so. I thought you were tougher than most eleven-year-old boys."

"He ain't," Bobby said. "He cries all the time."

"Well, he ain't crying now," Ruth said. "Maybe he's all done with that." She pushed on her knees and stood. Her back stiffened again and she laid her palm where it hurt. Billy turned and spit awkwardly onto the gravel. "You know," Ruth said. "I seen two gardeners in the woodpile this morning. One of them was about three feet long and I didn't even see all of it."

"Where was it?" Bobby asked.

"In the woodpile. Like I told you. Right up near the top."

Both boys turned to the woodpile in front of the shed.

"Go on," Ruth said. "Let me and your mother talk a minute."

When the boys had gone, Polly pulled a pack of cigarettes from her back pocket. "Randy left," she said.

"What happened?"

"Becky Wagner is what happened. Probably happened last time, too."

"You're better off, then."

"I don't feel better off."

"You are."

"I'm gonna miss his paycheck."

"You got your own paycheck."

"It's hardly enough to justify the paper it's printed on."

"So find a new job."

"Where?"

"What about Hinman's? They used to pay overtime on Sundays, from what I remember."

"What am I going to do with Lila and the boys?"

"We can work something out."

Polly put the cigarette between her lips and lit it and took a drag. "You watch them enough already. Besides, the manager at Hinman's gives me the creeps. He's only got that one eye."

"He only needs one eye to sign your checks."

"I guess. But I still don't see why he doesn't cover the other one up. Besides, he don't like me. He's always looking at me funny—out of the one eye he's got."

"All the guys look at you funny. That's just how guys look at girls like you."

Polly smiled a little and took another drag. "It's going to be hell," she said. "We were hardly making it before."

"Hardly making it is still making it."

"Right up until it ain't."

"You've got some time before that. You're younger than you think."

Polly crossed her arms and looked over at the boys. Ruth studied the oval-shaped scar on her cheek, hardly visible beneath the thick foundation. She thought back to the first time the caseworker drove Polly out to the house in the middle of the winter when the boys were still little and shy. The stitches were visible then and the caseworker telephoned Ruth beforehand to explain that Polly had been stabbed through the cheek with a pair of scissors and that the boys had seen it all. Ruth knew the man who had done it—knew his surname, at least. It didn't come as a surprise and Ruth figured Polly knew he was a snake when she picked him up. But she had two kids by then and no self-worth and she wasn't the first woman to fall under the weight of those circumstances.

"Why don't you talk to your caseworker," Ruth said. "It might be she knows of some new programs out there. Something to get your costs down for a while."

"I'm not doing that family unification bullshit. They make you live with roommates. They tell you you're getting support because you're living with people just like you. My whole thing is I got to get away from people like me."

"She might know of something else. Maybe something outside of town."

"I can't pull the boys out of school again."

Ruth turned toward the boys, who were taking turns holding up the blue tarp and pulling out split logs. She thought about how simple it seemed to her now. To move a child from one school to another. How simple a problem for a mother to have.

"I saw a place advertised in the paper this morning," Polly said. "It's almost half the rent we pay now. It's only got the one bedroom, but we done that before."

"Where is it?"

"Down on Cottage Street. Behind that old brick building."

"The sock factory?"

"I guess. I never knew what it was."

"No. I guess you wouldn't. It's been boarded up for some time now. At least it ain't far."

"No. It ain't far. I hate to move again, though. I hate the thought of it. Those boys haven't seen two seasons in the same house since they were born."

"That's not your fault."

"That's not how they'll see it. They'll blame me 'cause I'm the only one here to blame."

"They'll come to understand."

"I don't know."

"They will." A flock of geese moved loudly overhead. Ruth waited for them to pass. "You're doing all right," she said.

Polly nodded and dropped her cigarette on the gravel and put it out with her sneaker.

Ruth turned to the boys. "What do you say? You boys ready to get your hands dirty?"

The boys shouted something unintelligible and took off for the small shed nearly hidden behind the copse of birches.

MILK RAYMOND

IN THE AFTERNOON THERE WAS A KNOCK ON THE DOOR. MILK SAT AT the kitchen table with his boot on the spindle of the chair smoking a cigarette and looking through a stack of discharge papers.

Daniel sat on the couch wearing his goggles and trying to draw on a damp piece of birch bark he had found on the ground outside. He turned to Milk. "Who is it?"

"I don't know." Milk stood and went to the door. The blinds were drawn. He held his cigarette by his side and looked out the peephole. "Turn that television down."

Milk opened the door, and a woman holding a yellow legal pad smiled and pulled the pad to her chest. "Milk—Milk Raymond?"

Milk didn't say anything. The woman was his age—maybe a little older. She had a round face and dark cropped hair with a streak of it dyed blue and she wore purple cat-eye glasses.

"My name is Jett Oakley," the woman said. "I'm with the Family Services Division."

Milk held her eyes, and then he glanced at his boy, who was leaning over the arm of the couch, watching.

The woman pulled a business card from her pocket and handed it to Milk. The card was yellow with green text. It read: JETT OAKLEY:

Department for Children and Families, Family Services District Office—Bennington.

"Is it all right if I come in?"

Milk handed her the card. He stood there a moment and then took a step backward and pulled open the door.

"Thank you." The woman smiled and stepped into the house. Milk looked out at the empty road and the flurries that had begun to fall.

"Is this Daniel?"

"It is."

The boy remained seated on the couch. He had gotten into his pajamas when they returned from the gas station. Dark-blue ones with green flying saucers scattered around the arms, chest, and legs like polka dots.

"Hello, Daniel," the woman said.

The boy nodded.

"I like your goggles."

The boy was quiet.

"What's this about?" Milk asked.

"Can we talk in private? Maybe Daniel can play in his bedroom for a little while."

Milk took a drag from his cigarette and studied the woman. She wore an open knitted vest over a checkered shirt and several bracelets on both wrists. He turned to Daniel. "Why don't you go to your room."

The boy sat still.

"Go on. I'll come get you in a few minutes."

Milk watched Daniel get up slowly from the couch and start down the carpeted hallway. He looked back when he reached the end of the hallway, and when he saw they weren't going to start talking until he was gone, he went into his bedroom and closed the door.

"No school today?"

Milk shook his head. "Professional development day. I guess they couldn't fit it in during the three months they got off in the summer."

"That's always hard on parents. Is he in second grade?"

Milk nodded. "He's small for his age." He motioned to the kitchen table. "Go ahead and have a seat if you want."

The woman made her way to the table and sat down and placed the yellow legal pad in front of her. Milk took the discharge papers that were on the table and set them on the counter.

"Well, like I said before, I'm with the Department for Children and Families. I tried calling, but your phone is disconnected."

"I've been having trouble with it lately."

"I'm glad I caught you then." The woman shifted in her seat. "I'm here because our department got a call a couple days ago about an argument that took place at Two Twenty-Two Prospect Street. Apparently a window was broken. The police were called. My understanding is that the boy—Daniel—was at the house?"

"That's his grandmother's place."

The woman pulled a pen from her coat pocket. "Now, you understand, when we get a call like that, we've got to come out and make a determination as to whether the child is in any sort of danger. That's according to Vermont law."

"He's not in any danger."

"That's good. I'm glad to hear that."

"Might've been."

"What's that?"

"He might've been in some danger."

"At Martha's?"

"Martha?"

The woman looked down at her notepad. "Martha Gladstone. The boy's grandmother."

"I only ever known her as Marcy."

"I thought she told me Martha—but I could have misheard."

"You talked to her?"

"This morning."

Milk took another drag from his cigarette. "Well—there's your danger right there."

"What kind of danger might that be?"

Milk thought a moment. "I suppose neglect is what you'd call it."

The woman uncapped her pen. "Why don't you start by telling me about your relationship with her?"

"With Marcy?"

"Yes. Has she always been in Daniel's life?"

Milk scratched at his ear. "I figure she told you at least that much."

"I want to hear it from you."

Milk tilted his head back—trying to figure out how to begin. Trying to figure out just how much he wanted to tell. "Marcy is Jessica's grandmother. Jessica, as you probably gathered, is Daniel's mother—by blood at least."

"She doesn't live here?"

"No. I don't know where she lives."

"And what about Jessica's parents?"

"They died when she was little. She was living with Marcy when we had Daniel."

"And she continued to live there?"

"I got us a place as soon as I graduated. That's when I was working at the Jiffy Lube, but it ain't here anymore."

Jett continued to write on her legal pad.

"It was after a couple years working at the Jiffy Lube that we decided I should enlist. Daniel would have been about five then."

"And Jessica and Daniel stayed here in North Falls?"

"We decided Jessica and Daniel would move back in with Marcy while I was in basic and after that they'd come out to Fort Hood." Milk took another drag from his cigarette. "This was about May 2001, and I bet you can guess what happened next."

Jett looked up from her pad.

"I thought they were joking when they told me."

"How long were you gone for?"

"I deployed in April 2003." Milk looked out the window at a tangled chokeberry dripping rain from its branches. "Jess got restless, though. I don't think she liked sitting around with the other wives. Too goddamn hot over there, too." He shook his head. "A couple months after deployment—maybe June or July—she moved back home with Marcy. It was sometime after that when I got the letter. I don't know exactly when it was, because they don't give you letters until they get a whole stack of 'em. So you didn't always know when they were from. Sometimes you got them out of order and you had to sort of piece things together."

The woman nodded.

"Anyway, it was from Marcy, and she told me that Jess had gone and found herself a new boyfriend and a new habit to go along with him."

"What habit might that be?"

"Same habit everyone else has got around here." Milk took another drag from his cigarette. "I'll give Marcy credit for this much, though— she had the sense about her to tell Jess to leave Daniel. I don't know how she convinced her to do it, but she did." Milk tapped the ash from his cigarette into a cup.

"Sounds to me like you and Daniel were lucky to have Marcy."

"She took care of him until I could get my boots back in the States."

"When was this?"

"Five days ago."

"Five days?"

Milk nodded.

"And you came to see Marcy when you got back?"

"I came to see my son—but yeah, I saw Marcy. We agreed it would be best if she watched Daniel for a couple weeks to give me some time to get set up in my own place and to give Daniel some time to get used to the idea." Milk picked at his teeth. "Problem is—I didn't understand how Marcy was getting. I didn't understand the shape she was in."

"How do you mean?"

"After a couple days back, I went over there to check on Daniel. The three of us were sitting at the dinner table, and she started talking to people who weren't there."

"She was hearing things?"

Milk nodded. "Thought people were stealing from her, too."

"How long did this go on?"

"One night was long enough. I moved him into this place the next day. It ain't much, but it was available."

"This was two nights ago?"

"That's right."

"And you picked up Daniel then?"

Milk nodded. "I went over there and she starts yelling at me, accusing me of stealing her jewelry—and get this, her cat. But she don't have no cat. Got a name for it, though. You want to know the name of the made-up cat?"

The woman was quiet.

"Jesus. She named the cat Jesus. As in our lord and fucking savior."

The woman looked at her legal pad. "How'd the window break?"

"That was me. I won't run from it. I was pissed off and looking for an argument, and she gave it to me."

"Where was Daniel?"

"He was in the truck already." Milk tapped his cigarette on the cup. "The neighbors must have heard. That's how I'm guessing the trooper got called—except I wasn't there when he showed. I was gone by then."

Jett scribbled something else down on the legal pad. "I got the impression while I was over there that Marcy is maybe suffering from some early dementia."

"That'd be a word for it."

The woman turned over the pad and set the pen on top. "I'd like to see Daniel's bedroom. If you don't mind."

Milk looked toward the hallway. "It ain't much."

"It doesn't have to be."

Milk stood from the table. "The man that rented me this place said he'd clean the carpets before I moved in—he said he'd get the walls repainted too. But I told him I didn't have time for any of that."

"Maybe he could come back once you're settled."

"Maybe. I'm just glad the place had furniture. And the television. That was here too."

Milk reached the bedroom and pulled open the door. The blinds were still drawn, and Daniel was sitting on his bed holding the piece of birch bark.

"Hello, Daniel."

The boy nodded.

"I asked your father if I could see your bedroom."

The boy nodded again.

"Is this your bedroom?"

"Yes."

"Do you sleep in here alone?"

"Yes."

"I sleep on the couch," Milk said. "It's a pullout."

"That's good that he's got his own room. He's old enough to where he should have his own room."

Milk took another drag from his cigarette and wiped his brow.

The woman walked over to the closet. "Do you have a favorite toy, Daniel?"

The boy was quiet.

"A stuffed animal or something?"

"I haven't been able to get all his things from his grandmother's yet," Milk said.

"Well—I can help with that. He should have his things." The woman looked at the white fiberglass dresser that was chipped at the corners. "Does he have enough clothes?"

"He's got plenty of clothes. He's got clothes in the drawer there and his coat in the closet." Milk walked over to the dresser and opened the drawer for the woman to see.

"Good. That's good. I'm glad he has those things." The woman looked around the room again. "I always like to talk to the children alone for a few minutes," she said. "If you don't mind. Do you mind that?"

Milk rubbed his brow again with the hand that held the cigarette. "All right," he said. He stood there a moment looking at his boy. Just a little thing with one sock pulled half off his left foot. "I'll just be in the kitchen, Daniel, okay?"

The boy nodded.

Milk looked to the woman, who was smiling, and then left the bedroom. The door closed quietly behind him.

HE COULD HEAR their voices from the kitchen table, but he couldn't make out what they were saying. He heard Daniel laugh a few times, and every time he did it put Milk a little at ease.

After ten or fifteen minutes the woman came out of the bedroom alone. "May I sit?" she asked.

Milk motioned to the empty chair across from him. The woman sat down. She set the legal pad on the table. Several pages had been bent back and the page that sat open was blank. She looked toward the bedroom. "He's a good boy," she said.

"I know it."

"He seems to be doing well."

Milk was quiet.

"I know this is a strange situation," the woman said. "To come back and along with everything else to have to deal with this."

"It's not how I planned it."

"Are you on inactive duty right now? I mean, I don't know exactly how it works. I guess I'm wondering if they can call you back."

"I got a medical discharge."

"What was it for? The discharge—if you don't mind me asking."

"TBI. They give it to everyone now. It don't mean much."

The woman nodded. "Well, I'd like to come back. I'd like to see about getting Daniel some things from Marcy's—we might have some things at the office too. Anyway, I'd like to see you both again."

Milk looked toward the hall. "You want to check on him."

"That's part of it, but only a small part. Our office can help families—especially families in transition like yours."

Milk tapped his cigarette in the cup. "Transition," he said.

"That's right. Have you had any luck finding a job?"

"I haven't had much time to look since I been back—with Daniel and now this professional development day."

"Have you seen anybody? Anybody who can help, I mean?"

"Not since discharge. But that didn't help much."

The woman nodded. She studied her notepad and then leaned forward. "I'm going to give you two addresses that are hopefully going to make your life easier." She tore a piece of paper from her notepad and started writing. "The first is for the Veterans Outreach Center. The office is in North Bennington, and it's a good group of people—all veterans such as yourself. They can help you find a job that might work with your schedule, and they can help you with your disability claim if you got one or even help you get in touch with other veterans, if that's something you want. The second address I'm going to give you is for a woman named Ruth Fenn. She teaches art lessons at her house up the road from here, and she can help you if you get yourself a job interview or if you just find yourself in a jam and need someone to watch Daniel for a couple hours. She's been doing it a few years now and she only works with children I refer to her. She doesn't charge anything."

Milk stubbed his cigarette in the cup and took the piece of paper from the woman. He studied the name on it and tried to place where he'd heard it before.

RUTH FENN

THE LIGHT HAD GONE AND A STEADY RAIN POUNDED THE STORM windows. "Coming Back to Me" by Jefferson Airplane played over the radio. Ruth poured a small glass of bourbon and studied her reflection in the window above the sink and listened to the song. Her mother was asleep in the guest room with the door partially open. The dogs were fed and had fallen asleep in front of the woodstove.

Ruth tried to remember the last conversation she'd had with Elam. She remembered that he couldn't find his keys. He had called to her from the other room, and she'd told him she had seen them on the bench in the mudroom. She wondered whether his face would have conveyed something had she taken the time to go over to him rather than shouting. She went to her bedroom and sifted through Elam's closet and his dresser drawers, and then she stood in the middle of the room looking for a sign or a note or something else she might have missed. Elam's nightstand looked the same as it always had, with the iron lamp and the broken watch with the thick leather strap she had given him when he got his first raise from AAA Northern New England all those years ago. She studied his nightstand and then went over to it and pulled open the single drawer. A dog-eared drawing of a tree and a house with a big moon above it that Mathew had drawn and signed when he was seven was the only thing in the drawer. She put her hand on it. Felt the old paper and the smooth wax of the colored pencil and then shut the drawer and went to the telephone and picked up the receiver and dialed the Whistler.

"Hello?"

"Buddy?"

"This is Buddy. Who is this?"

"Buddy. It's Ruth. Ruth Fenn."

"Ruth?"

"Listen—I'm wondering if you've seen Elam."

"Hold on a minute." Ruth heard a click, and then Buddy started coughing and heaving on the other line. "Christ," he said. He sniffled and then coughed once more. "Sorry about that, Ruth. I got this bug moving through me." He coughed again. "Della called last night. Said Horace and Elam never came home. I don't know where they are. I haven't seen 'em."

"Any idea what they'd be doing together?"

"Beats the hell out of me. I'll tell 'em you're looking if I see 'em."

"Just Elam."

"What's that?"

"I'm only looking for Elam. And you don't need to go asking around."

"All right—but word travels fast around here. You know that."

"I know it. No need helping it along." Ruth waited for Buddy to say something, but he seemed distracted. She heard voices in the background. "I appreciate it, Buddy."

"Good luck, Ruth."

Ruth hung up the receiver. She paused a moment and then picked it up again and dialed Gordon Sadluck.

"Hello?"

"Gordon? It's Ruth. Did Elam stop in today?"

"I haven't seen him."

Ruth turned and looked out the window. The rain pelted the glass.

"Is something wrong?"

"I just couldn't remember if he said he was going deer hunting or not. I figured he would have stopped in the shop to get the reports if he had been."

"Well, he hasn't been in here."

"I must've misheard 'im."

There was a silence on the other end of the line.

"What about Horace?" Ruth asked.

"Horace?"

"Has he been in there?"

"No. I haven't seen him since last season." Gordon paused for a long moment. "When's the last you saw him—your husband?"

"I'm sure I just misheard 'im," Ruth said. "I'm sorry to bother you, Gordon."

"It's not a bother."

Ruth hung up the receiver. The sap boiled and popped in the wood-stove and the dogs stirred. Ruth watched them slowly relax until their chins were resting on one another again, then she went to the closet and got her winter coat and her good rain boots.

THE TOWN OF North Falls consisted of twenty-eight square miles positioned on a high plateau in the southern region of the Green Mountain range. It had the highest altitude of any village in the state, which meant the snow came early and it came often. It also meant that the first thing anybody noticed about the town was the church steeple. The rotting whitewashed wood and the slatted oval window and the copper spire all connected to the simple wood framing. It was the highest point in the state, and people liked to say it was closer to God than anywhere else in Vermont. Not that it did the town much good.

A wide brook ran through the center of town and divided the eastern and western hills, which were populated, mostly, by American beech and sugar maple. That was the second thing people noticed: the trees. The wooded backbone of the town. There had at one time been a bar-iron manufacturing plant, but the plant had closed down almost sixty years ago and the mountainous landscape combined with the rocky soil and the thick forests meant that few people farmed and most people logged, which was a good way for a poor town to stay poor.

Ruth's boots stomped out puddles of water held by wide ruts. A wet wind carried the scent of hemlock and pine. She had grown up in a cottage close to the center of town on a quarter acre behind a double stone wall shaded by old-growth maples. Her mother and father had bought the home after selling the hill farm in Rochester for pennies on the dollar. Her father hadn't known much other than farming, and so he built cider presses and did other odd jobs to pay the bills. He liked living in town because he could go on long walks and observe the other homes and trees that he was used to seeing only from a distance.

But Ruth's mother missed the privacy of the hill farm and she hardly left the house. So when Ruth got older, she walked with her father. He pointed out the homes that needed work and told her how he would fix them, and he pointed out the different trees and called them by their names. Ruth calculated one time that she'd probably walked half a million miles in her forty-eight years living in North Falls.

Della's house sat less than a mile south of Ruth's at the end of a wide crushed-stone drive. The moon was bright and shone on the two-story house, and Ruth could see that the paint was peeling, so the clapboard looked like it had been fashioned from birch bark. The chimney was crumbling and the flashing was torn and some of the shutters were missing. Gone to who the hell knows where. Della's truck was parked in the drive, and a school bus painted the colors of the American flag sat flush on the grass behind it as it had for the last fifteen years, ever since Horace bought it from the elementary school after the transmission tunnel locked up.

Ruth had met Della at a town potluck after both women were married but before either one of them became pregnant. They were an odd pairing in a lot of ways. Della was deeply religious, and Ruth believed the Bible made about as much sense as the Loch Ness monster, save for the fact that she could at least picture some handsome carpenter talking a bunch of nonsense with enough bravado that people started to believe it no matter how ridiculous it sounded. She'd seen that movie play out any number of times during her life. But Ruth and Della were both private women, and neither one of them had been born in North Falls. To some small degree they were both outsiders. It was probably those things, and the fact that they both wore blue jeans while all the other women wore gingham dresses, that got them talking during that town potluck and kept them talking well into the night.

Ruth started down the drive and made it three steps before the motion light snapped on, capturing the heavy rain, and a tall German shepherd sprang out from under the porch, growling and barking. Ruth stopped and watched the dog struggle to pull free from the metal chain that held him back.

The front door swung open, and Della stood there staring out at the drive. A moment later she turned to the dog. "Trigger," she shouted. "Goddammit. Quiet, boy."

The dog took to jumping in place as though it might out-jump the chain. Della went back inside the house and came out holding something in her hand. She tossed it under the porch, and the dog chased after it and disappeared.

"Come on," Della said.

Ruth came down the drive and climbed the sagging porch steps and followed Della into the home. The wood-paneled living room opened into the kitchen. A picture of Jesus walking on water hung above the kitchen table in a rose-colored frame. Some of the tile had been ripped up from the kitchen floor and stacked against the wall near the refrigerator. The hallway light was on, and Ruth could see down the narrow hall to William's old bedroom, where the door was closed and the NO TRESPASSING sign still hung.

They had found the two boys on the east ridge about a hundred yards west of Sandy Pond. The trails in the southwest section of the Green Mountain National Forest weren't well maintained, but you could find the ridge if you stayed close to the stream and followed it north from the Sandy Pond turnoff for about three miles to a fallen red maple that came out the side of a hill and stretched across the stream. Elam knew the area best. He had taken Mathew a couple of times to fish for brook trout and to camp on the ridge at night.

The morning they found the boys was hot, and the sun was high enough that it shone through the branches and in their eyes as they walked the stream. Still, the orange two-person tent was visible on the ridge. It was Elam who spotted it. The remnants of a campfire were outside, and the rain fly was up and secured to the gravelly soil even though it hadn't rained the night before. Elam was the first to reach the tent, and he pulled the zipper down and climbed under the rain fly and opened the side door. He called to Ruth to stay where she was, but Ruth didn't listen. She pushed right past him and pulled back the side door.

Her son lay on his stomach stripped of his clothes, his shoulders covered in purple bruises. William was on his back on the other side of the tent. His right eye had been ripped from the socket, which was caked in dried blood, and he had bite marks up and down his legs and around his genitals.

Ruth didn't remember seeing the needles or the beer cans, but she knew they were there. The medical examiner said the heroin had been laced with fentanyl and it could have been that or the loss of blood that killed them. Either one would have done the trick. The only fingerprints belonged to the boys, and the official story was that the boys had gotten drunk and then they had gotten high, and once they were high they had hallucinated and attacked each other. That was what the newspapers ran with. It was only when some people started to ask just where the hell two fifteen-year-old boys living in North Falls had gotten their hands on a bundle of heroin that the state trooper Leo Strobridge got it in his head to tell a reporter from the *Bennington Banner* that he suspected Mathew had loved William and that he had lured him into the tent with alcohol and drugs and that things had turned ugly. He sat right down at the Whistler and told his reasons for it. Told how the boys weren't known to hang out with each other and how the bite marks were mostly around William's privates and how they had found Mathew's ejaculate in the sleeping bag.

The bartender, Buddy Cole, heard most of it. Though he didn't need to because the whole thing was reprinted almost word for word on the front page of the *Banner* with a picture of Leo and the headline "Love and Violence: Responding Officer Describes the Grisly Scene in the Death of Two North Falls Teenagers." From there the *Burlington Free Press* picked it up, and they printed just about the same story with a couple more quotes from members of the community and one from a professor down at the college. Ruth knew Leo meant to distract the town from the fact that two fifteen-year-old boys had been camping out right under his thumb with a tent full of heroin, and she showed up one evening at his front door to tell him as much. He was wearing the same brain-dead cowboy hat he had worn in the black-and-white newspaper photograph, even though he was in the middle of supper. Ruth told him what she thought about him, and he told her that she was just upset and that grief had a way of making the truth never seem quite real enough. Then Ruth said something more, and though she couldn't recall what, it was bad enough that Leo's wife stood and started to clear the table.

Of course it didn't much matter whether the story was true or not; it stuck. William was the crown jewel of North Falls. A good-looking athletic boy who took after his father, who had played college ball at Southern Vermont before blowing out both knees and who, despite his later failings, held on firmly to his position as top turd on the North Falls wheelbarrow. Mathew was a different sort of boy altogether, and to some the story helped make sense out of someone they'd never been able to understand. It all sat just fine with Della, who made sure to get her own quotes in the paper in support of the story the town had come to believe. She told a reporter that William wasn't much like Mathew and that he'd only hung out with him on a couple of occasions because Ruth had told Della that Mathew was lonely and that he didn't get invited to things like the other boys did. Della said all that even though she knew it wasn't true. Even though when the two boys were out of school they were tighter than bark on a tree. It wasn't long before people came to see Mathew as some sort of predator, and those same people could only stare wide-eyed at Ruth or else avoid her like she carried some rare illness that just might be contagious to other parents.

Of course, there were people who couldn't help themselves. Ervine Schwartz, one of Horace's softball buddies and the father of the first baseman on Mathew's baseball team, went as far as to carry a used condom into church the week after Mathew's death and put it in the collection basket when Elam came to his pew. It was after Mathew died that Ruth saw a side of the town that had always been there but that she had never seen before—and once she saw it, like an uneven line in the wall-paper or a scuff mark on an oak table, it was all she could see. She never forgave Della for her role in it, the way she just abandoned Ruth and Mathew in favor of fanning the flames, and she didn't think she ever could.

"It leaked," Della said.

"What?"

"The refrigerator." Della motioned toward the corner of the kitchen. "That's why those tiles are piled up the way they are. Horace's been working on it. But it's still a mess." She opened the cupboard next to the refrigerator. "You still drink bourbon with water?"

Ruth wiped the rain from her forehead. "I'm not staying."

Della paused a moment and shut the cupboard door. She was wearing a long flannel shirt with the cuffs unbuttoned, and Ruth caught a glimpse of a scar running the length of her thumb that she couldn't recall being there three years ago.

"Where have you looked?" Ruth asked.

"I been to the Whistler. I already told you that. I drove up and down Main Street, too—seeing if maybe they'd had a wreck."

"Have you looked at the top of Holcomb Hill? At the lookout over the brook?"

"I looked up there—looked all along the brook. I made some calls, too. Nobody's heard a thing."

"Who'd you call?"

"Guys from the Whistler, mostly. Most of the loggers. I was getting set to go down there again. See if maybe I could talk to some of the guys I couldn't get ahold of on the telephone."

"You talk to Leo?"

"Not yet."

"Good. I don't want you to."

"That's not your decision to make."

"Fine. Keep Elam's name out of it."

"Like I said—I'm headed down to the Whistler. I'm not at the point of calling the police."

Ruth removed her glasses. She pulled the handkerchief from her pocket and dabbed her eyes. "What about the hospital?"

"I called. They got no record of either one of them—so that's good, I guess."

Ruth repositioned her glasses. "Does Horace still hang out and drink beers in that bus?"

"He's not in there now, if that's what you're asking."

"That's not what I'm asking. I'm wondering if maybe there's something in there that would tell you where he went."

"You think maybe he keeps a day planner in there—one of them leather-bound ones with the holidays listed out?"

"I don't know what he keeps in there."

"He hasn't been in there in some time."

Ruth thought to say something about how Della might not have any idea whether Horace had been in the bus or not. About how even when the boys were living under their roofs Horace had always done his own thing. But she stopped herself. "So what is it, then? What is it you think happened?"

"I've got no idea. I don't know what they were doing together, and I don't know where they are. I'm going to the Whistler because it's the only thing I can think to do. You can ride with me if you want—but I'd just as soon not work against you on this thing."

THE CENTER OF North Falls consisted of a four-block stretch of road lined with elm trees. The post office and the two-hundred-year-old general store were on the south side of the first block. Henry's Diner and the hardware store were on the north side. The footpath that led to the brook ran between the two buildings, and the grass there was worn and littered with plastic wrappers and rusted fishing hooks. On the second block was the town hall, with its flood-stained brick facade and faded flag hung from a steel flagpole. Across from the town hall, on a plot of elevated land behind an old Norway maple that had been damaged by fireworks during a town parade, was the church. After that was the library and the fish-and-tackle owned by Gordon Sadluck, who lived in the apartment above. Then, farther down the road, a little out of the way from the rest of the buildings, was the Whistler.

That was it. If you wanted something more, you had to drive down Main Street for thirteen miles until you reached the blinking traffic light in front of the gas station. If you turned onto Route 7 and headed south, you'd find a Donut Shop and finally Hinman's Grocery Store. There used to be a department store in the lot with the grocery store, but it had closed two summers ago, and if you wanted clothes that didn't come from a catalog, you had to drive another ten miles to Woodford. There were no police officers save for Leo Strobridge, the resident state trooper, who lived in a small house with a big old front porch on Wicket Street just behind the church.

The truck jumped over frost heaves. Della readjusted her grip. A preacher with a voice like a busted crankshaft pushed Bible verses through the rattling speakers.

"This weather can't seem to make up its mind," Della said. "I wish the snow would just get on with it already."

Ruth stared at the empty road that unfurled in front of them. The rain was still coming down and the wipers beat against the windshield. "I guess it'll be getting around," she said.

"What's that?"

"That our husbands have gone missing."

"I guess it will."

They entered the center of town and passed the post office and the general store where Ruth had been working as a teenager when she first met Elam. He had come up to the counter as she was adjusting the dial on her transistor radio and told her that if she put the radio in the window facing south and turned it to 1570 just after dark, she could pick up a man named Wolfman Jack all the way in Mexico who played the Rolling Stones and Jefferson Airplane and ate vinyl records live on air. She tried it that same day before closing the store, but all she picked up were Pentecostal preachers. Elam came into the store the next morning, and she told him about the preachers. He promised to return that evening to help her find the station, and he did. He showed up that evening and every evening after that.

"I heard Elam stopped drinking," Della said. "Heard he just drinks soda at the bar—has been that way for a couple months now."

"Had been."

"Maybe it still is."

The truck crossed the small truss bridge and slowed as it ascended the hill toward the Whistler. The lights were on in some of the old homes tucked along Main Street. Only one or two windows lit in each home. Smoke rising from the chimneys. Nobody hell-bent on wasting electricity, least of all in the beginning of November when the winter was just settling in.

"People are going to be surprised to see you," Della said.

"Life is full of surprises. Most of 'em a hell of a lot more interesting than me."

"Not in North Falls. In North Falls you're probably it."

The Whistler was a one-story building with horizontal clapboard siding. It sat low to the ground and looked more like a cowshed than a place that had been given a license to serve liquor and food. The only sign was a brass horse that hung crooked over the door, which didn't make an ounce of sense. Four motel rooms were attached to the rear of the bar. Larry Grogan lived in one with his mentally disabled son, and the other three were occupied from time to time by men who drove up from Hartford to run heroin and didn't bother making a secret of it.

Several pickups sat in the pea-gravel lot in front of the motel. A wooden sign with MOTORCYCLES ONLY spray-painted on both sides was propped up on the grass in front of the bar. Della pulled into a wide spot between two pickups and cut the engine.

"You thought about what you're going to say?" Della asked.

"What I'm going to say?"

"To the men inside."

"I'm going to ask whichever of them look capable of stringing together a sentence if they've seen my husband. It don't require a lot of thought."

Ruth got out of the truck and studied the Whistler. There was a time that her and Elam would come to the bar every Friday night. She'd never liked it much. There were too many drunks and too many fights. But there were also cold winter days, sitting at a table in the corner with Elam drinking beer and listening to whatever bad songs people played on the jukebox, when it could be almost comforting.

The door to the Whistler swung open as Ruth and Della approached, and blue light poured out onto the pea gravel. A big man with a full goatee stumbled out and unzipped his pants not two feet from the door and started pissing on the grass. Ruth recognized the man as Jay Brewer's son Mitch, though she hadn't seen him since he was a teenager volunteering in Mathew's T-ball league.

"Don't worry, ladies, I got a permit for this thing." Mitch moved his hips and watched the steaming line of piss paint a small circle on the grass.

"You sure you need a permit for a toy gun?" Ruth asked.

Mitch looked up and studied Ruth, and his face broke into a smile. "Holy shit—Ruth Fenn." Mitch tipped his head back and started laughing. He shook the last of the piss from his limp penis and stuffed it back in his pants and pulled up his fly. "In the goddamn flesh," he said. "I ain't seen you in a while." He wiped his palms on his jeans and stuck out his right hand.

"That's okay," Ruth said.

Mitch put his hands on his hips and shook his head. "Hell, Ruth, I was hearing maybe you built an underground bunker up there—locked yourself in for the duration."

"I did. But I guess I missed the Whistler too much."

Mitch laughed again. He looked over at Della and back to Ruth. "Some of the boys are in there," he said. "Jack Canfield and Harry Timblin—and Royce Peters. You remember Royce."

"I remember."

"We're celebrating," Mitch said.

"That so?"

"Yup. Rickie got herself pregnant." Mitch threw up his hands. "I'm going to be a father."

Ruth studied the scar that ran across Mitch's jaw. She remembered hearing about the accident. A couple of years ago he had been driving alone on Route 9 when a truck axle snapped and pirouetted through his windshield. He was lucky he wasn't dead.

"You don't get yourself pregnant, Mitch."

"I guess not. I guess I had something to do with it."

"Well, good. That's a big thing to have happen."

Mitch nodded and smiled like he knew it was. Like he knew it was the biggest thing that would ever happen to him—bigger than anything that he deserved to have happen.

"Is Cecil Higgins in there?" Ruth asked.

"He's in there, I think. I seen him about an hour ago, anyway." Mitch took a cigarette from his coat pocket.

"What about Elam—when's the last time you seen him?"

"Elam?"

"That's right."

Mitch snorted and wiped his nose with his hand. "A couple days ago, I guess."

"What about last night?"

Mitch shook his head. "I was over at Rickie's. Putting together a crib for the baby. Damn thing took me near all night."

"It gets harder."

Mitch nodded and lit his cigarette. He still looked like a boy to Ruth, though his hair was thinning and his shoulders had grown coiled the way they seemed to do on all the loggers.

Mitch had never shown particular interest in Mathew as a player, which made him just about like every other person in North Falls. But he'd been kind and patient with Ruth's boy. He had come to the funeral, too. Him and his mother. He was the only person from the league that did. Ruth hadn't forgotten that.

The rain started to come down harder. "Congratulations," she said again. "On the child."

"Grayson—David—Brewer. You remember that name. He's gonna be famous someday."

Ruth nodded. She knew Mitch believed it, too. Knew he believed he already knew everything there was to know about his boy.

NOT A WHOLE lot happened when she entered the Whistler. It might have gotten a little quieter, but for the most part people seemed to continue doing whatever it was they had been doing before she arrived. A wagon wheel fitted with Christmas lights hung over the bar. A small wooden stage was set up at the far end, and three people held cans of beer and danced by themselves to the loose chords of a beat-up guitar played by a man wearing a floppy-brimmed camouflage hat. Ruth took off her glasses and wiped her eyes with her handkerchief, and then she put her glasses back on. She scanned the bar looking for people she recognized. Just about all the men wore ball caps and shirts that said FLEMING LOGGING or else NORTH FALLS VOLUNTEER FIRE DEPARTMENT. A woman Ruth's age with tattoos running up her arms sat on a bar stool knitting something pink. Another man sat at a table in the corner of the bar with his head tilted back against an exposed beam and his eyes closed.

Ruth spotted Cecil Higgins sitting at a small table in the back with Eddie Ransom, and she left Della at the entrance and walked over peanut shells and spilled drinks to the table. Cecil saw her and stood and grabbed his tattered green snow hat like he was going to take it off, but in the end he just held his hand there on top of the thick wool.

"Ruth," he said.

Cecil had worked AAA roadside assistance with Elam out at George Milken's shop for close to twenty years before turning exclusively to plowing and driving trucks for HP Hood. The two continued to hunt together, and every now and then Cecil came by the house afterward for beers. He was always good company, but Ruth hadn't seen much of him lately.

"You don't have to stand, Cecil—I ain't the president."

"I wouldn't stand for that piece of shit." Cecil leaned forward and gave Ruth a hug. Then he stood back and studied her. He was a big barrel-chested man, and he wore a flannel shirt and open brown vest. His beard was thick and uneven, like it had been cut with a bucksaw. "What the hell are you doing here?" he asked.

Eddie Ransom was looking at her too now.

"I'm looking for Elam."

Cecil looped his thumbs around his brown leather belt. "I haven't seen him—figured maybe he'd be in later."

"What about yesterday?"

"I seen him yesterday—both Eddie and I did."

Eddie nodded. He was a thin man with a gray ponytail. He wore a twine necklace with a shark's tooth hanging from it like a little boy might wear.

"You see him leave?"

Cecil squinted his eyes like he was trying to picture what he might have seen. "I don't think so—I mean, we might've left before him. I don't remember. What's going on?"

"He didn't show up at the house last night."

Cecil looked directly at her. "Hell, Ruth."

"Horace didn't come home neither—that's why Della's here." Ruth turned to the entrance, but Della was no longer there.

"You two came here together?"

"Happy as a couple of toads in lightning."

Cecil scratched his beard. "They were talking," he said. "Elam and Horace. Sitting just over there at that table by the bar."

"You know what they were talking about? What the hell they might be doing together?"

"I don't know. I thought maybe they were patching things up."

Ruth studied the table by the bar. A young girl and a man were sitting there now. The man put his hand on the girl's cheek, and she pushed it away but laughed at the same time.

"He seem drunk to you?"

"Elam? No. He hasn't had nothing to drink for a few weeks now."

"Not even last night?"

Cecil shook his head. "I'd have noticed if he was drinking again."

Eddie nodded in agreement.

"Were they arguing?"

"Not that I saw. Like I said, I thought maybe they were patching things up. I tried to give 'em their space. I saw Jack Barlow go over there, though."

"Jack?"

"I know him and Elam don't like each other much. I suppose he was wondering what Elam and Horace were doing together. It wouldn't be like Jack to give nobody space."

Ruth looked around the bar. "Is he here tonight?"

"Not tonight. But you can catch him at the AA meeting on Tuesday."

"AA meeting?"

"Twelve o'clock—at the church. He don't miss 'em. I see that orange piece-of-shit truck parked outside every time I go to lunch."

"What the hell is he doing in the Whistler if he's going to AA?"

"Hell, Ruth, half the guys in here go to that shit. Mostly 'cause their wives make 'em."

A redheaded woman stood from the bar and walked to the bathroom. She caught Ruth's eye because she was young and pretty and there wasn't anybody else like that in the Whistler. Not even close.

"Who's that?"

Cecil turned as the woman slipped behind the bathroom door.

"That's the new girl Henry's got working for him. From Underhill—calls herself Rain."

"Rain?"

"Like from the sky."

"Well, why not," Ruth said. "Why the hell not."

"She moved into Jim Dalfino's old place last week. Henry gave her a job just like that."

"I'll bet he did."

"Said he could use the extra hand."

"I know right where he could use it, too."

Cecil laughed and pulled off his snow hat and ran his hand through his curly hair.

"Listen," Ruth said. "You don't know where Elam could be? He didn't tell you nothing?"

"Hell, Ruth, I'd tell you if he did. You know that."

Ruth nodded. She looked around the bar. "Horace's truck is still outside. Elam's is missing—but Horace's has been here since last night."

"You think maybe Horace's wouldn't start, then? Maybe Elam gave him a ride somewhere?"

"I don't know. But I'm thinking we ought to open it up."

"I can help you with that."

The redheaded girl came back from the bathroom, and Ruth watched her walk slowly up to the bar and put her elbows down on the countertop. She leaned over, and Ruth could see where her underwear came up past her jeans. Some of the guys started talking to her and laughing and pointing at something underneath the bar counter.

Mitch had moved to a small table in the corner. He was sitting there by himself with a beer in his hand grinning largely while the rest of the guys flirted with the redheaded girl.

"Mitch Brewer is having a kid," Cecil said.

"That's what I heard."

"He ain't but a kid himself."

"He's older than that."

"I suppose. Maybe he is. But I still remember him as a kid."

"I know it."

"He was a big ol' boy even then. I remember him loping around after balls. Elam used to joke that if he ever had to haul ass, it would take him two trips." Cecil smiled a little to himself and then pounded his beer and set it on the table. "Let's get that truck open."

The three of them pushed through the crowd. All of those people standing around laughing on a Sunday night like they didn't have a single care in the world, even though Ruth knew they did—most of them plenty more than just the one.

THE RAIN HAD turned to flurries. A man wearing a jacket with a mouton collar sat on a guardrail that hugged the road, holding a beer, looking toward the other buildings on Main Street in the far distance and singing quietly to himself. Ruth could see some of the yellow-lit houses on the other side of the road behind small yards, some that were well kept and others that had grown tall with weeds behind their chain-link fences.

Cecil's truck was a red Ford F350. He kept it parked on the patch of grass at the far end of the lot near the wooden motorcycle-parking sign. Ruth followed him past a couple of men who stood outside smoking cigarettes and leaning against the side of the Whistler.

"I suppose you called Gordon," Cecil said. "Not that Elam would be out in this shit."

"I called him. He hasn't seen 'em."

Cecil removed a trenching shovel from the bed of his truck. He opened the cab and pulled a stained rag and a long bar from behind the seat.

The wind blew, and Ruth took a deep breath. The cold winter air smelled fresh to her, even in the parking lot of the Whistler. She studied the crowded lot and tried to picture her husband there. Tried to imagine what he was talking to Horace about. Closed her eyes and tried to hear it. The wind blew again and turned the rain sideways.

"That's it there." Cecil pointed to the small single-cab powder-blue pickup, parked at the opposite end of the lot, across from the motel rooms, close to a telephone pole with weeds grown up around it. "You want Della out here for this?"

Ruth shook her head. "Ain't no need."

Cecil tried the handle of Horace's pickup, and when the door didn't open, he walked around to the other side and tried the passenger door. "Thought maybe we'd get lucky." He set the shovel and the long bar on top of the cab and put his boot on the front tire and moved his weight up and down a little, as though seeing whether the truck could hold him, and then he pulled himself into the bed and crawled up on top of the cab. "You hear about that truck that broke down in New Mexico? Lady pulled it off the highway and popped the hood and found a seven-foot python curled up on top of the engine block."

"Still alive?"

"According to the guy on the seven o'clock news, it was." Cecil rotated his legs so they hung down on each side of the side mirror. He laid the rag down over the door and then rested the shovel on the rag and used it to pry the door open. Eddie was standing off to the side having a smoke.

"You look like you done this before," Ruth said.

"I haven't always been the model citizen you see here before you."

The light in one of the motel rooms turned on and wavered.

"I was a Boy Scout—it's true," Cecil said. "But only for two weeks before I got caught diddling the Scout leader's wife."

"I don't believe that."

"It's true."

"Whose wife was that?"

"Perd Talham's. Her name was Lucy."

"Lucy Talham? Hell, Cecil, I think maybe you could've done better."

"I was thirteen years old. She could've been a notch in the side of a sycamore tree."

The light in the motel room wavered again, and a moment later the door opened and a man in a thick winter coat came out holding a lawn chair. He set the lawn chair in the gravel underneath the overhang and sat down and lit a cigarette.

"Who's that?" Ruth asked.

Cecil looked over at the man and then back to the truck. "You know who that is."

"I never seen him before."

"They're all the same." Cecil slipped the long bar in between the door and the frame and started moving it around.

Ruth could tell the man in the lawn chair was watching them even from across the lot. She couldn't see his eyes, but she could tell which way his head was tilted by the burnt-orange light of his cigarette.

"Got it," Cecil said. He pulled the long bar up through the space he had created with the shovel and climbed down from the truck. "Didn't even leave a scratch—not that it would've made a difference."

The man in the lawn chair stretched his legs out onto the pea gravel and rested the heel of one boot on the toe of the other as though he were poolside in some resort in the dead of summer. The light behind him wavered again.

"Someone else is in there," Ruth said.

Cecil looked back at the motel room. "Probably."

Ruth started toward the room.

"Ruth—they don't have nothing to do with this."

Ruth continued across the pea gravel. She smelled cigarette smoke and truck fuel.

"Goddammit, Ruth."

The plastic blinds were drawn closed in the room. The welcome mat outside the door was torn in places and covered with cigarette butts.

"Something I can help you with?" the man in the chair asked as Ruth drew close.

"I want to know if you seen two men here yesterday."

The man took a drag from his cigarette. Held it for a moment in front of his face between his red muttonchops.

"One of them is short with a bald head. Walks with a limp. The other is skinny and tall. Wears a Browning cap."

"I don't know nobody like that."

Ruth knocked on the door.

"Ain't nobody in there seen a thing," the man said.

Ruth knocked again. A boy that didn't look older than a teenager opened the door. He wore a flat-brim hat and a gray hooded sweat shirt and basketball shorts. He looked Ruth up and down but didn't seem like he was going to say anything.

"I'm looking for my husband."

The boy looked at the man in the lawn chair and then back toward the motel room. A black man was lying on the bed holding a remote and flipping through channels.

"Kennon—you married to some old woman?"

"Nope," the man said. He continued to stare at the television.

"I'm looking for a man named Elam and a man named Horace."

"Those are some fucked-up names."

"Elam's about six foot tall and thin as a whip. Wears a hat that says BROWNING on it. I want to know if you seen him yesterday."

"He ain't here."

"Horace is short and wide, walks with a limp like he's dragging a chain."

The boy held Ruth's eyes. "Are you deaf or just fucking old?"

Ruth felt Cecil's hand on her back.

The boy smiled at Cecil. "You looking for your husband too?"

Ruth peered past the boy. There were towels lying on the floor outside the bathroom. The trash underneath the side table was full, and more trash had gathered beside it. The man on the bed continued to flip through the television channels.

Ruth looked back to the boy in the doorway. He was tall and lanky. His face was smooth and unblemished save for his nose, which looked like it had been broken more than once. She turned to the man in the lawn chair. "What are these boys—sixteen?"

The man in the lawn chair took a drag but didn't say anything.

"You must be proud of yourself," Ruth said.

"Let's go, Ruth," Cecil said.

"You ought to listen to your friend there." The man flicked the ash from his cigarette onto the pea gravel.

Water dripped from the gutters. The damp mixed with the smell of smoke. Ruth turned back to the motel room. A bone-thin girl wearing just her underwear opened the bathroom door and quickly pulled it closed.

"Who else is in there with you?" Ruth asked.

"Time to go, lady," the man in the lawn chair said.

"Who is that—who else is in there?"

The boy turned to the man in the lawn chair. "You want me to get rid of 'em, Dwyer, or do you want to do it?"

The man in the lawn chair stood.

Ruth took a step toward the room. "That girl's not more than a child."

The boy pulled a six-inch blade from his pocket and held it close to his thigh.

"Whoa," Cecil said. He stepped in front of Ruth.

The boy glanced over at the man that had been in the lawn chair, and the man suddenly lunged at Cecil and wrapped his arms around his waist. Cecil grabbed the man's shoulders and the two wrestled. The man's leg struck Ruth's knee, and she fell to the ground and scraped her palms. She looked up in time to see the boy duck and drive the blade into Cecil's upper thigh.

"Motherfucker," Cecil yelled.

Ruth got to her knees as Eddie came from somewhere behind her and grabbed the boy around the neck and begin pulling and punching him at the same time. The black man came out of the motel room with his fists up. Cecil broke free of the man that had been sitting in the lawn chair and rushed the black man. The knife stuck straight out of his thigh, and blood poured down the front of his jeans. He slipped his fist through the black man's raised guard, and Ruth heard a sound like the hood of a car slamming shut. The black man's nose exploded and his head snapped backward and struck the metal door frame. Cecil pivoted and tackled the man who'd been in the lawn chair, just as the man was reaching for his pocket, and started pounding on his head. Eddie was on top of the teenager punching him in the face while the boy struggled. Ruth saw blood and heard footsteps rushing over pea gravel.

THE KNIFE WAS deep, but it had caught Cecil in the meaty part of the leg. Eddie pulled out a smoke and gave it to Cecil. One of the men from the bar brought out a shot of something and Cecil took it down fast, spilling a little on his beard.

"Son of a bitch," he said.

Ruth tore a section of Cecil's jeans. Someone behind her shined a light on his leg. "You got to get to Southwestern Medical," Ruth said. "I don't want to risk pulling it out here and springing a leak when we got nothing to close it up with."

"I'll take him," Eddie said.

Ruth nodded and slowly got to her feet. Her back hurt and she laid her hand on it. She could hear people talking now. Whispering and saying her name.

"Son of a bitch," Cecil said again. He spat blood onto the ground.

Ruth looked over at the motel. The black man had gone back inside and closed the door. The man in the lawn chair was still unconscious on the gravel. One of the men from inside the Whistler stood over him smoking a cigarette. Making sure he woke up and that he didn't do anything stupid when he did.

The boy in the hooded sweat shirt had run to his car holding his side and peeled out of the gravel lot weaving all over the road. Ruth overheard somebody say that it was Dottie Flaker's son.

Della had come out sometime in the middle of everything, and she sat in Horace's truck with the door wide open. She was holding something. Turning it over in her hand. Ruth watched her a moment and then caught a glimpse of what it was. Saw the bluish-black steel and wondered what Horace was doing with a gun that wasn't used to hunt.

"Son of a bitch," Cecil said, quieter this time.

MILK RAYMOND

In the evening after the two had eaten fish sticks for dinner and the boy had finally stopped asking questions about the woman from the Department for Children and Families, Milk sat on the couch smoking a cigarette and flipping through the stack of papers. There were insurance forms and lists of transition centers and home modification resources and workforce investment sheets, and every time he flipped to the next sheet he got more upset. He thought he was putting his life on hold when he enlisted. He thought he would come back to North Falls after serving his time and hit the play button again. He even thought that so long as he managed to keep all his limbs from being blown off, he might come back as something more than when he left. But that wasn't what happened. Instead he returned to a life that hadn't bothered to wait for him. He had a stack of papers telling him how to start a new life, but there wasn't a single one telling him how to get his old one back.

He set the papers on the cardboard box and leaned back on the couch. The television was showing a Boston Red Sox game from 1960. The one where Ted Williams homered in his final at-bat and then skipped out on the last three games of the series to go fishing in Maine. Milk watched Russ Nixon ground into a double play and then he put out his cigarette and stood and went down the hall to check on his boy.

The light was off in the bedroom and the door was closed. Milk listened for a moment and then quietly turned the doorknob. The quilt was on the floor between the bed and the wall, and the sheet stretched from one of the spindles on the headboard to the wall, where it was attached somehow. Daniel sat underneath the sheet, shining a flashlight down on a book with pictures of planets open in front of him. He wore his goggles and the pajamas he had worn all day with the flying saucers running up and down the legs and arms.

"How'd you get that sheet to hang like that?"

"Thumbtacks."

"And then it looks like you tied it around the bedpost here?"

Daniel looked toward the bed. "With rubber bands."

Milk nodded.

"Are you mad?"

"Mad? Hell, why would I be mad? I like it. It's a nice setup you've got in here. I used to make something like this when I was your age. It wasn't as good as this, though. I used to prop up a wiffle ball bat on my mattress and drape the blanket over it, sort of like an A-frame. Then I'd pretend there was a big storm outside and I was inside a tent in the middle of the jungle. I had a plastic knife I used to pretend to sharpen. Listening to them big animals out there in the dark. Thinking about what might try to get me—how I might fight it off."

Daniel held the head of the flashlight in his palm so that his hand glowed orange.

"They're showing an old Red Sox game on television. The last game Ted Williams ever played. Teddy Ballgame, they used to call him. Or the Splendid Splinter. That was another one. You ever watch the Red Sox?"

The boy shook his head.

"Some of your friends must—some of your classmates."

64

The boy shrugged. "Some people talk about the games sometimes."

"It's all we ever talked about when I was your age. I went to a game one time with my father before he died. We drove all the way to Boston in the morning so we could get there to watch batting practice. He was too cheap to get a motel, so after the game we drove the whole three hours back. They didn't win that game. They got blown out. It was a good time, though. We weren't anywhere near the field, but it was something to be in the same place with all those players. My father didn't like Boston. Too many people. He couldn't figure why so many people would live in the same place. Stacked up like sardines. I guess that's how come he settled on North Falls." Milk scratched at his chin. His beard was coming back, and he thought it was just as well. "You warm enough? You warm enough in here?"

The boy nodded.

"Tell me if you get too cold. We might have to get you some storm windows." Milk looked around the room. The walls were bare, and he thought it might be good to get some pictures hung. "All right," he said finally. He slapped his hand on the door frame and turned from the bedroom and then stopped before closing the door. He turned back to his boy. "Don't stay up too late. You got school in the morning."

The boy nodded but didn't look up from his book.

IN THE LIVING room Milk sat with the lights out and the colors from the television playing on the walls. He wondered how long it would be before the previous tenant realized he was paying for the cable Milk was watching. With one bedroom it was probably someone without kids. Maybe a single guy or someone recently divorced or an elderly person who hadn't moved out but died instead. If that was the case, he might get to watch cable for a while longer.

He pulled another cigarette from the pack and thought about Jessica. He wondered if she was watching the same Red Sox game, but figured it was just as likely she was passed out on the ground somewhere. He wondered if she thought about him or Daniel and figured she probably didn't think about Daniel. If she did, she wouldn't be able to stay away.

He knew it wasn't easy raising a child. He knew it must have been hard for those years he was away. But hard was one thing. Leaving your own child was another. Milk probably never would be much of a father, if his own father was any sort of indication. But he wouldn't ever leave Daniel. He wouldn't have left the first time if he had known what was going to happen.

He lit the cigarette and tried to push the thought of Jessica from his mind. It didn't matter where she was or what she was thinking about. She was extraneous information. That's what one of the gunners used to say whenever someone went on about something that had no bearing on the mission at hand. *That's just extraneous information*, he would say—*and extraneous information will get you killed*.

RUTH FENN

Ruth could smell it the moment she opened the door and stepped out of the cold and into the home. The fire in the woodstove had gone out and there was nothing to mask the smell. She flipped on the light and took off her coat and hung it on the nail. The dogs stood and stretched. Ruth went to the kitchen and removed the bottle of bleach and a sponge and a plastic trash bag from under the sink.

It was dark in the room save for the light from the television. The bed was empty and the sheets had been pulled back on one side. Ruth switched on the light and picked up the remote from the nightstand and turned off the television. The bathroom door was closed, and Ruth could hear water running lightly.

She pushed open the door. Her mother stood in front of the sink in her long flannel nightgown holding something under the water.

"What are you doing?"

"Quiet. You'll wake your father."

Ruth took a step toward her mother and saw the soiled underwear in her hands. "Jesus," she said. "I told you to throw them away. That's why I get them so cheap. Just throw them away."

"Quiet."

Shit was smeared on the white porcelain rim of the sink. The drain had clogged, and the water that pooled at the bottom was a brown rust color.

"That's enough," Ruth said.

Ruth's mother continued to scrub the underwear with the heel of her hand.

"Stop it."

"I ain't done."

Ruth turned off the water. "Stop."

Ruth's mother stopped.

"Set them down."

Ruth's mother set the underwear on the lip of the sink. Her palms were covered in feces, and there was some between her fingers and more on the front of her nightgown and on her chin. Ruth sat her down on the lid of the toilet and grabbed the towel from the ring beside the sink and ran it under the water. She held her mother's wrists gently one at a time and cleaned her hands and then her face. Her mother didn't put up a fight. She held still like a child who was scared somewhere past the point of squirming.

Ruth led her mother to the bed and sat her down on the mattress. She found a clean nightgown and helped her change and then she lifted her mother's legs onto the mattress and pulled the sheets so they covered her shoulders and then laid the quilt over her body faint as a dandelion's shadow. She gathered the soiled nightgown and the towel and the underwear and placed them in the trash bag and then she went to the bathroom and stuck her hand into the water and clawed the shit loose from the basket strainer.

"What are you doing?" Ruth's mother asked. "Is your father in there with you?"

"Quiet," Ruth said. "Quiet now."

When the water had drained, Ruth grabbed the sponge and began cleaning the sink. She took deep breaths through her mouth and tried not to be angry with her mother for no longer being the woman she was. She had always been difficult. She seemed to want something from the world but never said what it was and then seemed upset with everyone for not knowing. But she was strong and guarded and it hurt Ruth to see her so vulnerable. It felt like watching an old tree lose its bark.

Looking back on it, Ruth didn't think her mother had ever wanted children. She never could give herself to Ruth in the way required of a mother. It was something Ruth had grown up wanting. To be a good mother. Elam understood what that meant, and it was one of the reasons she fell in love with him. He had been born to a caring woman who raised four boys and kept her kind disposition even after she was diagnosed with breast cancer, even after the bills from the hospital started to stack up. Even after Elam's father took out a life insurance policy and sat down on the tractor in the barn one winter morning and pulled a ski mask over his head and shot himself with a twelve-gauge shotgun.

Ruth dropped the sponge in the trash bag with the other soiled items. She caught a glimpse of herself in the mirror. She had put on weight. She could see it in her face and in the way her shoulders and back and arms had become one solid slab. She could see her mother there too, pushing through and distorting her face like a tussock of pasture grass beneath trampled snow.

She left the bathroom and stood in the doorway and watched her mother, who had already fallen asleep. The smell of soap clung to the air. Ruth thought to open a window, but it was too cold. She turned off the light and walked to the kitchen, where she stuffed the trash bag into the garbage underneath the sink and washed her hands.

Woodstock ambled into the kitchen, his nails clicking on the pinewood floor. Ruth poured a glass of water and studied the dog. "I don't suppose nobody fed you, did they?" Ruth took a sip of the cold water and wiped her mouth. "I suppose that would be up to me." She set the glass in the sink and fed Woodstock from the container on the floor of the pantry, and by that time the other dogs had come around and she fed them too. They seemed content afterward and lay down by the woodstove licking their lips and waiting for it to be lit. She went to the front of the house and stood looking out the window at the moon and the leafless trees and the empty drive.

She thought about the gun in Horace's truck. Della had said it was for protection. "Protection from what?" Ruth had asked.

But Della just shook her head. "Oh hell, I don't know. That's just the kind of world it is now."

And maybe she was right. Or maybe it had always been that kind of world and people had just grown tired of pretending otherwise.

In the bedroom Ruth undressed. She removed her glasses and set them on the nightstand beside the lamp and climbed into bed and switched off the light. The rain had picked up and the wind rattled the loose windowpanes. After a moment Woodstock came into the room and lay down on the braided wool rug. Ruth listened to the rain and the rattling glass and the dog's nasal breathing. She listened to the sounds for a long while until each one became commonplace. But sleep never came, not completely. Heavy stones had begun to gather deep in her gut. She could feel them piling up like a boundary wall.

MILK RAYMOND

THE SOUND ENTERED HIS DREAM AND CHANGED THE IMAGE FROM shadows moving over rooftops to dirt skipping in front of him before he opened his eyes and realized what was going on.

"Shit."

He stood and pulled on his pants and his shirt. "Daniel," he shouted. "Daniel." He went to the window and pulled open the blind and saw the school bus idling on the road. The sky was overcast and raindrops covered the concrete drive, though it wasn't raining any longer.

The horn sounded again. "Son of a bitch. Daniel. Hurry up. The bus is here." He put on his boots and grabbed his coat and went outside into the cold.

The bus wasn't full size. It was short like the ones that carried special-needs kids. It was the same size as the bus Milk had ridden until he bought his 1985 Chevy Cavalier for six hundred dollars in the tenth grade. There weren't enough kids living north of town to justify a full-size bus. Milk was lucky a school bus came at all.

The cold wind blew off the road. When Milk reached the end of the grass, the driver opened the door and tilted his head a little. "Is he sick?" The driver wore a pink-collared short-sleeve shirt and a white hat that said ST. PETERSBURG.

"He'll be out in a minute."

"He's late."

"I know he's late."

"You need to get an alarm clock."

"I have an alarm clock. It didn't go off."

"Well, that's not my problem. That's not these kids' problem either." The driver reached for something on the dash. "I got a timer I keep in here for when kids aren't outside. I set it for thirty seconds, and I sound the horn at the beginning and then again halfway through. If they ain't out by the time the alarm goes off, then it's too late. I been doing this fourteen years. All the kids know to be on time with me. All the kids know about me before they even ride this bus. Their parents too. I don't know where you been."

"I said he's coming."

"It's already been thirty seconds since we been talking." The man put the timer back on the dashboard. His stomach sat on his lap and the top button of his shirt was unbuttoned and silver hairs like guitar strings came up over the fabric.

"Aren't you cold in that shirt?" Milk asked.

The driver looked down at his shirt as though he hadn't noticed it before and then he looked back at Milk. "You ought to forget about my shirt and worry about why it is you can't get your son up on time—why it is you're standing out here arguing with me. Why it is you . . ."

Milk looked toward the back of the bus, where the children were mostly quiet.

"Go on then," Milk said.

"How's that?"

"You heard me—fuck off."

The driver straightened in his seat. "Real nice," he said. "That's real nice—and in front of the kids too."

"Fuck you," Milk said. "You look like a marshmallow peep in that goddamn shirt."

Milk turned from the bus and headed back across the damp grass to the house. He heard the air being released as the door closed and then the rumble of the engine as the driver put the bus in gear and started down the road.

Inside Milk went for his cigarettes. Daniel came running out of his bedroom with his hair sticking out in seven different directions and his goggles swinging from his hand.

"Slow down," Milk said. "I'm taking you to school."

"I'm going to be late."

"You're not going to be late."

"The bus is leaving."

"Damn it, Daniel. Relax a minute. We'll get to school before the bus does."

"You don't know where it is."

"Where what is?"

"The school."

"Daniel. I was going to that school before you were ever born. It hasn't gone nowhere."

Daniel went to the window. His backpack was unzipped.

"Come on," Milk said. "Quit staring out the window and get your coat."

THE TWO RODE along Stump Hollow in silence. A beat-up pickup passed them heading north, and Milk thought he might wash his truck when he got back to the duplex. He tried to recall whether he had seen a hose coiled up outside.

When they turned onto Wicket Street, he flipped on the radio. Daniel held his goggles on his lap, and now and then he squeezed his eyes closed like he was trying to pass something through his digestive tract.

"What's going on?" Milk asked.

"Nothing."

They continued up past the last of the farms to the small brick school that sat at the back of a paved lot partially fenced in with split rails. There were already a couple of buses pulled up next to the school, and there were children getting off the buses and making their way to the big red double doors. Milk slowed the truck and pulled in behind one of the buses that had its stop sign extended underneath the driver's side window.

"This is where the buses park," Daniel said.

"Think of me like a bus."

"You're supposed to park with the cars."

"Jesus, Daniel. I'm only here a minute dropping you off."

Daniel opened the door without saying another word and jumped out.

"I'm picking you up, too," Milk shouted.

Daniel shut the door, and Milk watched his son rush to join the other children, who were all headed toward the red double doors. His hair was still sticking out in every direction and his backpack was pulled tight against his shoulders, whereas all the other kids had theirs hung loose off their asses. Milk spotted a couple of boys huddled close together talking, and after a moment one of them with a blond bowl cut and a Boston Bruins hockey jersey came up behind Daniel and started stepping on the heels of his shoes. Daniel stumbled a couple times, but he didn't turn around. Milk reached for the door handle but stopped himself. He watched the two walk for a little while before one of the female teachers came over and told the kid in the hockey jersey to knock it off. The teacher put her hand on Daniel's shoulder, and the two of them walked through the doors together.

RUTH FENN

Ruth supposed she had time. Della had been holding her meetings at the church over the noon hour for the last three years. For a while it was only Mondays, but Elam had recently told Ruth she was up to three days a week. It wasn't hard to believe. Della had always been a devoted member of the parish, and after William died she'd stuck to the church the way a dog sticks to a square of sunlight stretched across a cold floor.

Ruth walked along the side of the road. The late-morning light came down sideways, and she kept her eyes on the ground to avoid stepping in borrow pits and erosion channels or tripping over spots where the pavement had frozen and cracked and lifted like warped boards. It was cold, but it was dry, and the sun felt nice on the side of her face.

She continued around the bend just before Della's house and stopped when she heard the start of an engine. She could see the back of the police cruiser between the oak trees. The forest-green paint with the horizontal yellow safety stripe. The cruiser began backing out of Della's drive, and Ruth thought to step off the road and into the overgrowth where she might not be seen. But instead she stood perfectly still and watched the cruiser back out of the drive and rotate its tires and head south toward town.

A moment later Della followed in her pickup. Ruth watched the vehicles disappear. She'd known Della would seek out Leo eventually, and she felt some relief in her having done so. But she felt angry, too. Angry that Leo might feel like he was needed. She remained in the road with the wind blowing the skeleton leaves in tight circles, and then she continued toward Della's.

The curtains were closed. The long chain was gone, and Ruth wondered if the dog had gotten free and run off somewhere. She lifted her nose and tested the air as though she might be able to tell something from smelling it, but she only picked up the scent of rotten leaves and damp pavement. She removed her glasses and wiped her eyes with her handkerchief. The sky to the west was cloudy, and it looked like it might start to rain again. She studied the quiet road and the trees and the gently sloped hills in the distance, and then she started down the drive.

Elam's clouded image came to her mind. A warm fall morning two years ago. He was sitting on the front porch with a mug of coffee tucked between his legs and the horse races on the radio. He greeted her when she stepped outside. He picked up his mug and set it on the railing beside the radio and gave her a small peck on the cheek. He asked her to sit down beside him in the old rocker, and even before she agreed he started to wipe away the leaves that were caught between the slats.

The hills had turned the color of rust. She could hear the track announcer between stretches of static. Elam stared at the woods for a long time in silence until she began to think he might only want to sit beside her and look out at the changing colors and breathe in the sharp autumn air like they had done when they were young, before Mathew died and even before he was born.

But after several moments he turned to her and said he had been thinking they should try again. She must have looked confused, because he leaned forward and said *a child*. Ruth was fifty years old. Mathew had been dead just over a year. It didn't make sense. It wasn't even possible. But she didn't have to be so harsh. She didn't have to let on that it was such a foolish idea.

Elam had seemed happy. Blind as a water beetle to just what in the hell he was asking—but happy. That used to be enough for her. It used to be the most important thing to her, and she regretted not holding on to his happiness for a little while longer.

The school bus sat on the dead grass next to Della and Horace's house. The blue paint had faded on the hood, and she could make out the old route number. Brown curtains hung over the side windows, and sheets of plywood had been secured to the entry door. Two U-bolts clung to the plywood, and a bike chain had been looped through the bolts and secured.

Ruth wasn't sure what exactly she expected to find in the bus. She wasn't even sure she would be able to get inside. But she knew Della and Horace kept their distance, and she knew Horace spent a lot of time in the bus with the rest of his friends, smoking and drinking and listening to baseball. He had been doing it ever since William was born and Della finally got up the courage to tell him he needed a new place to carry on without waking the baby. And so Ruth thought there might be something in the bus that would give her some idea where Horace had gone or what he had been doing talking to Elam at the Whistler.

Besides, she didn't have any better ideas, and she was past the point of sitting around and waiting on something close to luck to find her. Ruth looked back again to the empty road and then started along the east side of the bus, searching for gaps in the curtains.

The thin whistle of a sparrow startled her, and she turned to the woods. The clouds had parted and filtered light shone down through the branches. The sparrow whistled again, and Ruth's eyes followed the sound to a trash heap several yards into the woods. The sparrow fluttered above the trash heap and settled on a branch.

Ruth continued along the side of the bus until she reached the rear window, where the same brown curtains had been hung. She looked back to the house. The pale-blue curtains were drawn. She was struck by the feeling that someone was watching her from behind them. But she knew that if there was, she would already have found out.

Two silver handles were positioned vertically on the sides of the rear window of the bus. Ruth got up on her toes and pulled one and then the other so they sat parallel to the ground. She pulled the handles toward her. The window popped open. She looked around for something to stand on and spotted a white plastic bucket by the trash heap and started toward it. The bucket sat upright about fifteen feet into the woods. It was filled with leaves and rainwater and dead mosquitoes. She tipped it over and watched the oil-colored water snake under an arched bush with deep-red berries. The trash heap smelled like rotten eggs mixed with something sweet. It wasn't compost, exactly. It was just a pile of trash, and she wondered what it was for.

She carried the bucket back through the woods to the bus and positioned it on the dead grass under the rear window. She tested the bucket with the edge of her foot and then stepped up onto it and pulled the window all the way open.

It was dark inside the bus. The air coming out smelled like warm beer and cigarettes. A couple of seats had been removed from the front driver's side and a rug had been laid on the floor. Ruth cursed herself and swung her arms over the window and pulled. She wasn't as young as she used to be. That wasn't something she needed to climb through the window of a school bus to find out, but it did reinforce the point.

She shut the rear window almost all the way and reached over one of the seats and pulled the curtain back to bring in some light. The seats were green vinyl and cracked with white spider veins. Some were torn, and straw-colored stuffing bulged from the openings. Others had been repaired and covered haphazardly in a glossy sealant. A thin layer of dust clung to everything.

Ruth made her way down the aisle. Cigarette butts were caught in the thick ribbed flooring. She checked the seats like a child who had lost her winter gloves, but most were empty save for a couple of beer bottles with their labels torn and a can of Rust-Oleum without a cap. She tried to picture Horace sitting here with a group of guys smoking cigarettes and drinking beer, but it was hard for her to imagine grown men sitting on a school bus. She wondered about the logistics. Did any of them sit in the same seats? Did they stretch their legs across the benches or sit facing forward? Did they sit in the front or in the back? She wondered if Elam had ever been inside the bus.

A small metal fan had been mounted on the dash to the left of the steering wheel. A faded pine tree air freshener hung from the stick shift. The rearview mirror was just a shell, its glass gone.

Ruth reached over the steering wheel and drew back the curtain. She could see all the way to where the road disappeared around the bend. She watched the road, expecting to see Della's truck appear, followed by the police cruiser, but when it didn't come, she drew the curtain closed. She turned from the window and stepped on the rug that lay behind the driver's seat where the bench seats had been removed and felt the floor bow.

She stood there a moment looking down at the slight seam that ran across the center of the rug. Then she lowered herself to the ground and pulled up a corner. The cheap cotton had succumbed to dry rot and nearly crumpled in her hand. Damp leaves and all-but-disintegrated pieces of paper stuck to the floor.

Ruth pulled the rug back to expose the seam running straight across the floor. She ran her finger over it and then pulled the rug into the aisle and dug her fingertips into the lip of the seam and lifted. A section of the floor came up easily, and the cold air came with it.

"Jesus Christ," she said.

She looked through the floor into a hole in the ground. A wooden ladder extended down the side of the hole like an oil-change pit. She couldn't see to the bottom, and her imagination started going places she wished it wouldn't go.

Ruth looked up at the dim light coming in through the curtained windshield. She thought for a moment that she might just forget about it. That she might close up the hole and move on like she'd never found it. But she knew she couldn't do that. Knew her mind wouldn't rest knowing the hole was there and not knowing what was inside it. She took a deep breath and got herself turned around and cursed herself for the second time that morning and started down the ladder.

Elam hadn't mentioned the child after that fall day. But something was different. It was as though the two were opposed in some way. They didn't talk save the few words that were necessary. Elam started visiting Mathew's grave more often. He left in the early mornings. Ruth knew when he had gone because he returned home smelling strongly of cigarettes and he was content to sit on the porch with his radio or watch the television. They no longer went to Mathew's grave together. It was something Elam seemed to want to do alone. It worried her how easily it had happened, and she wondered if it made Elam feel as hopeless as it made her feel.

Ruth reached the bottom of the hole and stepped cautiously onto the dirt floor. She looked back up at the school bus. The hole was just large enough to conceal her. The walls were roughly four feet apart from each other. If she reached upward, she could almost reach the opening.

It was colder in the hole. The air was stagnant and metallic smelling. She ran her fingers over the walls that had been reinforced with cinder blocks. As her eyes adjusted to the dark, she spotted a crumpled ball of aluminum foil in the corner. She picked it up and unraveled it. She studied the burn marks and held the foil to her face and smelled something like resin.

She wasn't so blind that she didn't know what the foil was for, but she couldn't see why Horace was climbing down into a hole to get high. She let the foil fall from her hands and stretched her arms out fully so that she touched each side of the hole. She thought about Mathew buried at the top of the hill behind her house, past the wide sweep of goldenrod underneath the slab of limestone, and her stomach turned over and sweat pricked on her forehead.

She climbed the ladder and closed the door and positioned the rug back where it had been and then sat down in the front seat of the old North Falls school bus and let her stomach settle. Sitting there, she couldn't help but think of Mathew and then of Elam.

For years she had tried to teach her students to see things that other people let go unnoticed. She had given them an assignment where they were required to observe an object. The only rule was that it had to be an object whose name they didn't know. She had them write down three words to describe it, and then she had them trade their three words with another student. Each student would have to sculpt something out of clay using the three words they were given. The game was designed to get the children to pay attention—to see things that went unnoticed. But for all her talk, she seemed in the end to have let her own son and then her own husband recede to some distant and unfocused point.

And she wondered how it had happened. Wondered what it was about them and about her that had let it happen.

RUTH FENN

THE SEVENTH-GRADE PLAY THAT YEAR HAD BEEN ON THE LAST DAY OF school on a hot June midweek. The Christmas plays were always announced in the school bulletin, but the summer plays were a surprise every year, and the children were pretty good about keeping it that way, treasuring in some small way that little piece of information they held.

Mathew generally played the lead. He was a quiet boy, but he enjoyed being on stage. It was different from baseball, where he tended to sit in the dugout and fill the water cups for the other boys and hope nobody asked him to grab a bat or glove and head out onto the field. Ruth thought it was the chance to be someone different that appealed to him. Maybe she should've been concerned, but she was only proud.

Ruth and Elam drove to the school in the early evening with the sun still high and bright. Elam had purchased a new video camera, and he planned to use it the way some of the other fathers had done in years past: standing in the back of the auditorium with the heavy camera propped up on his shoulder.

The sky was pure blue, and the old-growth trees were full and green and the light shone through their leaves and cast latticed shadows on the paved road. Mathew was already at the school, having stayed after to rehearse one last time with the new theater teacher, a younger man who had come from Boston and who had created a stir when he stood up at a town hall meeting to ask for more money for the art department and to preach the importance of sustainable theater in rural schools like North Falls. Prior to that day Mathew had been studying his lines on his own for months in his bedroom with his door closed, and Ruth was excited to see what he would do and also glad for it to be over so that he might go outside and play again.

The small parking lot was nearly full when they arrived. Most of the other men had come straight from work, and they wore clean clothes that they had stored in their trucks over steel-toed logging boots thick enough to stop coasting chains. Elam found a parking spot, and he and Ruth walked across the pavement, where they joined with several other families and funneled through the double doors and passed the student-made signs to the auditorium.

The school was hot, and two tall metal fans stood in the back of the auditorium, rotating and blowing warm air. Metal-backed chairs lined the room, and Elam and Ruth made their way to the front row, where they sat down and watched the small stage where the children would soon be performing.

They sat for some time with parents still streaming in and talking to one another and the principal of the school walking around the auditorium shaking hands and adjusting the fans and looking around to see if there was anything else that needed to be done.

When the show was almost ready to begin, Elam removed the video camera from its metal case and made his way to the back of the auditorium, where some of the other fathers had started to gather and pick out their spots. A moment later Della came into the auditorium and sat in the empty seat next to Ruth. The two waited and talked about getting together for lunch and a walk the next day and turned every now and again to observe their husbands, who stood next to each other underneath the EXIT sign.

The principal turned off the lights at six o'clock, even though the sun came in through the windows and lit the room. The crowd quieted save for a few young children.

When the curtain lifted, Mathew was alone onstage, standing just behind a shaft of sunlight holding a wicker basket with a stuffed dog and wearing a frilly blue dress and a dark wig and red lipstick. Some of the people in the crowd started whispering, and a couple of the men laughed and were quickly hushed by their wives. Ruth sat, staring forward at her son with his pale, thin legs and his dress that was a little too short and a little too tight.

And then he spoke. "Oh, Toto, I wish I could go somewhere over that rainbow. I just know there's more to the world than this." He spoke in a high-pitched voice with a slight accent of some kind, and more people began to laugh and cover their mouths.

Ruth didn't turn to see Elam or the rest of the crowd. She sat quietly and stared forward for the entire thirty minutes. Through the munchkins and the scarecrow and the trees and the flying monkeys and the wizard behind the curtain, played by William. When the play ended, she stood and looked for her husband, and when she couldn't find him standing against the back wall, she looked for Mathew. She went to where the children came down the steps to hug their parents and found him. One of the boys bumped into him, and he stumbled and fell on the ground, and his dress came up high on his legs and showed his white underwear. Some of the boys laughed, and a couple of the parents tried to quiet them. Mathew got up quickly, and Ruth went to him and adjusted his shirt and then told him to change with the rest of the children. She stood there in the auditorium and waited while the other parents either looked at her and tried to smile or else looked away. When he was finished, she walked him out through the parking lot, where some of the other children shouted things at him. Ruth watched him as it happened and understood that it wasn't the first time the children had shouted these things, but that it had happened before, possibly many times, long enough for Mathew to stop responding or even seeming to notice.

Elam was waiting in the truck, and he turned the key in the ignition as soon as the doors were shut. Ruth sat in the passenger seat with her feet crammed next to the camera in its big metal case. Mathew sat in the back seat. His lips were still pink where he had tried to wipe off the lipstick and his hair was ruffled from the wig.

"What the hell was that?" Elam asked.

Mathew was quiet.

"What were you supposed to be?"

"Dorothy," Mathew said.

"Do you know what people are going to say? Do you know what they're already saying?"

"I don't care."

"Jesus Christ—what are you turning into?"

"I'm not turning into anything."

Elam reached over the seat and slapped Mathew hard across the face. Then he put the truck in reverse and pulled out of the parking lot onto the narrow country road.

MILK RAYMOND

"How was it?" Milk asked.

Daniel set his backpack on the bench seat and pulled himself up into the truck. "Fine." He reached for his seat belt and snapped it into place.

"Just fine?"

The boy nodded.

"What did you do?"

"When?"

"Today. At school."

"I don't know."

"How do you not know?"

Outside the truck, some of the other children were playing tag while others stood around ignoring the teachers trying to herd them onto the buses lined along the blacktop.

"Can we go?" Daniel asked.

"Tell me one thing that happened at school, and then we can go."

Daniel sat there quiet for a moment. "One of the kids ran away during recess."

"Ran away?"

"Into the woods. He took off during Capture the Flag and wouldn't come back when Mr. Grant called for him."

"Did they find him?"

Daniel shrugged. "I don't know. They made us go inside."

"What's his name?"

"William Nelson."

"Like the singer?"

"I guess. He doesn't talk."

"He can't talk?"

"He can—he just doesn't. Hardly ever."

"Well, shit," Milk said.

"Can we go now?"

Milk started the engine. He put the truck in reverse and backed up a couple of feet so that he would clear the bus in front of him and then headed out of the parking lot. Once he reached the rutted road, the shovels in the truck bed began to clang together. Daniel turned in his seat.

"Shovels," Milk said.

"For what?"

"I need your help getting some dirt for the drive. It's supposed to snow in a couple days. You can't wait until the last minute or else the whole town will be trying to get dirt."

The town garage was located just past the firehouse on a stretch of property used to store plows in the winter and host flea markets and classic car shows in the summer. Milk pulled into the drive and followed it down to where the piles of dirt were spread. He backed the truck up to one of the piles and shut the engine.

The garage stood in a clearing just beyond the last dirt pile. It wasn't really a garage. It was an old agricultural shed with tin siding. There were orange snow plows parked behind the shed, and some of the straight blades were detached and sat in the dead grass.

Milk got out of the truck and lowered the tailgate. He pulled himself up into the bed and grabbed a shovel. Daniel got out of the truck.

Milk stood on the edge of the gate. He adjusted his grip and speared the dirt. He lifted a shovelful and flung it into the bed of the truck. The dirt sprayed across the plastic liner. After a moment Daniel put his hand on the tailgate.

"Use the tire," Milk said.

"What?"

Milk stopped shoveling. "The tire—step onto it and pull yourself up into the bed."

Daniel looked at the tire. He approached it cautiously and stepped onto it and pulled himself up so that he was standing on the tire with both feet. He remained there for a moment, and then he swung his right leg over the side of the truck followed by his left and stumbled into the bed.

Milk shook his head. "You won't get points for form."

The boy stood and untwisted his jacket. A murder of crows leaving the mountains for the valleys counted numbers out over the woods.

"Grab a shovel and come beside me."

The boy did what he was told.

"When you lift, lift with your legs, not your back."

Daniel speared the dirt and lifted a shovelful and dropped the dirt into the bed of the truck.

"Good." Milk watched him for a moment and then went back to shoveling. "Your mother keep dirt on the drive while I was gone?"

"No." The boy wiped at his face.

"Did she keep it clear at least?"

"She had someone come over and do it one time."

"What? Shovel?"

"He had a Jeep with a plow."

Milk lifted another shovelful. He looked toward the trailer and saw an old man step out wearing a brown snow hat and coveralls. "She say anything to you when she left?"

The boy shrugged.

"It's all right to tell me. I won't tell her."

The boy stabbed the dirt. "She got into a fight."

"With who?"

"Grandma."

"What kind of fight?"

"They were yelling at each other. Grandma slapped her in the mouth and Mom hit her back."

"Jesus. What were they fighting over?"

The boy shrugged. "I was supposed to go with Mom. She had me put my stuff in a cardboard box. But then she and Grandma started fighting. He had to come in the house and break it up."

"Who did?"

"I don't know. The guy with the plow."

"She was seeing this guy?"

"She went out at night with him sometimes."

"And he broke up the fight?"

"Mom was yelling, and he came inside and pulled her away. She said she was gonna come back for me. Grandma just kept crying."

"What's this guy look like? The one she was seeing."

"I don't know. He was old. Older than you."

The man from the trailer started toward the truck.

Milk looked over at his boy and then stood there holding the handle of his shovel upright like a walking stick.

"How's it going?" the old man asked.

"We don't need much more," Milk said.

"Oh, I ain't worried about that. We got plenty this year. People are getting their dirt from Breznick Farms. Paying ten cents a pound. Breznick is claiming it's a special kind of dirt. Probably somebody pissed in it and called it blessed is all. I just thought I'd check if you needed anything."

"We're all right. We're almost done here."

The old man nodded. "It ain't no rush. I like to see a man working with his son. Most boys don't like to work. Wouldn't know a piece of hard work if it jumped up and bit them in the ass. I known plenty myself. My old man had me shaving ladder rounds before I knew how to write my name. Never paid me a cent for it neither. His biggest fear was raising a boy up to be spoiled. There weren't nothing worse than that is how he felt. He was probably right too. He usually was. The kind of right where you don't always know it until years later." The old man coughed up something and spit. "All right," he said. He turned to Daniel. "It's good of you to help your father."

Daniel didn't say anything, and the old man nodded to himself a couple of times and headed back to the trailer.

Milk watched the man and then turned to his boy. Daniel looked like he was thinking about something, as though there was something else he wanted to say to Milk about his mother. But he just regripped the shovel and speared the dirt with more force than Milk would have thought him capable of generating.

THE SUN HAD almost set when Milk pulled up in front of the duplex. The bed was filled with more dirt than they needed to cover the small drive and the two concrete steps, but it felt good to get outside and to get his muscles stretched. He looked over at his boy and saw that he was asleep.

He let the truck idle. He thought he should carry his boy inside, but decided Daniel was too old for that. He watched the last of the light play on the wet branches of the trees in the woods behind the duplex and then he shut the engine. He was about to wake his boy when he saw something move from behind a tree in the woods. He studied the tree and saw a black bear emerge. The bear scratched at the bark of another tree and then sniffed at it and pulled something from the trunk with its teeth. It chewed on whatever it had pulled from the bark and then paused and turned and looked in the direction of the truck. It remained that way for a long moment and then began lumbering toward the vehicle. Milk looked over at his boy. His eyes were still closed, his head still pressed against the window. He turned back to the bear. The bear looked to be about three feet tall and its ears were cocked forward. Its head dipped and rose as it walked so it looked as though it was rolling toward the vehicle. Milk straightened his back. He reached out and locked the door and then thought how ridiculous of a thing it was to do. As though the bear might pull on the door handle. The bear stopped in front of the truck and looked Milk dead in the eyes and then started around to the passenger's side of the truck with its head held high. Milk looked at Daniel still asleep with his head against the glass window.

"Daniel," Milk said.

The boy opened his eyes and looked at Milk.

"Pull your head away from there."

The boy sat up.

"Listen to me. There's a bear."

Daniel turned to the window and immediately pushed his back against the seat.

"It's fine," Milk said. "He don't want nothing from us."

"What's he gonna do?"

"He ain't gonna do nothing. He's just sniffing around a bit, and then he's going to get bored with us and head back into the woods."

The boy studied the bear.

"Look at him," Milk said. "It's a sight, ain't it? Wild as hell. All teeth and muscle."

The bear lumbered around to the bed of the truck, and then it rose on its two back legs and brought its paws down on the tailgate. The truck shook, and Daniel gripped the seat cushion.

"It's all right," Milk said.

The bear sniffed the piles of dirt, and then it lowered itself from the tailgate and started around to the driver's side but kept on going. Milk watched the bear trample through the flowers in the small side yard and head into the woods.

"See that," Milk said. "You just got to keep calm. Wild animals like that don't want nothing to do with humans. Mostly they want to be left alone. It's rare they ever attack."

"What happens if they do?"

Milk turned to Daniel. Wide-eyed and still pressed against the seat. "Well then, boy, you run like hell."

RUTH FENN

Ruth heard the truck from the kitchen while she was warming up a pot of soup for her mother. She grabbed her coat and stepped outside and closed the door behind her.

It had begun to rain again, and Della cowered a little as she crossed the drive and came up the porch steps. "Can I sit?" she asked. Ruth nodded toward the porch chairs, and Della went to the farthest one and sat down and wiped the rain from her brow. "Aren't you going to sit?"

"I'm fine standing."

Della was quiet a moment, and then she stood. "I called Leo."

Ruth looked out toward the birches, the white bark dull and stressed by the wind and rain. She thought inexplicably of Elam stepping out from behind the trees, waving his arms as if to tell her to call off the search. That his disappearance had been a joke and that it had gone too far.

"I didn't tell him about Elam. I only told him that Horace went missing and that his truck is still at the Whistler. I would have told him about Elam if I thought it would help. But I figure the only thing he'd do is come talk to you. And you don't know nothing—so that wouldn't help."

"He'll come here anyhow. It won't take him long to figure out they were together."

"That may be. He says the first thing he's gonna do is put out an all-points bulletin. I guess that means he's going to send a message to all the officers across the state with a description of Horace. And then he's going to get a couple people from the state police barracks in Shaftsbury to start calling around to some of the hospitals and shelters. He says there's not a whole lot more they can do for a grown man. It's different for a child."

"I suppose it would be."

"Still. It's good that people will be looking."

The wind blew and swung the wooden birdfeeder that hung from the crossbeam of the porch roof. Ruth had hung the bird feeder a few years back with the hope of attracting mourning doves. Their cooing had always comforted her. But mostly it brought squirrels, who stole the seeds and scampered across the roof.

"There's something else I wanted to say. I reached out to you after everything that happened. With the boys, I mean. I wanted to talk. I tried to call, but I couldn't get ahold of you. So I came here and Elam answered the door. He said you didn't want to see me, and I asked him to tell you about the support meetings at the church. I've always hoped he gave you that message."

Ruth looked out toward the birches again and thought back to the funeral for Della's sister, who had been found in her 1962 Studebaker with a wooden potato masher shoved in the exhaust pipe. Ruth sat in the first pew beside Elam and Mathew. Right next to Horace and Della. The preacher spoke first, and when he finished Della walked up to the lectern and said some words. Ruth couldn't recall exactly how she started, but she remembered how she ended. Della laid into her sister. Called her weak for not giving herself to God in times of trouble, as though there wasn't a thing in the world that couldn't be fixed by look-ing up to the sky and extending a hand. Ruth thought the people in the church would be furious, but when she looked around, most of them were nodding in agreement. Ruth understood then that there was something different about those who put their fate in God's hands and those who didn't. And probably there was something different about Della, who seemed to go a step further and put the fate of the people around her in God's hands, too.

Della's religion hadn't been an issue all those years they were friends. Mostly they didn't talk about it. Both women became pregnant soon after they met, and they had Mathew and William within a week of each other. Ruth supposed that had a lot to do with their friendship. The two also had a way about them that was honest. They weren't afraid to complain about things or talk about things with each other that a lot of women kept quiet about. Things like money and sex and boredom. It was Della who had talked Ruth into returning to work after Mathew was born. Who made her feel it was all right for a woman to want things. Of course it seemed unbelievable now. And maybe there had never been any honesty to it. Maybe all her bold talk was just another sort of lie.

The wind picked up and the bird feeder started to swing again. Ruth watched the string twist around itself.

"Have you got more to say? Is there something else you want to tell me?"

Della was quiet. "No."

"Okay then. Thanks for telling me about Leo." Ruth turned from Della and pulled open the door. She closed it behind her and stood in the darkened hallway and waited for the engine to start and then fade away. When it did, she removed her coat and hung it on the nail. She went to the living room, where her mother sat on the burlap chair with the television muted.

"What was that about?"

"Elam didn't come home the other night."

"I know that. I'm not blind."

"I know you're not."

"What the hell has it got to do with that woman?"

"Horace has gone missing too. He went missing the same night. The thought is they're together."

"That don't seem likely."

"People saw them together."

"You sure he's gone?"

"Who?"

"Horace."

"I told you. That's what Della says."

"Well, she's a liar."

"Not about this. I don't think she's lying about this."

"Horseshit."

"It don't matter. Elam's gone. I don't need for her to tell me that."

Ruth's mother narrowed her eyes. "That woman is the reason the whole town thinks your son is some sort of monster. She could've put all those rumors to rest."

"I know it. It isn't that I've forgotten."

"It seems like maybe you have."

"I haven't."

"Fine, then. Don't listen to me none. Don't expect no help finding him, though."

"I don't."

"How's that?"

"I don't expect no help."

"Good. Because you won't get it. Not in this town and certainly not from her."

Ruth took a deep breath. The television flashed to a man in a blue parka leading cows down a dirt path. "I'm going to the shed."

"Now?"

"Yes. I've been out walking and I'm tired and I need to relax, so I'm going to the shed."

"Fine. Take that old dog with you. He keeps trying to lie on my feet."

"It's probably because he's cold."

"Probably. But it won't be me to warm him up."

"No. I guess it won't."

THE RAIN STARTED coming down harder and at a slant. Ruth crossed the yard with Woodstock following closely behind. The shed was a sixteen-by-eighteen timber-frame structure with plank siding and large windows. Potted plants surrounded the shed—most of the pots cracked and the plants all dead.

Ruth opened the door and flipped on the light. A large oak table sat in the center. A smaller table sat against the back wall, underneath the largest window. On the side of the shed facing the drive were an old cast-iron double-basin sink and an electric space heater. On the other side were the kick wheel and the twenty-six-liter oven.

Ruth hung her coat and turned on the space heater. She removed her shoes and socks even though the floor was cold. She liked the feeling of the hardened clay on her bare feet. She went to the old blue Dansette and placed *Crown of Creation* on the platter, and then she went to the cupboard and removed a block of clay. She set the clay on the small table and removed the plastic and kneaded the clay and pounded it into a ball. She filled a bowl with warm water and carried the bowl and the clay to the kick wheel. Woodstock lay down beside her.

Ruth had built the wheel thirty years ago. The frame consisted of four-by-four uprights and two-by-four cross members. Two flywheels were attached to a long spindle and supported by a lower socket and an upper bearing. It was close to three hundred pounds, and sitting in the shed it looked like some sort of medieval torture device.

She had gotten the idea from an American Indian art magazine she had seen at Hinman's Grocery Store. She had been drawn to the brown slip jug on the cover, and then she had been drawn to the photograph of a woman standing in front of a woodshed shaded by white-flowering dogwoods. But mostly she had been drawn to the idea—almost obsessed with the idea—of building a small shed in the woods. A place she could go to.

Ruth had read the article that accompanied the photograph and then she'd called the North Falls Library and had the librarian order the book referenced in the article from the library in Burlington. When the book arrived, she brought it home and told Elam that she wanted to build a shed and a pottery wheel. He asked her if she knew anything about using a pottery wheel, and she told him she would figure that part out.

The wind blew the thin birch branches, and they scraped the side of the shed.

Sometime after Mathew died, Ruth had been cleaning the dishes when Elam came into the kitchen and asked her if she was going to start the divorce proceedings. It shocked her and she couldn't think of how to respond. Elam met her eyes and then left the kitchen without saying another word, and they never brought it up again.

The rain pounded the roof and ran down the window in narrow rivulets. Ruth placed her left foot on the bottom wheel and flicked her ankle until it began to spin. She wetted her finger and caulked the bottom of the clay so that it stuck to the wheel. Most people used automatic wheels, but for Ruth the kick wheel felt right. She had more control and was more apt to remember the importance of changing speeds. She appreciated the quiet, too. The automatic wheels whined and groaned. The kick wheel was all but silent.

She locked her elbow on her knee and began to center the clay. She wetted her hands and glanced at the simple shelves on the wall opposite the wheel. Most held books, but one shelf held a photograph of Elam standing in front of the partially built shed. His face was covered in a dark beard that he'd let grow from the end of one baseball season to the start of the next. He held a cigarette in his right hand and squinted his eyes at the sun.

Ruth didn't have many pictures of Elam. There were some at the beginning when they got married. And some more when they began to fix up the house. But at some point she stopped taking pictures. At some point it seemed enough that she saw him every day and that it might always be that way.

When the clay was centered, she made a hole in the middle with her thumb and began to pull the walls. She and Elam had drifted a little before Mathew died. But that was what couples did. Thirty-five years was a long time to be with someone. Parts got closer. But other parts got further away. You drifted even from yourself. She thought back to the day she took the photograph. She remembered telling Elam to take the cigarette out of his mouth, and she remembered setting the camera down in a shady spot in the grass after she had taken the picture and helping Elam lay the remaining rafters across the roof of the shed. She remembered the sun that day and the smell of dry earth and wood. But mostly she remembered the way she and Elam worked together. How comfortable it had been. How easily they communicated with one another.

Ruth reached into the bowl and splashed more water onto the clay, but the clay was already stiff and she couldn't seem to do much with it. She couldn't seem to do much with anything.

MILK RAYMOND

In the morning Milk got in the truck and made sure Daniel was buckled, and then he pulled out onto the road, which was covered with a light snow so that the pavement was only visible where the treads had dug down.

"Did you call the school?" Daniel wore his goggles and his winter coat with the polyester hood that scratched every time he shrugged or tilted his head.

"We don't need to call the school."

"Grandma always called."

"We don't need to call."

They moved along the road lined with green pines. All the other colors had turned to shades of gray, like tangled patches of fur.

"I need a note. For tomorrow."

"Fine. I'll write you a note."

"I'll get in trouble for missing school if I don't have a note."

"I said I'll write you a note." Milk adjusted the vents. He had considered dropping Daniel off in the morning, but he didn't know what to expect at the Veterans Outreach Center. He didn't need help with his paperwork; he only wanted help finding work. But he figured that's probably what most guys wanted, and he didn't know if he would have to wait a long time to see someone and then have to sit around and fill out applications or even take some sort of aptitude test like they'd made him take when he entered the military. He didn't want his boy at home waiting on him. He was worried that someone from Social Services would come by the house while he was gone.

They passed a narrow hill littered with old stones where flowers grew from the clefts. "What's your favorite subject?"

"In school?"

"Yes—in school."

"I don't know. Reading, I guess."

"What do you like to read?"

The boy shrugged.

"I can't hear you."

"I don't know."

"You must like to read something."

"I guess."

"So what is it, then?"

"*Wolf and Sheep.*"

"*Wolf and Sheep*?"

The boy nodded.

"What's that?"

"It's about a wolf and a sheep that are best friends."

"The wolf and the sheep?"

"Yes."

"Don't the wolf want to eat the sheep?"

"They're best friends."

The woods broke, and Milk passed a home with a yellow station wagon sitting outside on chocks. He slowed the truck and went around a bend in the road marked with a metal guardrail and a sign with a black arrow indicating a sharp turn. The trees behind the rail were tall and dark and their limbs poked through the utility wires.

"Wolves and sheep can talk where I'm from."

Milk looked over at the boy. "Where's that?"

"Planet Mador—they can talk there. All animals can."

"Planet Mador?"

"That's where I'm from."

"I thought you were from Vermont."

The boy shook his head.

"I never heard you talk about being from nowhere else before."

The boy shrugged.

"You got any pictures—of this planet Mador?"

"We don't take pictures there."

"What do you do, then?"

"We take videos."

"How come I never seen none of them?"

"Our videotapes don't fit the machines here. They're a different shape."

"They wear goggles on planet Mador?"

The boy nodded. "For protection. It's closer to the stars than planet Earth."

Milk looked to the boy and back to the road. "How long you figure you'll wear yours, though—now that you're here on planet Earth?"

The boy didn't say anything.

"You figure you'll wear them when you get your first job? What about when you're old enough to start going out to bars and playing pool and meeting girls? What about the first time you're alone with one—a girl? You figure you'll wear them then?"

Daniel was quiet. He turned to face the window.

"I'm just giving you a hard time," Milk said. "Men like to give each other a hard time—you need to be able to take it."

"I can take it."

"That right?"

"I popped a kid in the nose one time."

"Who's that? A kid in your class?"

"Gordon."

"Why did you do that?"

The boy shrugged. "His dad was in the war. His last name's Beckwith."

"Beckwith?"

"He said he was in the Army."

"I didn't know no Beckwith. There were a lot of guys out there from all over the country—we weren't all in the same group. It's not like school."

The boy continued to look out the window.

"Did he hit you back—this Gordon?"

The boy nodded.

"Did it hurt?"

The boy shook his head.

"Good. The key is to be able to take it as good as you give it."

Milk slowed as he passed the gas station. He studied the large window but couldn't see much past the posters for cigarettes and hot dogs and lottery tickets. He stopped at the blinking traffic light and then turned east onto Route 7. The snow had started to fall. Just light flurries. Barely visible.

"You miss your mother at all?"

The boy didn't say anything.

"It's okay if you do."

"A little."

"What do you miss about her?"

"I don't know."

"What's that?"

"I don't know. Just her being here, I guess."

A metal rake lay in the middle of the road, and Milk crossed the yellow line to get around it. In the distance a burgundy-colored Ford was pulled over on the side of the road and an old man with a ball cap stood in the road next to the truck looking at the front tire.

Milk glanced in his rearview mirror and slowed the truck. "Roll down your window."

The boy hesitated and then grabbed the lever.

The old man wore a blue winter coat and a cap that said MILLER LUMBER. Milk put him at seventy years old.

"You look like you're having some trouble," Milk said.

The old man put his hands on his hips. Behind him, a border collie sat in the driver's seat looking out over the steering wheel.

"It's the goddamn lug nuts," the man said. "Rusted over, I think. I can't get 'em to budge."

Milk looked in the rearview mirror at the empty road. "Hang on tight," he said. He drove a little farther and pulled to the side of the road so that his tires were up on the grass. "Anybody ever show you how to change a tire?" he asked Daniel.

The boy shook his head.

"No. I suppose not. I suppose that would've been my job."

Milk shut the engine and pulled the key from the ignition. He got out of the truck, and a moment later Daniel followed.

"They won't budge," the old man said again.

"Maybe the two of us can get 'em turning."

"I don't know. They're real stuck. Son of a bitch. My wife will worry if I'm late."

Milk walked to the front of the truck. The tire iron lay on the pavement. He bent down to look at the lug nuts, and a blue Honda with a lowering kit drove by, hugging the right lane.

"Sons of bitches," the old man shouted at the car.

Milk watched the Honda head south down Route 7. To the north the road was empty. He picked up the tire iron and secured the lug nut and pushed. It wouldn't budge. Milk repositioned himself. He set his knees on the pavement and then looked back to where his boy was standing in the grass. "Grab my gloves," he said. "In the utility box."

The boy went to the truck and Milk studied the lug nuts. Then he studied the road already covered in dirt and salt and flurries.

"The cold don't help," the old man said. "Cold as hell and it ain't even December."

"I'm guessing you don't have a sledgehammer."

"I'd have used it if I did."

Milk nodded. He looked over to his truck and saw that the boy had climbed inside the cab. His shoes came out the passenger's side door. Milk got up and went to the truck.

"Did you look in the utility box?"

The boy didn't say anything.

Milk went to the bed and popped open the metal case. "Right here," he said. "You know what a utility box is, don't you?"

Milk pulled the gloves from the box and slammed it shut. He carried the gloves back to the truck and kneeled down on the cold pavement. He put on the gloves and checked for vehicles and then positioned his hands on the tire iron and pushed down toward the pavement. The lug nut loosened a little. He moved onto the next one and then the next. By the time he was done, he was breathing pretty heavy and he didn't have them anywhere near off.

Milk looked at the road again. "You got the keys?"

The old man looked at Daniel and then pulled the keys from his pocket. "Her name's Dixie," he said. "She don't bite unless you try to take her duck."

Milk got in the truck, and the dog pressed herself against Milk, panting and drooling on his neck. There was a toy duck on the passenger seat. Milk swung his arm over the back of the seat. "Go on," he said. But the dog didn't move. She just started licking his face. "Christ." Milk put the truck in reverse and backed up quickly about fifteen feet. The dog's legs stiffened. Milk then put the truck in drive and shot forward quickly about the same distance and slammed on the breaks. He pulled the key from the ignition and opened the door. When he stepped out of the truck, the dog shot past him like water through a busted dam.

"Dixie," the old man shouted.

The dog went straight for the road. She crossed the first lane and then the second lane and then started south like she was running toward town.

"Dixie," the old man shouted again.

The dog got about a hundred yards down the road, and then she turned around and started running north along the side of the road. Vehicles were passing. A station wagon blew its horn.

The old man looked like he might have a heart attack. He stood on the side of the road with his fingers jumping around like he was playing the piano.

The dog stopped on the other side of the road and looked toward the old man.

"Dixie," the old man said. He took a step toward the road.

An eighteen-wheeler was coming from the north. The old man turned toward it and then looked back to the dog. He put his hand up as though to tell the dog to stay right where she was. The air breaks hissed and the eighteen-wheeler rolled by, and Milk held his breath until he saw the dog sitting on the other side of the road.

The vehicles kept coming, and Daniel took a step out onto the road.

"Daniel," Milk said.

There was a break in traffic and the old man continued to call for the dog, but the dog just sat there tilting her head.

Daniel took another step into the road. He bent down a little and slapped at his thighs.

The dog looked at Daniel and then started trotting across the road. Milk watched for traffic, but the road was clear and the dog reached Daniel, where she dug her nose between the boy's legs and then rolled over in front of him. Daniel scratched at the dog's stomach with both hands.

"Come on, Daniel," Milk said. "Away from the road."

Daniel stood and the dog followed him back to the old man's truck.

DRIVING THE TRUCK had loosened the lug nuts, and Milk removed the tire. He put on the new one and tightened the lug nuts while Daniel watched from his truck.

Milk put his gloves back in the utility box. Then he went to the old man and told him he was all set.

The man shook Milk's hand. "I appreciate it," he said. "And thank your boy again for me. My wife tells me I got no reason to take that dog with me everywhere I go. I'm too old to run around after her and she don't listen to me none."

Milk looked out at the road. Vehicles passing by now.

"You military?" the old man asked.

Milk faced the man.

"Your sticker there." The old man pointed to a sticker on the back of Milk's truck that a recruiter had given him when he was in high school.

"I was a motor transport operator in Iraq."

"How long you been back?"

"Six days."

"Six days—shit. How are you getting along?"

Milk shrugged. "It'll be fine soon as I can find some work. I've about blown through my hazard pay paying the first and last on an apartment."

"It's getting harder to live out here. You got these people coming from New York City buying homes and tearing them down and rebuilding summer homes twice as big with twice as many bathrooms. Something in the city water's got everybody shitting twice as much as the rest of us." The old man shook his head. "I'll tell you what," he said. "I got a lumberyard just east of here in Wilmington. I can always use help in the winter. Why don't you come on by tomorrow and I'll get you set up. I can't promise nothing past this winter—but it'll get you started."

"I can't take a job from you."

"Sure you can. They ought to have jobs lined up for you boys, as far as I'm concerned. Oh, wait a minute." The old man scratched at his ear. "Tomorrow won't work. I got to be out at one of the sites tomorrow. How about you come by on Thursday—four o'clock. All you got to do is take this road north." The old man faced north and pointed. "You're going to pass a gas station. After about three miles you'll reach Bennett Hill. Take a left on that and just follow the son of a bitch for about six miles. You'll pass a torn-down barn and then you'll see a small building on your right. That's the office there. The yard is a couple miles out. You'll see a sign out front."

"I'll be there," Milk said.

"All right," the old man said. "Thanks again for the help."

Once Milk was inside the truck, he turned and faced Daniel. "You okay?"

The boy nodded.

"I didn't know you liked dogs."

"Did you have one in Iraq?"

"What? A dog? No. We didn't have no dogs."

"My teacher said some people that were in the war get dogs."

"That's true—afterwards. Some people do, I guess."

The boy looked out the window.

"Let's get home," Milk said.

"We're not going anymore?"

"No. I got what I needed for now. Besides, I want to show you something I found last night."

Milk started the truck. He looked in the rearview mirror and saw the old man. He didn't look like he was in a hurry to get anywhere. He was just sitting in his truck wrestling around some with that dog.

BACK AT THE house, Milk led the boy around the side of the duplex to the red angled doors of the storm cellar. "This is ours," he said. "You ever been down in one of these?"

The boy shook his head.

"Well, you're going to start doing stuff now. You're going to start learning about stuff."

Milk bent down and pulled on the door handle. The steel door popped loose. He lifted the door, and some dirt fell onto the grass. He went to the other side and lifted the second door. The door made a loud creaking sound.

"We can fix that with oil," he said. "That's what you do when there's a door that squeaks. You put some WD-40 on the hinge."

The boy looked down into the cellar.

"What I got to show you is down there," Milk said. "This cellar ain't it."

A vehicle pulled into the drive in front of the house. Milk couldn't see it from where he stood, but he could hear it idling. He had parked his truck in the garage. There was only one spot and it was supposed to go to the other tenant. But Milk was paying rent too, and he had a nice truck that didn't need to be sitting outside where it would collect salt from the passing vehicles and rust.

"I'll hit the light when I get down there," Milk said. "You ain't scared, are you?"

The boy shook his head.

"Good. I'm glad I don't have no scaredy-cat for a son."

Milk started down the wooden steps. "I came down here last night looking for a breaker box. You know what that is, don't you?"

The boy didn't say anything.

"It's where all the power comes from. I was trying to figure out why our washer and dryer don't work. I thought maybe the power had been turned off."

Milk reached the bottom of the steps and pulled the string that hung from the ceiling. The cellar was probably fourteen by twenty feet. It wasn't much to look at. The walls were stamped concrete, save for the piece of Sheetrock that separated Milk's half of the cellar from the other tenant's half and a partial wall that came out a few feet. Eight or nine solid plastic chairs with bright nickel-chrome legs, the kind that belonged in a high school classroom, were positioned in front of one of the walls. Milk didn't know what the chairs were doing in the storm cellar, but the chairs weren't what he wanted to show the boy. What he wanted to show the boy was under the workbench.

The boy started down the stairs. He moved slowly, and when he reached the bottom, he just stood there looking up at the ceiling. "Is this under my room?"

Milk looked up at the wood beams and hot water pipes wrapped in yellow fiberglass insulation. "I don't know," he said. "It could be." He tried to picture the layout of the house, but he couldn't remember where everything was. "It don't matter," he said. "This is what I wanted to show you."

Milk led the boy to the workbench. The surface of the bench was crowded with scrap wood, and over the bench was a piece of wood that came down from the ceiling and held plastic jars full of nails and screws. "Look under here," Milk said. He bent down and pulled a black tool bag from the bottom shelf. He set the bag on the floor and opened it. It was stuffed with electrician's tools—wire strippers and crimping tools and meters and testers. "And look at this." Milk pulled a pin nailer from the crowded bottom shelf and set it on the floor next to the tool bag. "See all this stuff down here? This is probably five or six hundred dollars' worth of tools. I never had nothing like this before."

The boy stood staring at the tools.

"You know what this is?" Milk rolled out an air compressor that sat against the wall next to the workbench.

The boy shook his head.

"What's that?"

"No."

"Well—this is an air compressor. You hook up this pin nailer to it, and the air compressor builds enough pressure to fire these nails off like a gun. You don't got to do nothing but pull the trigger. What do you think?"

The boy didn't say anything.

"We can use this stuff. We can get it cleaned up a little down here. Have us a whole workshop. There's a couple things in the apartment that need fixing, and I was thinking of a couple projects we could work on. I used to love doing stuff like this. I missed it over in Iraq. I got to work on the vehicles some. But that ain't the same. There's nothing like fixing up your own space. Building stuff that didn't exist at all until you built it."

Milk looked over the tools on the bottom shelf. He reached in and pulled out a circular saw. He studied it for a moment. "You ever use one of these?"

The boy shook his head.

Milk stood. He unwrapped the cord and blew the sawdust from the blade. "You want to see if this bad boy works?"

The boy shrugged.

"Here—help me clear this scrap wood from the table."

Milk and Daniel moved the scrap wood from the table to the ground in front of the partial wall.

"Now take one of them pieces of wood there."

Daniel grabbed a piece of old crown molding.

"Not that one. One of those flat ones."

Daniel picked up a two-by-four.

"Set it on the table here."

Daniel set the wood on the table.

"You learn to use these tools and you won't ever have to ask anyone for help. You'll save yourself a ton of money too." Milk slid the wood so that a couple of feet hung over the table. "Hold the end against the table there."

The boy pressed the wood against the table with his left hand.

"Not like that. With both hands."

The boy hesitated and then held the wood with both hands. Milk studied him for a moment. "Do you want to try the first cut?"

The boy shook his head.

"Come on."

"I don't know how to do it."

"I'll show you."

The boy shook his head.

"All right," Milk said. "You're going to have to learn eventually, though." He positioned the blade a couple of inches from where he planned to cut the wood and turned on the saw. The noise exploded in the quiet basement, and Daniel let go of the wood and jumped backward. His foot came down on the pile of scrap wood, and he turned to steady himself and slammed his face into the side of the partial wall.

"Jesus Christ," Milk said. "What the hell was that?"

The boy held his face with both hands.

"The blade ain't anywhere near you."

The boy lowered one hand. Milk could see tears running down the boy's cheek from underneath the palm of his hand. "Let me see it," Milk said.

The boy took a step back.

"Goddammit, Daniel." He heard something behind him and looked up at the cellar doors. A large woman stood looking down at them. Milk raised his arms. "What?" he said.

"That your truck in my garage?"

"You're goddamn right it is."

The woman looked over at the boy. "Is he all right?"

"Mind your fucking business, lady." Milk could hear the boy sniffling. A dull pain shot through his temples and settled behind his eyes. "Goddammit," he said. He turned back to the boy, who was still holding his eye. "Come here," he said. "It's all right. Just come here."

THAT EVENING MILK couldn't sleep. His head ached, so he went outside for a smoke. He didn't need to smoke outside, but he wanted to feel the cold and see the night sky. His body shivered as he adjusted to the temperature. He wore his coat and his jeans and his boots, and the sky must have been cloudy because the stars were scattered few and far between like crumbs on a mess hall table where only a handful of soldiers sat. He took a drag and looked around at nothing.

That's what he'd first thought about Iraq. A whole lot of nothing. A country in the middle of nowhere that didn't mean a damn thing. But that's only how he thought of it at the beginning. After a while it became obvious it was much more than that. It was everything. The whole of human existence stretched out as far as it could go and then stretched even further beyond that.

Milk took a long drag from his cigarette. He stuck his hand in his pocket and felt for the truck keys. He looked back toward the bedroom window, where the blinds were drawn, and then he took one last drag and put his cigarette out on the concrete step.

He took the truck slow out of the drive and didn't turn on the headlights until he could no longer see the duplex. His night vision had kicked in by then, and when he turned on the headlights, everything seemed so bright he almost turned them back off.

He headed south toward the center of town and wondered about some of the men in his platoon. He had no intention of seeking them out. To combine one life with the other would be like a bad science-fiction movie where two species were bred together. Nothing good ever came of that.

He followed the empty road past tall trees that made dark walls against the night ceiling until he reached the center of town, where the diner and the other shops were lit up and the streetlights shone like suspended fortune-teller globes. He thought about stopping by the Whistler but didn't feel like sitting on a bar stool and risking conversation with someone who remembered him. He just wanted to drive for a while. It felt good to move. It felt like he might be headed somewhere worth heading.

He turned on the radio and heard a woman singing a song he didn't recognize. He pulled down the visor and removed a disc from the mesh case he had bought back in high school and put the disc in the stereo. Merle Haggard's voice cracked through the speakers. He turned up the volume and headed over the truss bridge, turned right onto Steadman Road toward the tree farms and orchards. The road was wider than the

road that ran through the center of North Falls and it ran straight for
several miles, so that in the far distance he could see the glow from the
grocery store. He shifted in his seat and listened to Merle talk about a
good man gone to waste. He pressed his foot down on the gas and watched
the broken yellow line go solid. He checked the rearview mirror and saw
the headlights of a vehicle in the far distance. He turned up the volume
some more. *I never go around mirrors. Cause I've got a heartache to hide.*

He thought of his boy in his fort reading his book about planets.
He'd known a sapper in Iraq who could name every constellation. Rae
Brakeman. His father was a celestial navigator in the Navy and Rae had
memorized the stars as a child. Three months into a twelve-month stint,
his wife gave birth to a baby girl. As a sort of memento she sent Rae an
expensive telescope, a rigid six-foot contraption. Rae treated that telescope as though it were his actual newborn child. At night he draped it
in his flak jacket and duct-taped a protective insert to each side. Lying
there in his cot inside the walls of the canvas tent with the telescope
beside him, he would go on and on about the stars he had seen over the
Iraq desert that were too far south to see from his home in Minneapolis.
He even talked about taking his little girl to Iraq someday, when the war
was over, to see the stars. They named her Lyra Celeste Brakeman.

He was a hell of a soldier. A track star in high school that set state
records. Stick-thin and fast as the wind. But in the end it didn't matter.
Not fast enough.

Milk listened to Merle and pushed his back against the seat. The
vehicle in the distance had gotten closer. He studied the headlights and
knew it wasn't a police cruiser, and so he pushed down on the gas and
watched the needle cross one hundred. He rushed by a tree farm—the
trees smaller than he thought they ought to be for this time of year. He
tried to picture Lyra Brakeman all grown up. He saw her as having curly
golden hair and a small nose and blue eyes.

The needle crossed one hundred and twenty, but he hadn't created any distance from the vehicle behind him. He thought of what his boy had said about the man in the Jeep that came for Jessica. He tried to recall if there had been a vehicle behind him when he was driving through town. He studied the headlights and the darkened outline of the vehicle. A big SUV of some sort, but he couldn't make out the model. He pushed the truck up to one hundred and thirty. The SUV seemed to be getting closer. He looked ahead to where the road turned into a two-lane road, and when it did he moved into the left lane and slowed the truck a little, hoping the SUV would pull alongside him, but the vehicle followed him into the lane. He continued along the road and then moved into the right lane. The SUV followed. He studied the dark just above the headlights in his rearview mirror, but he couldn't see the driver past the bright lights. He looked ahead to the distant lights of the grocery store, and suddenly he applied his brakes and pulled into the breakdown lane. He watched the vehicle roar past him, and though he couldn't see the driver, he saw what he thought was the Jeep logo above the license plate. He sat there with the engine idling and the trees on either side of him and the overcast sky above and waited for two brake lights to appear in the dark, but they never did.

RUTH FENN

THE LAST TIME SHE HAD BEEN INSIDE THE CHURCH WAS FOR MATHEW'S funeral. She hadn't grown up going to church, and so it wasn't something she missed or gave much thought to. But Elam had attended regularly as a child, and he continued to attend on his own even as an adult. All that stopped after Mathew died. After the congregation made it clear he wasn't welcome.

In the distance the low-slung mountains were just visible, all the color gone from them and nothing left but white and gray. There weren't many vehicles parked along Main Street, and there were no people on the sidewalks. In the distance Ruth could hear the rumbling of a motor along Wicket Street. She crossed the road and came up the stone steps that someone had covered with sand and salt and studied the long steeple and the copper spire.

Elam had been missing three days.

She didn't know what she would say to Jack Barlow when she saw him. She knew Cecil had seen him talking to Elam and Horace at the Whistler the night before they disappeared, but Cecil had also said they didn't talk long, and she wasn't sure she could trust anything Jack had to say regardless.

The church was musty smelling. A corkboard hung from the foyer wall with various flyers tacked under colored-paper letters that spelled

121

JESUS GIVES NEW LIFE. A glass font filled with holy water hung from the chipped wood door frame underneath a metal cross. Ruth could hear faint voices coming from the basement.

Ruth had never asked Elam to go to AA, even after those nights he spent passed out on the bank overlooking the brook. He had hardly drunk before Mathew died, and she couldn't bring herself to blame him for it afterward. Drinking to deal with pain was as old as cursing God for the same. Besides, she wasn't much better. She had stopped looking for work after the light factory closed and all but locked herself inside their home. She thought from time to time of moving to another part of the country, but it felt too much like leaving Mathew. And so she chose to stay and wait like a mother whose child wasn't dead but had only gone missing—as though she needed to sit by the telephone or by the window in case he called or came back.

Still, something had changed a couple of months back when her mother fell coming up the porch steps. It had taken all the strength Ruth had to get her up the stairs and into her bed, where she could get her comfortable and call Dr. Kellogg to come see if anything was broken.

Ruth didn't think her and Elam were ever going to get back to holding hands and watching the leaves turn. But they were going to need each other if they meant to go on with their lives. They might not have wanted it that way, but there had been a time both of them did, and she still remembered that time. The morning after her mother fell, when Elam showed up at the house still smelling of alcohol, she told him that if he came home again after having spent the night passed out somewhere, he wouldn't get past the front porch.

THE MEN CAME out the side door talking and laughing, their boots crunching the frozen grass. Ruth spotted Jack walking toward his truck with a man she didn't recognize. She ignored the stares and waited until Jack finished his conversation, and then she stepped down onto the road and made her way toward the orange pickup truck that bore the word CHEVROLET across the tailgate in faded block lettering.

"Good afternoon, Jack."

"Ruth."

Jack Barlow had deep wrinkles that framed his mouth and eyes. He wore a black coat and a brown Stetson hat with a bronze two-sided ax pinned just below the pinch.

"Cold as a booger, ain't it," Ruth said.

"It wouldn't be confused for Florida."

Ruth watched Jack's breath drift out in front of him. "I'll cut to it," she said. "I heard from some folks at the Whistler you might've talked to my husband the other night."

"Who'd you hear that from?"

"Cecil."

Jack laughed a little and turned toward the lot. Most of the men had gotten into their vehicles. Only a few remained, standing on the sidewalk smoking cigarettes and talking. "Go on and get in the truck, Ruth. If we're gonna talk, I'd just as soon not stand out here in the cold."

The truck smelled like cigarettes and diesel fuel. A figurine of a bent-over woman wearing nothing but a red sliver between her ass cheeks sat on the dash. Jack pulled a cigarette from his coat pocket without producing the pack. "You mind if I smoke?"

"It's your truck."

"That's the way I see it. But you'd be surprised how many people don't." Jack drew a match. A thick vein ran down the side of his neck. "I heard about Elam. I'll tell you right now, I don't know where he is."

"I only want to know if he said something to you."

Jack slung his wrist over the steering wheel. "I seen him there at the bar, and I went over to see if his boss had made up his mind on the new ball field. He didn't know nothing about it."

"What else did he say?"

"Nothing."

"What about Horace?"

"Horace neither."

"Do you know what they were doing together?"

"Don't know and don't really give a shit. Like I said, I thought Elam might know which way George Hodgkins was voting on the new ball field. I would've asked Horace the next day—what he was doing with Elam, I mean. But he didn't show for work."

The flurries started to gather on the windshield, and Ruth could smell the damp weather mixed in with the cigarettes and diesel fuel.

"They're thinking of naming the new ball field after Horace's boy," Jack said. "If it gets approved, that is. It was my idea. I think he deserves it. That boy was a natural. He could've been better than his father."

"He was fifteen."

"Old enough so's I could tell." Jack took a drag and tapped the ash into a sawed-off plastic cup that sat in the console holding some kind of brown substance. "I don't ever recall your boy playing. I mean—I know he was on the team. But I don't recall him playing."

"I didn't come here to talk about Mathew."

"No. That's right. You came here to talk about Elam. But that sail is cut pretty much from the same cloth, ain't it? People said Elam didn't get to be the way he is until after Mathew. But even when we were growing up, there was something off about him. Like trying to put a square peg in a round hole. He used to have that terrible stutter. Of course you remember that. You couldn't hardly get him to speak, he was so afraid he'd lose his words and have to set off trying to catch them. I remember sometime about the fourth grade this handicapped girl moved into town from somewhere up north. Bertie Ann Peas. She got to following the bunch of us around town. Sometimes she'd come to the sandlot and just sit in the grass and watch us play ball. One time she overheard Elam talking and that was it—she got to copying him and wouldn't let up. Like a dog latched on to the end of a rope. Used to follow him around stuttering, 'E-e-e-elam. C-c-c—ome h-h-h-ere. P-p-p-lease.' He never said nothing to her. I thought he might get mad, but it seemed like maybe he was sweet on that dumb little girl."

Ruth opened the passenger door.

"Della already came asking about Horace," Jack said. "She came asking about your husband too. It seems the two of you are talking now. I suppose you could've just asked her and saved yourself some trouble."

Ruth got out of the truck.

"Listen, Ruth." Jack pointed his cigarette. "I don't know what's going on with Elam. But you got balls to come asking about it. It seems to me you're trying to cash in on some goodwill you ain't got."

Ruth shut the door. A few of the men were still standing outside on the sidewalk, and they watched quietly from a distance, and when she passed they made their way over to where Jack Barlow said something and started laughing, and then they all laughed along with him, like laughter was something Jack Barlow had caught and they were all picking at it like coyotes over a small carcass in the middle of the woods.

RUTH FENN

Wʜᴀᴛ sʜᴇ sʜᴏᴜʟᴅ ʜᴀᴠᴇ ᴅᴏɴᴇ ᴡᴀs ᴄᴏᴍᴇ ɪɴ ᴛʜᴇ ᴇᴠᴇɴɪɴɢ ᴀғᴛᴇʀ Cecil returned from work. But after three days she couldn't just sit around and wait, so what she did instead was walk directly from the church to Cecil's house.

The only person there was some stick-thin blonde standing on the concrete steps shoving a corn whisk broom through the letter box.

"It works better if you put it on the floor," Ruth said. "Move it back and forth a little."

The woman looked at Ruth and then went back to doing whatever it was she'd been doing.

"Or you might consider a duster. They got them long ones with the lamb's wool."

"Do I know you?"

"Probably not."

The woman pulled the broom from the letter box. The cover flap clanged shut. She was at least twenty years younger than Ruth, but something worse than time had aged her. Her eyes were sunk deep into their sockets and the skin around her mouth had drawn tight.

"I'm looking for Cecil Higgins," Ruth said.

"He ain't here."

"I guess you don't know where I can find him."

The woman shrugged. "Work, I guess."

"I probably should have figured that."

"Probably." The woman leaned the broom against the letter box and pulled a pack of cigarettes from her shirt pocket. "You some kind of ex-girlfriend or something?"

"Girlfriend?"

"That's right. I don't care if you are."

"No. I haven't been nobody's girlfriend for a long time."

"I hear that." The woman lit her cigarette and took a drag. "I left my bottle of Old Heaven Hill inside on the counter. Come back for it."

Ruth looked at the green single-story house. The windows in the front were curtained.

"I don't figure I'll wait around all day, though. I got the bottle from a guy outside Southwestern Medical. He said it was expensive. Maybe it was. Maybe it wasn't."

"And you figure that broom will get you inside?"

"It's the only thing I could find out back that might. Unless I throw a rock through the window. But . . ." The woman's voice trailed off. She blinked at Ruth over her cigarette. "Why are you huntin' Cecil? He got something of yours?"

"I owe him an apology."

The woman nodded her head like she could understand how that might be. "This is my last day in this hellhole." She pointed a finger to the sky and turned it around in a tight circle. "I'm moving in with my sister. She lives down in Sessoms, Georgia. Right in the middle of a two-hundred-acre pine forest. Ain't nobody out there but her."

"Sounds nice."

"It is. There was this one time, though—about ten years back—when one of them single-engine planes came down right out of the sky and nearly crashed into her living room. Pine trees saved her life. She stepped out her front door and there it was. The plane all torn up into a million pieces. Four of them people dead and hanging from tree branches. But then my sister spotted this little girl still strapped into her seat. Both her legs broke but otherwise fine. She don't remember a thing is what they say. Some kind of shock, I guess."

"I hope for her sake that's true."

"She ain't the only one. World is full of 'em. Sole survivors, they call them, and some of them get together, like a club or something. What I wonder, though, is if you took all them sole survivors and put them on a plane and that plane went down—would all of them survive?"

"You probably couldn't get them on a plane. That'd be your problem."

"But if you could—I wonder what would happen then."

"I don't know. Somebody's luck runs out, I guess." Ruth looked toward the house. An open woodshed stood beside it with the wood stacked high underneath the roof. Ruth remembered hearing that you could tell a lot about a man by the way he stacked his wood. But she couldn't remember what exactly. She turned to the letter box. "You sure Cecil don't have no spare?"

"Hell. If I knew something about a spare, I wouldn't be messing with this broom, would I?"

"No. I guess not. It just seems to me that Cecil is the type to keep a spare. My guess is if you lifted them cinder blocks in front of that woodshed, you might find something more than earthworms."

The woman took a drag from her cigarette. She came down the steps and walked over to the cinder blocks and tipped over the first and then the second. "I'll be damned," she said. She bent down and picked something off the ground and turned to Ruth. "You sure you ain't no girlfriend?"

THE INSIDE OF the house was the same as Ruth remembered. Some of the hackberry bushes along the side of the house had grown tall and were visible through the window. The woman pulled two glasses from the cupboard and set them on the orange countertop.

"What's your name?" she asked.

"Ruth."

The woman filled the glasses with Old Heaven Hill and handed one to Ruth. "I'm Pearl Atkins. My sister—the one I was telling you about—her name is Linda Fay Atkins. She got her name from our mama. I don't know where *Pearl* come from. I asked my mama one time and she said from dirt, same as me. That was about as nice as she could be." The woman raised her glass to her mouth and paused. "Hold on a minute." She held her glass out toward Ruth. "Here's to sole survivors."

Ruth raised her glass, and the two women took a sip.

"You been living in town a while?" the woman asked.

"If forty-eight years is a while."

"Hell yes it is. I was born in Georgia. A little town called Helena. You wouldn't know it. Only thing people know about Georgia is the devil went down there."

"That may be. But they say he settled here."

"Do they? Well, I only been this far north a couple years now, and you might be right. You got nine months you can't go nowhere 'cause of the snow and two months you can't go nowhere on account of the mud. Then you got one month where you can go anywhere you damn well please, but it only takes you a day to find out there ain't nowhere to go."

"People learn to stay home some."

"I guess that's right." The woman finished off her whiskey and poured some more.

"How's his leg?" Ruth asked.

"How's that?"

"Cecil. How's his leg."

The woman studied Ruth a moment. "Oh hell," she said. She started to laugh. "You're the crazy bitch that stabbed that old cocksucker."

"I didn't stab him—I just got him stabbed."

"That's why you're huntin' him, then?"

"That's it. I been calling, but I can't get no answer."

"Well, don't let him milk you for nothing. It don't seem to bother him all that much. He can still do everything he could do before he got stabbed, if you know what I mean."

Ruth took another sip of whiskey. The house smelled like burned wood. The wallpaper was peeling in spots, and the floors had been sanded down so many times there were big gaps between the boards. She regretted not coming to Cecil's sooner. He'd always been good to her and Elam.

"You know what that girl's doing now?" the woman asked. "That little girl I told you about survived the plane crash? My sister kept tabs on her for a while. Last she told me the girl had dropped out of high school and was working the produce aisle at the Piggly Wiggly. You believe that?" The woman took another sip of whiskey. "She ain't done nothing with her life."

RUTH CAME HOME to find two shingles on the ground. She stood in the middle of the drive feeling half past worn out. In the distance she could hear the drumming of a red-bellied woodpecker. She studied the roof and then went inside and put on her sneakers with the good soles and her fleece cap with the fold-down ear flaps. The one Elam thought made her look like an Eskimo. She went to the garage and got the ladder and carried it to the side of the house and secured the rubber feet on the flat ground to the east of the porch with the head leaning against the crooked eave.

The sky had broken, but the temperature remained colder than the underside of a concrete pillow. Ruth thought of Elam and the time he tied one end of a rope around his waist and the other around the chimney to clear snow from the roof. Mathew had been six years old at the time, and he stood outside on the drive with the snow falling and watched his father like he was some sort of superhero born from the hills of Vermont.

Ruth turned to the woods and without thinking stuck her thumb and forefinger in her mouth and whistled as loud as she could. Then she took a step toward the woods and did it again. She watched the wind move a little in the high branches and pictured Elam walking the tree line with Mathew swaddled in his arms, talking him to sleep, and felt tears well in her eyes. She wiped them away and turned back to the roof. She gripped the sides of the ladder and set her foot on the first rung, hoping it was just a couple of loose shingles and not a hole.

She paused when she heard an engine. A black pickup truck turned off the road and came up the gravel drive. The paint was unscratched and the tires looked brand-new. She studied the cab but couldn't see past the tinted glass.

The truck stopped at the top of the drive, and a young man opened the door and stepped out. He wore a Red Sox cap pulled down tight and kept his chin high like he was trying to lift something heavy with it.

"I'm sorry to bother you," the man said.

"I don't know as you're bothering me yet."

The man patted his coat pocket and pulled out a piece of yellow paper. "I got a paper here with your name on it. A woman named Jett Oakley recommended I find you." He stuffed the paper back in his pocket. "This is my boy—Daniel."

The man looked back to the truck and motioned for his boy to come out. The boy got out of the truck and shut the door and stood close to it. He wore an oversized coat the same color as the man's, and he had a large black eye.

"Hello, Daniel."

The boy nodded.

"It looks like he took quite the shot."

"He did. Got it when we were working with a circular saw." The man wiped the underside of his nose. "It don't look good, I guess."

"No, it don't."

"Bad luck."

"Isn't that something?"

"What's that?"

"Bad luck."

The man looked to the boy. "I guess," he said. He waited a moment and then pulled a cigarette from his pocket. "I knew I'd heard your name before. I couldn't place it until now—but I knew I'd heard it."

"That right?"

The man nodded once. "My wife told me about your boy. She heard about it on the television. Your boy and that other boy. I was overseas when it happened."

"You got anything else you want to say about it?"

"No. I'm sorry about it is all. We used to camp up there some for the Scouts."

Ruth took a step away from the ladder. "You said Jett sent you?"

"Yes ma'am. She said you help people out sometimes—when they got job interviews and things like that."

"You got a job interview, then. Is that what you're saying?"

"Over at Miller Lumber."

"Where's that?"

"Next town over. Wilmington."

"Only lumberyard I know of is Russ's out by the baseball field."

"The guy said it wasn't far from here. Just down Bennet Hill a piece."

"Well, that may be. My husband would know better than I would."

Milk took a step forward. "Problem is, I don't want Daniel sitting in the truck during the interview. I don't want them thinking I don't have no one to watch him."

"But you don't."

"Not yet. I'll work that piece out, though."

Ruth looked over at the boy. He was studying the ladder, and she thought that was a good sign. That his interest was in what Ruth was doing rather than who she was—who his father might be trying to leave him with.

"Jett said you might be able to help on sort of a temporary basis."

"I might."

"Said you don't charge nothing for it."

"Sometimes I do, sometimes I don't."

"Well." Milk looked over at the boy. "I guess that's what I'm asking. I guess I'm asking for some help."

"I'm not a babysitter."

"What are you, then?"

"I'm a teacher."

The man lit his cigarette and nodded. "There are some things Daniel could stand to learn."

"What kinds of things?"

"Lots of things, I guess. He don't know nothing but how to watch television. That's his mother's fault."

"Well, I work with clay. I'm not sure that's what you had in mind."

"Working with your hands is good."

"I try to teach other things, too. My students are polite and they learn to observe things—to see things most people let pass unnoticed."

"He's pretty shy."

"He wouldn't be the first boy to be shy."

The man took a drag from his cigarette. "Clay," he said. "Like the statues in the museums? The ones without hands?"

"I mostly do ceramic wares and things. Bailed jugs and lidded jars. But the children do sculptures like the ones you're talking about. They all got hands, though—the ones I remember." Ruth looked to the boy. "Most of the children prefer animals. Or monsters. Some kids only make monsters. Can't get them to make nothing but monsters. Your boy, though—he looks like maybe he likes animals. That'd be my guess."

"I don't know. We never kept no animals."

"You ever work with clay, Daniel?"

The boy wiped his nose. "Some," he said.

"Did you like it?"

The boy nodded.

"Well, that's what I do here. I work with clay. Do you want to see where I do that?"

The boy nodded.

"Is that all right with your dad?"

"That's fine by me."

Ruth started over the dead grass toward the woodshed. Her shins burned from all the walking and her back felt like it was locking up on her. She could still hear the woodpecker in the distance, but she could hear the ticking of the truck engine as well and the footsteps of the boy and his father on the frozen ground as they followed behind her.

She guessed the boy's father was in his late twenties, and she wondered what he had done to get himself involved with Jett. It was usually the mothers that came to her. She couldn't remember the last time Jett had sent a father. She couldn't remember if it had ever happened at all.

"My husband and I built this shed together. I made sure to put in a lot of windows. I like it when the light comes in. I like to be able to see the trees while I'm working. Of course, we got nothing but trees around here." Ruth opened the door. "You don't got to wipe your feet."

The boy entered the shed and stood in the middle. He focused his eyes on the twenty-six-liter oven with the built-in fan.

"That's for when you're done," Ruth said. "You put the clay in there to harden it."

"Like a kiln."

"That's right. That's exactly right. You got one of these at school?"

The boy nodded.

"I got another one out back—behind the shed. It's a wood-fire kiln. A bourry box is what they call it. I don't use it in the winter, though."

The boy went over to where several white smocks hung from a nail in the wall. He kept his arms close to his sides like he was afraid he might knock something over. "We have these at school too," he said.

"Some people like to wear them. But you don't have to. That part is up to you."

"You do all these?" Milk asked. He pointed toward the shelf at the sculptures and the plaster masks.

"Most of those belong to my students. The one on the end there is mine, though."

Milk walked over to the shelf and picked up the sculpture on the end.

"I did that one when we were making portraits so the kids could have something to look at."

"Damn," Milk said. "It could be in a museum."

"I doubt that."

"You could make some money off it at least."

"Not in North Falls. Not unless you fashioned one end so it'd scrape ice off a windshield or made it big enough to plug a stud cavity. Then maybe you could sell it next to the hand warmers in the gas station for about ninety-nine cents."

The man studied the sculpture. "Who is it supposed to be?"

"It's not supposed to be no one."

"Well, it's real good. It seems like it ought to be someone."

LATER, AFTER THEY had gone through the rest of the shed and the boy had even got the wheel spinning just to see how it worked, Milk and Ruth stood surrounded by the withered birches, talking in the half-light.

"I don't like to charge nothing," Ruth said. "But I got requirements. You can think of them like payment if you want."

"Requirements?"

Ruth looked toward the boy, who sat in the passenger seat, fiddling with the seat belt. "You show up on time. Every time."

"I can do that."

"Every time," Ruth repeated. "If you don't know when you'll be back, that's fine—that's what you tell your son, and then you get here when you get here. But if you tell him you'll pick him up at five, you better be here at five or else we're done. A boy's got to be able to expect things."

Milk dropped his cigarette on the gravel, rubbed it out.

"Also, you show up sober or he don't go home with you."

"Shit," Milk said. "You're talking to the wrong guy."

"I don't know who I'm talking to. That's the point."

"Well—that ain't a problem." Milk looked back at the truck. "He's real shy."

"You said that already."

"He's a little strange, too."

"All children are strange. That ain't no crime."

"No. I guess not. I don't know. He's been with his mother for a while."

Ruth studied the man. His winter beard was coming in and the underside of his chin was pink. "It takes some time," she said. "It takes some effort. You might not think it should—you being father and son. But it does. That's true for most everyone."

MILK RAYMOND

MILK FOLLOWED THE RUTTED ROAD. THE SUN SPLIT THROUGH THE clouds in the distance and obscured the hills.

"What do you think?" he said. He glanced over at his boy, who sat with his hands folded on his lap, staring out the window.

"I don't know."

"She seems nice, don't she?"

"I guess."

"What's that?"

"Yes."

"And what about them clay sculptures—doesn't that seem like it would be fun?"

"Yes."

"I don't know why she said that bit about animals."

"I like animals."

"I know. But you could make monsters, too. It's not like you're a kid who won't make monsters."

Daniel was quiet. He started to put on his goggles.

"Let's leave those off a minute."

Daniel lowered the goggles to his lap.

"You might even make some friends," Milk said.

"I've got friends."

"I'm not saying you don't. I'm just saying you might make some more." Milk steered around a wide pothole. "You could invite them over. Some of your friends."

"What would we do?"

"I don't know. You could show 'em the workbench—show 'em the tools."

The boy was quiet.

"Or watch a movie. I could order us some pizzas."

They passed an unpainted barn with busted windows and sections of ripped-away siding. Milk glanced at the gas gauge and saw that it was less than a quarter full. He watched the red needle for a moment and then looked back up at the road and picked up speed. When he passed the bright-blue duplex, he felt his boy's eyes on him.

"I need gas," he said.

He followed the road through the center of town and passed a spare section of woods where he could see the brook and an outcropping of bedrock. He continued until the shoulder narrowed and he reached the gas station. Then he turned on his blinker and pulled into the lot and came to a stop in front of the pump closest to the building.

Milk got out of the truck and took in the smell of gasoline. He looked through the window between the large advertisements and saw that the girl was working the counter. He unscrewed the cap and removed the nozzle from the pump and lifted the lever. He hit the regular-grade button several times until it finally lit up, and then he put the nozzle into the tank and pulled the trigger.

An eighteen-wheeler rumbled by on the road. He watched the numbers on the pump rise and concentrated on the sound of the gas moving up through the hose and let go of the trigger when the number reached ten dollars. He put the nozzle back on the pump and secured the cap and opened the driver's side door. "Wait here," he said.

Milk shut the door and made his way across the puddles that had formed on the lot and pulled open the door to the gas station. The bell rang.

The girl looked up from the counter and smiled. She wore a gray long-sleeved shirt. "You come back for another Chiller?"

"What?"

"Another Chiller."

Milk looked over at the plastic machine. "No. I just need some cigarettes."

"Well, we got those too." The girl watched him for a moment. Milk saw that she wore a silver eyebrow ring he hadn't noticed before. "What kind you want?"

"Wildhorse."

The girl turned from the counter to the rack of cigarettes on the wall. Milk studied her body. He guessed she wasn't more than twenty years old.

"You want reds or yellows?"

"Reds is fine."

The girl searched the rack and pulled down a pack. She turned and placed it on the counter.

Milk pulled out his money clip.

"What's your name?" the girl asked.

"Milk."

"Milk?"

Milk nodded. He took out a ten-dollar bill and set it on the counter.

"I never heard that name before."

Milk shrugged.

"I like it, though. It's different." The girl didn't make a movement for the money. "You from around here? I never saw you before the last time."

"I been gone a few years."

"Where you been?"

"Iraq."

"Damn. You're in the military? I hear it's pretty crazy over there."

"It's a shit hole."

The girl laughed. "That sounds about the same as here."

"It's not the same."

"I only been out of the state one time."

"Yeah?"

"Yup. Went to South Carolina with my aunt."

"How'd you like it?"

"South Carolina?"

"Yeah."

"Better than here. They got beaches. And it's warm. It don't snow there—not ever. I didn't do nothing but lay on the beach in my bathing suit the whole time."

Milk looked toward the window. He could see his boy sitting in the passenger seat fiddling with something under the dashboard. "Maybe I should get another one of them Chillers," he said.

The girl smiled and came out from behind the counter and made her way to the machine. Milk followed her. She wore the same black pants tucked into tall camel-colored boots.

"You want the same kind?" the girl asked.

"I think so."

The girl grabbed a cup from the stack. She put the cup under the spout and pressed it against the lever. The machine made a gurgling sound, but nothing came out. "Shit," she said.

"It's all right," Milk said. "I don't need it that bad."

"I got more in the back."

"It's all right."

"Wait here," the girl said. "It'll only take a minute."

The girl went behind the counter and disappeared into the back room. Milk stood by the machine studying the blue and red straws and picturing the girl. There were no girls like her in Iraq. Not even prostitutes like they had in Vietnam. The only girls Milk saw that looked anything like her were the ones he conjured up in his mind while taking long showers.

He looked at the display of air fresheners. There was one of a pine tree and one of a Magic 8-Ball and one of an American flag. He lifted the American flag from the hook attached to the grid wall and saw that it was made in China.

"Hey."

Milk looked up. The girl stood behind the double doors, motioning for him to come to her. He looked out the window at his boy and then put the flag back on the hook.

The back room was the size of a small bathroom. It was lined with shelves holding cardboard boxes. Inside the room was a door to a separate room that looked even smaller. Through the window in the door, Milk could see a desk and a file cabinet. The girl pulled open the door and went inside and Milk followed. When he got inside, she grabbed the collar of his shirt and pulled him down to her and started kissing him on the mouth.

Milk could feel himself getting hard, and he pressed his body against hers and backed her up to the desk. She pulled back for a moment.

"How long you been home—from Iraq?"

"Seven days."

The girl shook her head and pulled Milk toward her and started kissing him again. She began to pull down her pants, and Milk tried to help her with one hand while unbuckling his belt with the other. When her pants were down, he turned her around so that her hands were on the desk, and he pulled the thin piece of fabric to the side with one hand and guided himself into her with the other. She made a sound like the wind had been knocked out of her, and then she started breathing heavily. He grabbed her tits and then the damp between her legs and then he grabbed her waist with both hands. He felt his heart racing and sweat moved down his forehead and into his eyes. He ran his fingers up her neck and felt the tiny clasp of the chain necklace she wore. He closed his eyes and thought about Jessica and how he used to pick her up at her grandmother's house before Daniel was born and drive her out to the pond, where they would hop the gate and sit on the edge of the dock and look across the water at the large homes and imagine that they might live in one someday. He thought about the last time they went to the pond. Before he deployed. Jessica had bought him a gold chain with a pendant that said ALWAYS UNDER THE SAME SKY. It was supposed to make him feel like they would never be far apart, but it made him feel just the opposite. It made him feel small.

He let go of the girl's necklace and grabbed the back of her neck. The first naked woman he'd seen in Iraq was in a field behind a bombed-out mosque while he was casualty collecting with the rest of the men. Picking up pieces of dead soldiers and tossing the pieces next to rolled-up body bags. The smell of piss and cordite clinging to the air. He came across a headless shape with its stomach unzipped and its legs drenched in blood. It looked different from the other gore, and he grabbed the leg and saw what was different.

He tightened his grip on the girl's neck and pushed himself harder against her backside. He felt himself going soft. He tried to push the image of the body parts drenched in blood from his mind, and when he finally did he saw Jessica again, sitting on the dock, but he could smell the cordite and the piss and decay. It seemed to hover over the water like a fog. He felt his chest grow heavy and he continued to push against the girl's backside, but he was only slapping his body against hers.

"Hey," she said. "Hey."

Milk opened his eyes and took a step backward. The cold air swept over him and he looked down at himself.

"What's wrong?" the girl asked.

Milk started to pull his pants up. "How old are you?"

"What?"

"You ain't more than a kid."

"What are you talking about? You know I ain't no kid."

"What are you, sixteen?"

"I'm twenty-two. What the hell's the matter with you?"

"Bullshit," Milk said.

"Hey, you don't got to be embarrassed. It don't mean nothing."

"I ain't embarrassed. I just ain't attracted to bony-ass sixteen-year-old girls."

"Fuck you."

Milk turned from the girl and pulled open the door.

There were no other customers in the store, and Milk went straight for the exit. He left without grabbing his cigarettes or his ten-dollar bill or turning back to see if the girl was following.

"What took so long?" the boy asked. He had put his goggles back on.

Milk's hands were shaking. He started the truck.

"It's cold," the boy said. "The heat wouldn't turn on."

"That's 'cause the truck wasn't running. Don't you know nothing about how things work?"

The boy was quiet.

Milk turned up the radio and put the truck in drive and peeled out of the lot. He got the truck up to sixty and then seventy once he hit a straightaway. He steered the truck over the center line where the road was smooth and pushed it to eighty. He felt his boy tense up—saw him push his palms against the seat. There were no other vehicles on the road, and Milk steered the truck back over the yellow line and slowed her down.

RUTH FENN

RUTH WAS TRYING TO APOLOGIZE FOR NOT SAYING ANYTHING WHEN Elam hit Mathew that night after the school play. At least that's what was on her mind when she turned down Schoolhouse Road and stopped in front of the old two-room schoolhouse.

It was warm, but there was a fine summer breeze in the air. Ruth and Mathew were on their way home from clothes shopping at the department store. Mathew sat in the passenger seat of the truck, drinking the last of his ice cream from a waxed paper cup. Ruth was listening to a Stevie Nicks cassette tape. She had her left hand out the window holding a cigarette.

The schoolhouse sat on a small plateau above the road, surrounded by trees and green ferns. It was where Ruth and Elam and everyone else in North Falls had gone to school up until 1958, when the town built the new public school to serve North Falls and the two neighboring towns. Ruth remembered when the schoolhouse was put on the market and how strange it had been to see her school for sale. The man who bought it was Jim Luchs, an attorney who used it as an office for several years until it was sold to the state and put on the historic register. The way Ruth heard it years later was that Vermont was the first state in the nation to authorize public education and that the little two-room schoolhouse had been one of the first of its kind in all of America.

Ruth came to a stop in front of the school and finished her cigarette with the truck running and the window rolled down. Then she flicked the butt onto the paved road and opened the door.

"I want to show you something," she said. "Come on and follow me."

Mathew hesitated and then got out of the truck. He looked like a little version of Elam. Ruth always noticed it in the summertime when he wore shorts and his knees stuck out from his thin legs like smoothed knots on a branch. There were times she tried to see herself in Mathew and it bothered her that she had to strain, but then he would do something small, like blink his eyes when he got excited or hold his hand over his chin when he was nervous, and she would see it and her heart would swell.

"Where are we going?" Mathew asked.

"I told you. I want to show you something."

The sun was coming down, and it shone in slanted lines through the branches of the trees that surrounded the schoolhouse.

"This was my school," Ruth said. "You might not think I was ever as young as you, but I was."

Ruth headed up the steep drive to the white clapboard schoolhouse with the stone foundation. The building was in good shape save for some rust on the metal roof and some paint chipping on the low belfry that sat on the roof ridge facing north.

Ruth pointed to a wooden railing running along the west side of the four concrete steps. "This wasn't here," she said. "Someone must have added that on."

Above the door was a semicircular gable window. Two more double-hung wooden sash windows flanked the door. Ruth went up to one of the windows and peered inside. She stood there a moment, and then she lowered her head and started around the side of the schoolhouse.

The woods that surrounded the school had started to choke the small side yard, and the two of them brushed past ferns and tangled weeds. Four large windows ran the length of the sidewall, and through them Ruth could see the small cloak room and then a larger room with a recessed stage alcove and a blackboard.

Ruth wasn't sure what she hoped to accomplish by taking Mathew here, but she thought guilt put wings on your feet and ideas in your head and there was no use fighting either one of those things.

"We weren't allowed back here," Ruth said. She stopped to light a new cigarette and then said, "We didn't have recess like you guys have now. They kept us cooped up in that classroom all day long."

Big chest-high woodland ferns stretched out in front of them. Mushrooms crowded the shaded spots under pine trees where the ferns wouldn't grow. A squirrel rustled the branches of a hemlock and then darted down its trunk.

"Your father didn't know about this place," Ruth said. "Nobody knew about this place." She smoked her cigarette and continued through the woods for several yards before she stopped. "Well, goddamn," she said. She pushed past a group of ferns with cinnamon-colored spores grown up through the middle until she reached a pile of rocks ten yards out and nearly as tall as her. "Rockslide."

"What is it?" Mathew asked.

"This was the entrance."

Mathew stood staring at the rocks.

"Right under here." Ruth pointed to the face of the pile. "I wanted to show you inside there. But it's all covered up now."

"Inside where?"

"The cave."

A breeze picked up and shook the ferns. The light turned a dusty yellow.

"I used to come out here in the middle of lessons sometimes. There was a little window in the bathroom above the sink, and I'd lift myself onto the toilet seat and climb out."

Ruth looked back toward the school. The building was still visible from where they stood—the rear wood door and the small framed opening leading to the crawl space.

"This cave runs at least a quarter mile long. Pools of water in parts and gravel in other parts, just like an old road. I never could see much inside. I could only feel what was there and smell it." Ruth put her hand on one of the rocks and shook her head. "I'd walk this cave in the dark and imagine it was a road leading somewhere different from here. I'd spend the whole walk imagining someplace on the other side, until I started to believe I might just come out there. But I always turned around before I reached it. I guess part of me knew there was nothing there. Now it's all covered up."

Mathew studied the pile of rocks that blocked the cave entrance. His mouth twitched, and it seemed to Ruth like he wanted to say something. But no words came out. He just stood there staring intently at the rocks like he was trying to see inside the cave to that other place.

RUTH FENN

THE WIND BLEW THE VENT DAMPERS ON THE SIDE OF THE HOUSE. Ruth sat at the kitchen table, listening to the clanging sound and watching the window where the sun had gone down. All that was visible was her faint reflection and the shadowed outlines of the tall trees, like rows of paper dolls.

She thumbed the chip on the rim of her mug and thought to call the Shaftsbury barracks. Leo hadn't come around asking questions, and she wondered if he assumed Horace had run off and had only tried to comfort Della by telling her he would do something about it.

"I'd like to see him," Ruth's mother said. "I'd like to see my grandson."

Ruth looked to her mother, who sat in her rocking chair in the living room with the quilt draped over her lap. "Mathew's not here," she said.

"I know he's not here. I'd like to go see his grave."

"It's cold. It's a long walk and it's cold."

"Not right now. But sometime. Sometime before the snow."

"We'll go in the next couple of days."

"I'll go myself if I have to."

"You don't need to do that."

"He's my grandson."

"I know. I'll take you."

Ruth's mother was quiet. She rocked slowly in her chair. The vent damper clanged shut again, and Ruth took her thumb from the chip in the mug and stood.

"I've got to make a phone call."

Ruth went to the hallway table and picked up the receiver and dialed Cecil's number. She stood in the dim light and waited as the phone rang, and after it had rung several times she set it back down in the cradle and hesitated and then let go. She studied the mail that had accumulated on the table. The envelope on top was addressed to Elam. An advertisement for Johnson Woolen Mills. She recalled how Elam had bought her a necklace through the mail for their anniversary years ago. It was just about the ugliest thing she'd ever seen. Large geometric shapes made from brass and colored with turquoise and white powder. She couldn't figure out why he thought she'd wear a thing like that. But he was so pleased to give it to her. He told her it came from New York, and he handled it with such care while he was showing it to her. She wore it just about every day after that. It was ugly as horse dressing but he had picked it out just for her.

When Ruth returned to the kitchen, Woodstock was lying underneath the table. Ruth picked up her mug and carried it to the sink.

"I don't remember the last time I saw him," Ruth's mother said. "I don't remember the last time I saw my grandson."

"It was in the fall."

"Last fall?"

"Two falls ago."

"That's too long."

"It's a long walk," Ruth said again. "It's a long walk up that hill. And then you've got to get over the stone wall."

Ruth's mother continued to rock in her chair. Her gray hair bunched behind her head like a loosely woven nest. "Where do you think he is?" she asked.

"Who?"

"Elam."

"I don't know."

"Who do you keep calling, then?"

"Someone he knows—someone we both know."

"Does he know something?"

"No one knows anything."

"What does he think? Where does he think Elam is?"

"I don't know."

Ruth's mother continued to rock in her chair. "He's lost then—or else missing."

"What's the difference?"

"Whether he knows where he is—whether he knows what he's doing. That's the difference."

"I don't know what he knows."

"You don't ever know somebody completely, do you? You can know a lot. But not all of it."

Ruth went back to the kitchen table and sat in the chair. She removed her glasses and set them on the table and began to massage her forehead.

"Take your father," Ruth's mother said. "I told you he had a heart attack helping that woman push her station wagon out of the ditch."

Ruth kept her eyes closed and listened.

"And that was true. But I didn't tell you that he had been driving the station wagon."

Ruth opened her eyes.

"I suspected something was going on. But I wasn't sure about it. I probably could've figured it out. But I don't think I wanted to know."

"Jesus."

"She called me. The woman. She called me soon after it happened. And then she came to see me. You were in your bedroom, and we sat and talked on the porch."

"What did she say?"

"It don't matter. She was a nice woman. I remember that. I remember being happy that your father had found such a nice woman."

"Jesus Christ," Ruth said.

"Oh, stop it. There's no use getting bent out of shape over it."

"Bent out of shape?"

"That's right. It's long over." Ruth's mother stopped her gentle rocking. "I don't mean to suggest that Elam's done the same. That's not what I'm saying. I'm only talking about how you can't really know somebody. But you already know that—so I guess I'm just talking. I guess I'm just saying things because I'm old and I got nothing else to do with my thoughts."

RUTH FENN

THEY HAD DRIVEN HOME FROM THEIR FIRST APPOINTMENT ALL THOSE years ago in what the forecasters called a weather event. Rain and hail and forty-mile-per-hour wind gusts that shook Elam's truck. The sky resembling some sort of complicated tapestry.

Elam had driven slowly. He fidgeted with the steering wheel and neglected a cigarette. The wipers beat against the glass, and he kept turning to Ruth and then turning back to the road. They were in North Falls before either one of them spoke.

"Mathew," Elam said.

"How's that?"

"That's his name." Elam looked at Ruth and smiled. "What do you think?"

"I think we don't know if we're having a boy or a girl. You comfortable calling a girl Mathew?"

"It's a boy," Elam said. "I know it. I can feel it."

"That's them pork biscuits you had this morning."

Elam shook his head. "I knew it the minute you told me you were late. The name came to me right then."

Ruth shook her head, but she smiled too. She thought of Elam in the doctor's office wearing his oil-slicked cap and dragging mud through

155

the carpeted hallways. Out of place with all the other women. Staring at the wall most of the time so as not to embarrass her but then asking the doctor all those questions she could tell he had been thinking about.

"I got to show you something," Elam said. He turned up Mill Road, where mowed pastures stretched on both sides of the pavement, and then he turned onto Holcomb Hill and followed it straight.

"Where are we headed?"

"I'll show you."

"You taking me to that old make-out spot?"

"It ain't an *old* make-out spot. It's still a make-out spot if you want it to be."

"We've gotten into enough trouble with that kind of thing, haven't we?"

"I'm not asking you to make out with me. That's not why I'm going there."

Ruth studied the road through the wipers. The way the pine boughs reached over the gravel and then pulled back against the wind, the way the road narrowed and seemed to grow steeper.

"You won't make it all the way up there."

"I'll make it."

Elam continued up the road, uneven like a washboard. The tires slipped off rocks and splashed puddles of muddy water. The engine moaned, and he continued up the road until it leveled off, and then he pulled the truck under an old oak tree in front of a large boulder and shut the engine but left the wipers going.

He scratched at his beard and leaned his head back against the seat. Ruth looked out over the rising brook and at what she could see of the rest of the town.

"I never made it up here much as a teenager," Elam said. "I was working most of the time. Besides, there wasn't no one I wanted to bring up here until now."

"I don't believe that."

"Well, there was this one girl. But that ain't the point. I just don't want to go home quite yet is all. I want to remember this day. I want to take the time to stop and remember how it feels."

The two were quiet for a long while. Just the sound of rain and wind.

"I been saying it in the shower," Elam said. "Mathew. Repeating the name out loud. Just to hear how it sounds. Just pretending. Just talking to the water."

"You ain't nervous?"

"Sure I'm nervous. But I can see the mother you'll be, and that takes the nervous away."

Ruth turned from Elam and wiped quickly at her eyes. "You sure you didn't take me up here to make out?"

"I only want to sit with you. That's all I ever want. To be sitting next to you."

"You will be," Ruth said. "I'll make sure of that."

MILK RAYMOND

THERE WERE GUYS WHO SHOULD HAVE BEEN MESSED UP MORE THAN they were. Milk knew one guy who got hit when a mortar round fell from the sky and exploded, sending a piece of shrapnel two inches long careening through the bridge of his nose and into his brain. The man had a two-inch piece of government-issued steel sticking out of his prefrontal lobe, but the only thing wrong with him was that he couldn't blink his left eye. The guy should have felt like the luckiest man on earth. But all he did was complain and talk about how he might as well be dead. Might as well, Milk thought. And maybe he was now. Milk hadn't kept tabs on him. He thought he remembered the guy being from North Dakota or some other place like that where Milk didn't think anybody lived outside of cows and prairie dogs. But then people probably thought the same of Vermont. He'd met one guy in boot camp who didn't even realize Vermont was a state. Thought it was some kind of capital, like Washington, DC.

Milk tore a long piece of duct tape from the roll. He secured it to the wall so that the edge of the tape sat even with the floor, and then he tore another piece and stuck that piece next to the first. He continued until the tape ran the length of the wall and then he stood. His knees were sore from being pressed against the concrete. He looked around at the sepia-toned basement.

One of the things he hated most about Iraq was the sandstorms. There was something about the way they swallowed you. The way you felt like even the landscape was against you. There were stories of soldiers who went so crazy with the taste of sand crunching between their teeth that they would step outside the tent and fire rounds into the shrieking winds. People lost their nerve.

Milk stuck a screwdriver under the lid of the paint can and popped it open. The smell was strong, but it was too cold to open the cellar door, and so he pulled his undershirt over his nose and spilled the paint on the ground at the far side of the basement. The paint was bright blue. It was the same color as the floor of the room where he used to take shop class in high school. Milk grabbed the roller and did his best to spread the paint over the floor. He stopped when he had covered three-fourths of the floor, and he stood in the unpainted section beside the workbench where he had gathered the chairs. He figured he would paint the rest the next morning when the painted section was dry enough to move the workbench. He wished he had a fan to turn on, but he figured things would dry quickly enough in the cold.

As he studied the blue paint—sections of which were already beginning to dry—he heard footsteps over the floor above him. He looked toward the ceiling at the sheets of plywood. The footsteps stopped and then started again. He waited to hear the toilet flush, and when it didn't he figured he ought to go upstairs and check on his boy. Find out what he was doing walking around in the middle of the night. Maybe he was hungry. Milk hoped he was. His plan was to get some meat on the boy's bones, and the best time to eat when a boy's trying to bulk up is late at night when he's just going to lay there in bed with the food sitting in his belly.

Milk went up the steps and pushed open the metal door and stepped into the cold. Moonlight blanketed the pavement. He patted his shirt pocket but must have left his cigarettes inside the duplex. He went around the side of the building and pulled open the front door and entered the house and saw the light from where the boy slept spilling out on the hallway floor. His cigarettes were on the kitchen table, but he left them there and went down the narrow hallway toward the bedroom.

He found his boy naked from the toes up stuffing his sheets behind his headboard. "What the hell are you doing?"

The boy stopped. "Nothing."

"It ain't nothing. You're doing something. It's *what* I can't figure out."

The boy remained facing the bed, his pale butt like a dried stone on a riverbed.

"Well?"

"Nothing."

"We already been down that road."

"I had an accident."

"What kind of accident?"

His boy was quiet, and then it hit Milk. The smell of piss. "Are you kidding me?" Milk raised the crook of his arm to cover his nose. "Why didn't you use the bathroom?"

"I didn't wake up."

Milk lowered his hand. "I gotta potty-train you too now. Is that it?"

"No."

"No? 'Cause it looks to me like you pissed your bed. Is that something someone does if they're potty-trained?"

The boy continued to stare at the bed.

"You got clothes at least, don't you?"

The boy stood still.

"Go on," Milk said. "Take something from the drawer there. Hurry up."

Milk felt his muscles tighten. There were little boys in Iraq that would piss themselves sometimes when you cleared a school or a house.

You told them you weren't going to hurt them, but they just yelled and cried and yelled some more and then they pissed themselves. The soldiers called them mushrooms—as in, *we got two mushrooms over here*—because the piss would start out small and then expand across their pants like a mushroom cloud. Milk watched his boy get dressed. "What were you planning on doing with those sheets?"

The boy's shirt was on inside out and his eyes were red. "I don't know."

"Wait here," Milk said. He went to the kitchen and removed a trash bag from the cupboard. "Put them in here," he said. "Then put the bag outside. In the morning we'll take it to the laundry. There ain't nothing we can do about it tonight." The boy took the plastic bag from Milk, and Milk stood in the doorway. "You know I'm working my ass off for you down there, don't you? Or don't you have any idea about that?" He gripped the door frame. "Getting that workshop set up for you so you won't be so helpless the rest of your life. And you're up here pissing your sheets." Milk patted his shirt again and then remembered the cigarettes were on the table. "I mean, goddammit. Is helpless what you want to be?"

RUTH FENN

IN THE MORNING RUTH WALKED TO THE FRONT OF THE HOUSE WHERE the sunlight poured in through the double-paned windows and pulled open the door. She stood there with her face cold, looking at Cecil, who stood on her front porch looking about the same as he always did, save for his right leg being a little thicker where she suspected a bandage was taped underneath his blue jeans.

"I owe you an apology," Ruth said. "I tried calling."

"Never mind that."

Cecil's truck was parked in the middle of the gravel drive. The plow light was attached to the top of the cab.

"What is it?" Ruth asked.

"I found something."

"Found what?"

"I'll take you out there."

"Is it Elam?"

"It ain't Elam."

"What is it, then?"

"I'll show you."

Ruth looked out at the truck again.

"Come on," Cecil said.

"Have you told anyone?"

Cecil shook his head.

Ruth stood in the doorway for another moment. "I'll get my coat."

THE MORNING WAS bright and clear. Cecil drove slowly and winced a little every time he had to push down on the brake or the gas.

"I'm sorry about your leg."

"You already said that."

"It seems like it might be worth two apologies."

"It wasn't you who stuck me in the leg with a six-inch buck knife."

"I pretty well brung it on, though."

"Well, you pissed off some cowhead son of a bitch—but that ain't really all that hard."

Ruth removed her glasses and took the handkerchief from her pocket and wiped her eyes.

"Those eyes don't seem to have gotten any better."

Ruth settled herself and put her glasses back on. "Not without surgery."

"Surgery ain't a cheap-sounding word."

"No, it's not. It's an expensive-sounding word." Ruth looked out the window at the passing trees and the partial stone walls and the leaves blown to the side of the road. "I think Horace was using again."

"Why do you say that?"

"I just got a feeling."

Cecil shifted the truck into second gear as they turned around a sharp corner and started up the hill past a broken-down barn.

"You don't seem surprised."

Cecil shrugged. "Whole town's using. You can't walk around the Whistler without stepping on plastic bags. Nobody's even careful about it anymore."

"You know where he kept it?"

"Where he kept what?"

"What he was using. I don't imagine he left it out in the open for Della to find."

"I don't know. I don't know nothing about that. It wouldn't be like Della to say nothing anyway. She'd just close her eyes and pray about it would be my guess."

Ruth took off her glasses and rested them on her lap. "I broke into his bus a couple days back."

Cecil turned to Ruth.

"I know it. But I found a hole inside."

"A hole?"

"Went straight through the floorboards and led to another hole in the ground. That one about twelve feet deep."

"What the hell would he need a hole like that for?"

"Keep his heroin."

Cecil shook his head. "That's like storing an ice cube in a freezer room. Besides, it's not something you just hold on to."

"That's what I thought at first. But then I got to thinking it might not be only *his* heroin."

Cecil turned to Ruth and then back to the road. "You think he was selling?"

"Would it surprise you?"

"I don't know that it would surprise me. I don't know that I would believe it either."

"What about Elam?"

"What about him?"

"Do you think he could be involved? Do you think Horace and him could be working something together?"

Cecil shook his head. "No. Not Elam. Come on. You know that, Ruth."

A blue truck was parked on the side of the road above the brook. A man in brown waders leaned over the side and lifted a tackle box from the bed. Ruth watched him until she saw his heavily bearded face and then turned away.

"If Horace were, though. If he were selling, I suppose he'd be working with the guys at the motel. And I suppose that hole would be as good a place as any to hide what they were selling."

"I suppose," Cecil said. "But I just can't see it." He lit a cigarette and kept his other hand tight on the steering wheel. The radio went to a commercial, and it was only then Ruth realized the radio had been on at all. "High winds been coming down from the northeast," Cecil said. "Power outages being reported up in Mudhill—they're saying three feet of snow in North Falls by tomorrow night."

The truck rattled over the frost heaves. They passed a hobby farm where behind a split-rail fence a group of cattle huddled in a circle to keep warm. A small cluster of sumac hung over the road. The wind-blown leaves caught in the thin branches. Ruth straightened her back a little. "Are you really gonna keep driving like this and not tell me where we're headed?"

"We're just coming up on it here."

Cecil followed the road round a bend marked by a yellow sign with an arrow nailed to the trunk of a tree. He slowed the truck and pulled into a dirt drive and came to a stop in front of a wooden gate that marked one of the paths into the forest.

"I saw the tracks from the road." Cecil let the engine run and pointed to a plot of tall weeds under a canopy of hardwoods about twenty feet from the gate.

The truck wasn't visible from the road, but if you were looking in the right direction, if you had someone pointing it out for you, it wasn't all that hard to find. Ruth grabbed the door handle.

"Hold on," Cecil said. "It might not even be Elam who left it here."

"What does that mean?"

"It just means we don't know what we're looking at."

Ruth opened the door. She pushed through weeds and swiped away low-lying branches. She ducked under the long limb of a maple, and when she reached the truck she pulled open the driver's side door.

The bench seat had three spots of blood spreading out like the seat had begun to rust. There was blood on the steering wheel and another spot of blood on the door handle.

Cecil came up next to Ruth and stood looking into the truck. "Came upon it late yesterday. I spent most of the night searching the woods. I wanted to see if there was somebody needing help before I came for you."

"Or a body."

Cecil spat onto the ground. "Or a body."

There was some dirt and bits of gravel and a paper coffee cup on the floor of the truck next to a couple of red ratchet straps, but other than that the truck looked empty. "What is this, then?" Ruth asked. "What the hell is this?"

"I don't know."

Ruth reached into the truck and pulled open the glove box. An empty pack of cigarettes and registration papers spotted with oil. She closed the glove box and faced Cecil. "And you still don't think they were involved in something?"

"It might not even be Elam. Could be somebody stole the truck."

"And then what? Where does that leave my husband?" Ruth shut the door. She looked into the thick stands of maple and beech. "It was dark," she said. "When you looked?"

Cecil nodded. "About one in the morning."

"Maybe you missed something."

"It's a lot of woods."

"I'll look again."

"Ruth."

"You don't need to help. You've done plenty."

"What about calling Leo?"

Ruth wiped her eyes with her sleeve. "I got somewhere I want to look first."

"I already checked where they found your boy, Ruth. There ain't nothing there."

"I'll check again."

"Fine," Cecil said. "I'll call Carl and Eddie, at least. We'll start a few miles out and work our way back." He started for his truck and then turned back. "Don't get too far out there, Ruth. You can maybe make three or four miles and still get back. The temperature's going to drop. Besides." Cecil looked toward Elam's truck and shook his head. "You just got to be careful."

THE GREEN MOUNTAIN National Forest stretched more than four hundred thousand acres. Some of it was marsh and pond. But the wilderness that immediately surrounded North Falls was thick forest. Third-growth beech and ash and birch and maple. Steep hills and a massive ridgeline that cut through the wilderness like an artery delivering blood to the rest of the forest. Ruth could see a narrow shaft of light coming through the open canopy and shining down on a skid trail where several large stones were sprawled across the path.

She swatted branches like steel tines from her face and headed deeper into the woods. The ground was hard and uneven. Trees had fallen every which way—deadfall from the storms the previous winter. She came upon the remnants of a crumbled stone wall and continued up the incline to where the ground leveled. She breathed heavily and looked back in the direction of the truck to see that she'd only gone a few hundred paces.

When they found Mathew, they had entered the forest from the Sandy Pond entrance about a half mile up the road from where the truck was. So while Ruth didn't know the woods well, she knew enough to know that the stream was about a half mile west of where she stood, and if she followed it for another mile or so north she would come to the spot where they'd found her boy. She stood listening but couldn't hear the sound of running water. She was too far. She removed her glasses and wiped her eyes and headed north.

HER FIRST THOUGHT had been that Mathew and William were murdered. It was only later that she wondered why she hadn't thought of an animal. The boys were alone in a tent in the middle of the woods, covered in bite marks deep enough to pierce their skin. There were bears around in the summer, and coyotes. Some people had even been reporting seeing catamounts. A week earlier Ruth had read about a high school girl who was jogging down Haystack Road when she saw one in a tree, and so the story should have been fresh in her mind. But she thought first of murder—of some hermit whose quiet might have been disturbed by the boys.

The other thing that came to her was an image. It came in a flash but didn't clear up until several days later. A group of children standing in a circle in the woods. Pale and faceless as little moons. They were looking down at something, and Ruth came to believe it was her boy. She didn't believe in things not born from this world, but she wanted to believe those children existed somewhere and that they were helping Mathew.

The flurries started to fall, and the sky turned the color of dusted stone. Ruth balled her fingers and tucked them inside the sleeves of her coat. She kept her eyes on the ground and navigated between tall trees, but all she saw were rocks and leaves and pockets of untouched snow.

The woods seemed to insulate her from the world. There were sounds, but they weren't the sounds of human life. She thought of her husband visiting the spot where their boy was found for some unforeseeable reason, and if he was there and unharmed, there would be hell to pay. Hell to pay for scaring her and for making her walk these same woods looking for another body.

She pushed through a tangle of low branches, and when she was clear of them she could see the stream in the distance. She looked north but could not yet see the ridge or the fallen tree.

She continued along the stream at a steady pace and then slowed, not sure that she wanted to get where she was going. She took to noticing things she hadn't the first time around. Ferns protected by big hemlocks. Steep banks carved out by water. An old pine growing on a rock, its roots wrapped around the stone like an eagle's claw.

She continued for some distance before spotting the downed red maple that stretched from the top of the ridge to the stream. A section of the tree had split and was near hollow inside, and there was fungus growing along the hollow parts. She was exhausted, but she climbed the stony ridge and stood in the clearing where the tent had been. There was nothing there now. She scanned the surrounding woods and closed her eyes and pictured Mathew.

She had come to understand that Mathew and William loved one another. Whether they were lovers exactly didn't seem to matter. She understood that they had cared for one another and that they had found comfort in one another. It brought her some peace now, but for three years she had carried the guilt of having turned from it. She had treated her son like a tanager that she could hear but not see. Content to know he was there but afraid to flush him out from the thick foliage where his color might be glimpsed.

She told herself that she had only been worried about him. And that was partially true. From early in his life, she had been scared to death of what the world might do to a boy like Mathew. But her fear had kept her from accepting him. And it seemed so foolish now. Not to embrace her own child. She wished she could tell him she was wrong. She hated that he might have died feeling unwelcome. As though he had carried inside him a blinding light that made people turn away.

Ruth heard footsteps over the snow. She opened her eyes. The wind swelled and the pines whistled and she lost the sound. She held her breath, but it was gone.

The sky seemed to be coming down on her. The flurries piled on her shoulders and clung to her hair. She heard footsteps again. The sound of crunching leaves. She looked around the woods. Nothing but tall trees. Some of them almost two hundred years old. Her eyes moved from tree to tree. No telling what they had seen. But none of them were talking. She couldn't hear a damn thing.

RUTH FENN

Ruth returned to Elam's truck out of breath. She stood for a moment with her hands on her hips—letting her heart slow—and then reached under the trailer hitch and pulled out a small plastic box. She removed the spare key and went to return the box but hesitated when she caught a glimpse of the aluminum toolbox mounted in the bed.

The toolbox was unlocked. The hasp was closed and the padlock hung from the loop, but the shackle was slightly uneven with the body. It wasn't like Elam to leave it unlocked, not unless he had opened it recently and the padlock had frozen to the point he couldn't get it closed again.

Ruth put the spare key in her pocket and pulled down the tailgate. She climbed into the bed and stepped over fresh snow and knelt down in front of the toolbox. She pulled the padlock from the loop and flipped open the hasp.

The toolbox was mostly full. She dug through battery cables and light sticks and several metal tools whose utility she didn't recognize, and then she leaned back on her heels and studied the contents feeling like something was missing.

"I'll be damned," she said. She slammed the toolbox closed and got down from the bed of the truck. She opened the driver's side door and looked around the truck again and then pulled the seat forward. A silver space blanket lay folded behind the seat. She lifted it and a couple of Sterno heaters, and a half-drunk bottle of whiskey fell from the blanket. She pulled the blanket to her nose and smelled Elam—cigarettes and loam.

She climbed into the driver's seat and shut the door and turned it all over in her head. Elam was coming back to the truck to sleep at night. She was sure of it. It didn't explain the blood and it didn't explain where he was coming from or why he didn't just come home, and that worried her. She figured whatever he was doing was bad enough that he wanted to keep her out of it, and she felt ashamed for allowing him to think he could. She knew she had brought it on herself by keeping her distance. But that wasn't how it was going to be anymore. They'd promised themselves to each other a long time ago, and if he wouldn't come back to her on his own, she was going to force his hand. It was a gamble, but if she took his truck and left him without a place to sleep at night in this cold, he wouldn't have a choice but to come home to her, or at least he'd know she'd found him and was asking him to come home.

She looked out the window at the woods. "Whatever this is," she said to the young beech trees still holding their leaves, "it's gone on long enough." She put the key in the ignition and got the truck to start after holding the key for several seconds and pumping the gas. Cold air pushed through the vents. News radio played quietly. She clicked off the radio and backed the truck over stiff weeds and then got herself turned around and pulled out onto the paved road.

SHE HEADED EAST and turned onto Putnam Road and followed it past broken split-rail fences and one-hundred-year-old homes. The pale sun followed in the rearview mirror like a stray dog. The town looked abandoned in the cold winter morning. Nobody out in the fields or driving the roads. Only Elam's truck moving against the steadfast quiet. She approached Steele Road and made a quick turn.

The Flakers lived in a post-and-beam house with a stone chimney and a large garage with four square windows attached to the side. Dottie Flaker was the boy's grandmother. A stout woman who'd taught the second grade when the school was located behind the First Methodist Church. Lou Flaker was a wiry man who had worked just about every job there was in his lifetime. Last Ruth heard, he had taken on woodworking and was selling pieces out of his garage and at flea markets on summer weekends.

That would have been several years ago. Ruth didn't know what the Flakers were doing now, save for housing a grandson who was supplying heroin to half of North Falls.

She was careful to park Elam's truck on the side of the road at the bottom of the driveway under an old oak tree. She glanced in the rear-view mirror at the empty road and then got out and started up the drive. Her boots crunched the gravel, each step like the spade of a shovel biting into the ground.

A Honda with tinted windows and an oversized exhaust was parked in front of the garage. Fart pipes, Elam called them.

The wood of the door was marked with low vertical scratches, like some animal had tried to claw its way in. A welcome mat like the one at the Whistler sat on the ground dusted with cigarette butts. Ruth raised her fist and knocked. The door rattled.

Somebody was in the house. She could hear them moving around. Someone said "Shit," and another voice asked a question, and then she heard the creaking of stairs and someone said, "I don't know." A moment later the door opened.

Johnny Flaker stood in the doorway in his jeans and no shirt. A gold necklace hung down from his bony shoulders.

"What do you want?"

"I got to talk to you," Ruth said.

Ruth could see into the house. Piles of clothes lay on the hardwood floor next to slumped cardboard boxes. The door that led to the basement was open and the light was on below.

"You got to get off my property is what you got to do."

"You can talk to me. Or I can call down to my friend to come up here. The one you stabbed in the leg."

"That big son of a bitch?" The boy looked past Ruth. "Why ain't he up here?"

"I told him to wait at the bottom. I didn't think his temper could take looking at you."

"Shit," the boy said. "Tell him and his temper to come on up here."

Ruth turned from the boy and started down the drive.

"Hold on," Johnny said. "What the hell do you want? I got shit to do."

Ruth stopped. She wondered if the boy's grandparents were dead. She and Elam used to read the obituaries every Sunday morning, but they had canceled their newspaper subscription after Mathew died. She turned back to the boy. "You knew the men I described. Horace at least. I could tell."

The boy licked his teeth. "That's what this is about? Your husband ran off and you expect me to know where he's gone to?"

"He ain't my husband."

"What is it to you, then?"

"He was with my husband. Both of them are missing. And I don't think they run off."

The boy laughed. "I don't know where he's at."

"You've seen him, though."

"The short one. With the limp. I seen him a few times. I don't know the other guy."

"When was the last time you saw him?"

"Couple nights before you came up, I guess."

"A couple? Not the night before?"

"I said a couple. He was asking for Dwyer. He wasn't there, though."

"Dwyer's the one in the lawn chair? The man with the red muttonchops?"

The boy didn't say anything.

"You sold to him? To Horace?"

"I sell to anyone that's got money to pay."

Ruth looked past the boy. "I knew your grandmother," she said.

"Everybody knows everybody in this hellhole. What's your point?"

"I knew your parents too. Years ago. When you weren't doing much more than sucking on a pacifier. I wonder what they'd think of what you're doing now."

The boy laughed. His teeth were white and straight across his mouth like a picket fence. He scratched at the back of his neck and studied Ruth for a long moment. Then he smiled and shook his head and pulled out a small plastic bag from his pants pocket that looked like it held a clod of dirt. He opened the bag and licked his thumb and stuck it into the bag and brought it to his nose and breathed in and out slowly, and then he shrugged. "You see anybody here who cares?"

When Ruth didn't answer, the boy turned to the staircase. "Kelly," he shouted. "Come up here a minute. I got something for you." He turned back to Ruth and held out the bag. "First time is free," he said.

"That's the only time, though, ain't it?"

The boy started to laugh. "That's like some poetry-type shit."

Ruth started down the drive. She heard the girl come up to the door and ask Johnny what he wanted. But Ruth didn't turn around. She heard Johnny say something and close the door. She remembered the night his parents were killed. She'd seen the car after, in the tow lot, folded like an accordion with the other car's license plate melded onto the engine. Maybe it was better for them that they were gone and didn't have to see what had become of their son. But then, things might have turned out differently if they were still alive.

Ruth got in the truck at the bottom of the drive. The flurries were coming down slowly. She knew it was here, then. The first snowstorm. Some people pointed to sparrows or the direction of the wind or the way dogs started sleeping against walls, but Ruth knew it wasn't any of those things. The first big winter storm in Vermont announced itself by the speed at which the snow came down from the sky—when it wasn't in a hurry, when it fell like it was going to be around for a while.

Inside the truck, her eyes watered. She felt like she had gone somewhere past tired and her body was stuttering on fumes and her mind was worn down flatter than a plate of piss. She turned on the radio. The same news radio that had been on when she first started the truck. She hadn't known Elam to listen to news radio. But then there were things about him she didn't know. And it seemed to her that not knowing things had become about as common as sitting her bare ass down on a cold toilet seat.

She put the truck in drive and pulled onto the road. She hoped she was doing the right thing. Hoped that by taking the truck, she was forcing Elam home and not into some more dangerous fate. She wouldn't bet on her decisions anymore, but she figured she had to keep making them just the same.

MILK RAYMOND

It was full light when Milk arrived at the small cottage with the Betty Boop windmills and wood cutouts in the front yard. Jessica's grandmother was on the porch in her nightgown, pushing a broom over the concrete steps. The grass was overgrown and the leaves unraked. There was mold growing on the side of the stone birdbath, and some of the mesh had come loose from the chain-link fence at the south side of the lot.

Milk waited in his truck with the engine idling. He had come home to find a note on the door from Jett informing him that she would be visiting Marcy to get some of the boy's things and that if he wanted to be there to help pick some toys out he could. Milk looked over at his boy, who watched Marcy from the passenger seat. He glanced at the clock and then the rearview mirror. Milk knew Jett wanted to be there to make sure he didn't do anything stupid, but he wasn't going to do anything he'd regret, and besides, he was already running late for his interview.

"You wait here," Milk said.

"I want to come in."

"Wait here." Milk shut the engine and got out of the truck and headed toward the house.

179

The flat stones that served as a path to the concrete steps were cracked and barely visible underneath the tall grass. The curtains were drawn closed, and mail had collected in the wall-mounted mailbox.

Marcy didn't look up until Milk reached the steps. When she did, she had a worried look on her face, and she held the broom close to her chest with both hands.

"I'm just here for some of the boy's things," Milk said. "I don't want to get into it with you."

Marcy shook her head.

"I won't be but a minute."

Milk came up the steps. Marcy took a small step backward and pulled the broom closer to her chest.

"I'm going inside now," Milk said.

Milk moved past Marcy and opened the door. The house smelled like something had crawled inside the walls and died. There were ten or fifteen empty cans of tomato juice stacked on the coffee table.

"Fucking hell," he said.

He went to the boy's bedroom. The bed was made and his toys put away in yellow bins, save for a worn plastic box of wildlife discovery cards that sat open on the floor. He opened the closet doors and grabbed some clothes from the top shelf and stuffed them into a wicker hamper that sat in the corner of the closet. He looked around the room and picked out some toys and stuffed them into the hamper. He spotted the poster of the solar system above the bed and pulled the tacks free from the wall and put them in his pocket and then rolled up the poster and set it on top of the laundry basket.

He left the boy's bedroom and stopped at the door of what had been Jessica's room. He set the laundry basket on the ground and peered into the bedroom. There were clothes piled on the floor and the sheets were pulled back. The blind hung crooked over the window. He went to the nightstand and pulled open the drawer and found empty bottles of pain pills.

"She's already gone."

Milk turned and saw Marcy standing in the doorway holding the broom.

"Who?"

"You're too late. She's gone to be with her boy. I know you never wanted that. You only wanted her. Well, she's wised up now. She's had a reckoning."

"What the hell are you talking about?"

"She's gone. That's what the hell I'm talking about." Marcy mumbled something unintelligible. Her eyes began to dart back and forth.

"I've got all I need," Milk said.

"Get the hell out of my house."

"I'm leaving."

Marcy stood shaking her head. Her eyes suddenly flashed something different. "You won't take her from me," she said. "You won't." She raised the broom and started toward Milk. She got four or five steps before her knee struck the side of the bed and she lost control and fell hard. The broom skidded across the pine floor.

Milk reached down to help her, but she made a fist and swung and struck Milk's leg weakly. "Get out of here," she shouted. Spit hung from her bottom lip, and her nightgown had fallen from one shoulder and exposed her sagged breast. "You won't take my granddaughter. You won't take my Jessica."

Milk pushed past Marcy and grabbed the laundry basket and continued down the hall and out the front door. Jett was getting out of her car when he stepped outside.

"Milk," she said.

"She's crazy," Milk said. "She don't know what she's saying."

"Who? Marcy? Is she all right?"

"No, she ain't all right. She needs help."

Milk opened the truck door and set the laundry basket inside and then he got into the truck. He started the engine and left Jett standing in the driveway. He pulled onto the road and glanced in the rearview mirror and saw her starting for the house.

RUTH FENN

Ruth parked Elam's truck in the gravel turnoff at the bottom of the drive so that her mother wouldn't see it. She sat there with her back aching and tried to pick up more of the scent of her husband on the steering wheel and in the seat, but all she smelled was damp and cold and something close to burning plastic.

She came up the porch steps and entered the quiet home. The light shone in through the window, and she stood there in the hall for a moment contemplating her next move. Wondering what Elam would do if it were her that had gone missing.

When she reached the living room, she heard an engine and returned to the front door in time to see a black pickup truck with tinted windows tear up the drive like it was trying to outrun the cold. It surprised her a moment, and then she remembered the young man and the boy and the interview at the lumberyard. She stepped outside and put her hands in her coat pockets and waited. The truck came to a stop, and the man got out and started toward her and then turned back to the truck and opened the passenger door and told the boy to hurry up. The engine ticked and steam rose from beneath the hood.

"I'm sorry," the man said. "I know we're late. We had to pick up some of Daniel's things."

"It's fine."

"I know you said—" The man's voice trailed off.

The skin around the boy's eye had improved, but it still looked like a piece of fruit that had been left out in the sun too long.

"I hope it's still all right. I don't think this will take long. It's right up the road like I told you—up on Bennet Hill."

"It's all right." Ruth looked at Daniel, who stood in the middle of the drive with his jacket twisted and only partially zipped. He wore blue jeans stained below both knees, and the laces of his sneakers were untied and traveled in opposite directions. He held a book close to his chest.

The boy's father walked around the truck to the driver's side door. He thanked Ruth again and got into the truck and backed down the drive without saying goodbye to his son.

"He's in a hurry, I suppose," Ruth said.

The boy didn't say anything. He stood there hardly more than nothing. Like a shadow cast into a narrow crevice. And then he cowered a little, as though trying to hide from even that.

"What book have you go there?" Ruth asked.

The boy pulled the book from his chest. "It's about frogs."

Ruth's mind went to Mathew. An afternoon in August when Mathew was six or seven years old. Ruth was sitting in her chair in front of the tube television. The temperatures that week had broken local records. Hotter than a tin can in hell is what most people were saying. The television wasn't on, but Elam had set a little metal fan on top, and from it he hung a cloth that had spent all night in the freezer, so it was about the coolest place in the house save for the basement.

She heard Mathew that afternoon before she saw him. Just a distant whining like an engine that couldn't get started. A moment later he came busting through the screen door and straight to his room, crying like someone was squeezing the tears right out of him.

Ruth got up from the chair and followed after him. She didn't bother with knocking. She just went straight into his bedroom, where he sat on the edge of his bed with arms clenched across his stomach. His face was pink from the sun, and she could see on his collar where he had wiped the snot from his nose. She grabbed hold of his tiny arms and unclenched them and looked him in the eyes and asked him what was wrong. He just looked down at his lap and kept on crying, and so she sat right beside him on the bed and waited there until he wanted to talk.

It took him a moment, but soon enough he got going. He told her how he had gone over to Brad Hall's house and how Nick Solomon was there too. He told her how the two of them had been collecting toads all morning and how they had a good two dozen of them in a cardboard box in the grass behind Brad's house. Mathew wiped at his nose as he told how Nick was standing next to the cardboard box and how Brad was standing about twenty feet from Nick with his back to the trailer holding a plastic bat. How Nick was picking toads out from that cardboard box and tossing them underhand at Brad, who cocked his elbows back and swung hard enough that his back heel dug out clumps of grass from the ground.

Some of the toads exploded on impact. Others Brad managed to get ahold of just right and launch over the tops of the white pines that surrounded the property. Mathew kept wiping his nose while he told Ruth. Told her how Nick held up his stained palm and laughed about how the toads were pissing themselves in his hand. Like they knew what was coming—like they could somehow foresee it.

"My dad said I could bring it," Daniel said. "He said it would be okay."

"Of course," Ruth said. "Of course it's okay. Come on. Let's get out of this cold."

The gravel crunched under their boots. Thin stalks of twinflowers bent in the wind. When they reached the shed, Ruth turned on the light and flipped on the space heater. The heater glowed orange and the fan buzzed.

"I normally get it warmed up beforehand. It don't take long though. Are you cold?"

The boy shook his head.

"You got a nice jacket there, it looks like. Did your father get that for you?"

The boy shrugged his shoulders.

"Well, it's a nice one." Ruth stood in the middle of the shed with her hands on her hips. Her mind kept returning to the truck in the woods. She wondered if she should call Leo and tell him about it. She wondered if there was any good it might do, but told herself she needed to wait for Cecil—give him time to find whatever he might find. Besides, she needed to give her attention to the boy. She knew it was important to do that much. "What are you working on in art right now?"

"Watercolors."

"That's good." Ruth went to the cupboard where she kept the clay. It smelled like damp paper. "What else are you doing in school? Do you have a subject you like?"

"Reading."

"Reading. That's good. My boy liked to read. He liked science too. He was always reading about astronomy." Ruth thought back to a time just before Mathew died. When she had gone through his room looking for clues as to what was bothering him and found a book on his desk with a leaf marking a page about black holes. She recalled sitting down at his desk and reading the marked page. Trying to imagine what it was that drew him to that book and that page. Trying to imagine it when she should have been asking him about it.

She removed a block from the shelf. "Have a seat," she said.

Daniel came around the table and dragged one of the chairs back. The seat was covered in dried red paint, and Ruth's heart skipped a beat when she saw it, even though the paint had been there as long as she could remember.

Daniel sat down in the chair, and Ruth unwrapped the clay and set it in front of him. She stood there a moment gathering her thoughts, and then she sat down at the table across from him.

"I wonder if you're excited or if you're nervous," she said. "Or if you're thinking about your father or wondering about me." Ruth looked out the tall window. "I used to go on long walks with my father, and on our walks he would give me a nickel for each one of my thoughts. It got to add up to something."

The boy was quiet.

"It's okay if you don't want to tell me what's on your mind just yet. I've put you on the spot. I had a thought of my own, though. The first time I saw you, I was thinking to myself that this little boy has a talent. I'm not sure what it is yet exactly. It might be working with clay. Or it might be doing something else—like drawing with charcoal. It might even be drawing one specific thing, like a frog. But I was sure of it the first moment I saw you." Ruth paused. "I'm excited to find out what it is—your talent. That's the other thing I was thinking. I'm excited to find that out."

Ruth studied Daniel a moment more and then stood. "All right," she said. "Now there are all sorts of tools we use when working with clay. And there are all sorts of things we do to prepare the clay—to make it easier to work with. But I don't want you to think about any of that right now. What I want is for you to do whatever you feel like. You're probably not used to hearing that. But that's what I want. There's a kind of freedom that comes from not overthinking things. And I can't

teach you more in an hour than you'll learn in just a few minutes playing around without any ideas in your head."

Ruth filled a small bowl with water from the tap and set it on the
table. "Just get your hands dirty. Use the water if the clay is too hard.
You can try to make something or not—that part is up to you. In a
while I'll show you all the tools and I'll teach you some techniques. But
for right now you can't do nothing wrong. Does that make sense?"

"I think so."

"Good. Would you like a smock?"

The boy looked over at the smocks that hung on the wall and shook
his head.

"Okay, then. How about some music?"

"Okay," the boy said.

"You got any particular type of music you listen to?"

"I don't know."

"Well, let's find out what you think about Grace Slick."

Ruth went over to the small desk where she kept the blue Dansette.
She removed the record from the sleeve and looked over at Daniel, who
had begun to tentatively touch the clay. She set the record on the platter
and lifted the needle and placed it just before "Two Heads."

The flurries had started to come down quicker, and they stuck to
the window. She studied the birches and thought again of Elam and the
truck and the spots of blood and the clearing in the woods. After a
moment she went to the sink and washed her hands. "Your dad said you
never kept no animals. I've got dogs. Sometimes they wander in here.
Do you like dogs?"

The boy nodded. He worked the clay with his fingers.

"I've got a couple students who really love dogs. Billy and Bobby are
their names. Their mother's name is Polly. You'll probably meet them
some time."

"My mother's allergic to dogs," the boy said.

"Is that so?"

"She's allergic to a lot of things."

"Well," Ruth said. "Some of us are. Some of us can't hardly stand our surroundings."

The boy continued to work the clay.

"I'm sure she's managed, though."

The boy was quiet.

RUTH WAS SITTING at the table with Daniel, taking him through some wedging techniques and coming to recognize and appreciate his unusual calm and focus, when she glanced up and saw Elam in the drive. Something sharp twisted in her gut like a knife, and she shot up from her seat, but it only took her a moment to realize it was just her mother wearing Elam's old field coat. Ruth told Daniel to hold on for a minute and went to meet her mother.

"What the hell are you doing out here?" Ruth asked.

"I was wondering the same about you—out here in the woods like some wild animal."

"I'm not in the woods."

"Looks to me like you are."

"Where did you get that jacket?"

Ruth's mother looked down at the brown field jacket with the torn pocket and then settled her gaze on Ruth. "Got it from the closet. It's colder than Billy-be-damned, if you hadn't noticed."

"I've noticed."

Ruth's mother craned her neck. "Who is that? Who have you got in there with you?"

"A student."

Ruth's mother studied the shed.

"Come on," Ruth said. "Let's get back to the house."

Ruth's mother didn't move.

"Come on," Ruth said again. She put her hand on her mother's shoulder and turned her gently to break her gaze.

"Cold as Billy-be-damned," her mother said again. "Out here like some wild animal."

Ruth led her mother over the dead nettle grass and the gravel drive. When her mother reached the porch steps, she walked up them gingerly, making use of the railing, and then she sat down in the old rocker and produced a pack of Elam's cigarettes from the coat pocket.

"What are you doing?"

"Having a smoke."

"You don't smoke."

"The hell I don't."

"Not in twenty years, you haven't."

"It'll come back to me."

Ruth's mother put the cigarette in her mouth. She struggled with the match but finally got the cigarette lit and took a long drag. She closed her eyes a moment and then opened them and held the pack out to Ruth. "Go on," she said.

Ruth didn't move.

"Come on."

"You're going to freeze out here," Ruth said. She studied her mother. Her thin, veiny hand on the arm of the chair.

"What's his name?" Ruth's mother asked.

"Who?"

"Your student."

"It doesn't matter."

"It's a secret, then?"

"Daniel."

"Daniel. How old is he?"

"I don't know. Eight or nine, maybe."

"He looks like Mathew."

"A lot of boys look alike at that age."

Ruth's mother took another drag. "I wonder what you're doing," she said.

"What does that mean?"

Ruth's mother waved her hand at the shed as though that explained everything.

"I've got to get back," Ruth said.

"Of course you do."

Ruth watched her mother.

"Go on, then. Nobody's stopping you."

"You're going to stay out here?"

"I'm going to finish this cigarette. And I might have another after that."

"Jesus Christ."

"Jesus ain't got nothing to do with it."

Ruth held her mother's eyes and then turned back to the shed. She could see Daniel watching through the window, his small face a little distorted. She wondered where the boy's mother was—whether she was fighting for him or even looking for him. And then she thought of Elam and of Mathew, and how a person could be lost and still not missing, or else missing and not lost—and how she wasn't sure which of those was worse.

MILK RAYMOND

Milk headed north past the gas station and the blinking light and then turned left onto Bennett Hill Road. He followed the road past old homes and fields and barns and stretches of deep woods. He kept a lookout for the Miller Lumber sign, but after a while all he saw were tall pin oaks. He slowed his truck and came to a stop in front of a small shed with a restroom sign. The snow was coming down steadily.

A state tag was stapled to the trunk of one of the pin oaks. He looked across the road, but all he saw were more pin oaks and some white pines farther back. He continued north. The woods broke, and he passed a vacant lot bordered by cinder blocks stood up on their sides. At the back of the lot was a building with a hipped gambrel roof that was mostly rotted.

Milk watched the thick woods that crept right up to the road until eventually he passed a wooden sign that told him he was leaving Wilmington. He looked in his rearview mirror and swung the truck around and started back the way he had come. He watched the woods made up of black and green and white. His windshield wipers pushed away the flurries. The heat sputtered and the tips of his fingers were cold.

He reached the vacant lot and put on his turn signal and pulled into the drive. He got out of the truck and stood there studying the lot. The snow covered most of the grass. Some pieces of trash lay on the ground. A large piece of yellow egg-crate Styrofoam and a barrel tipped on its side, rusted with white lettering spray-painted on top of the rust.

A chain-link fence stretched behind the building but stopped several feet shy of the woods. The windows were boarded up, but there were gaps between the boards. Milk went to one of the gaps and peered inside. Weeds had grown up through the floor. He saw a dirty sock and a broken beer bottle on one of the few remaining planks.

He followed the building around to the back, where he spotted a second door with a wooden sign over the door that said MILLER LUMBER. The door was closed and the curtains were drawn over the small windows.

Milk knocked on the door. He stepped to the side and tried to peer in through the curtains but couldn't see anything. After a moment the door opened and the old man stood there in a heavy Carhartt sweater and his Miller Lumber hat.

"Shit," he said. "Come on in out of this."

Milk stepped inside the small room. He felt the heat blowing around him immediately. There was a worn leather office chair pushed back from a small desk covered with maps and scraps of paper and a portable radio and a liter plastic bottle of Coke. A framed picture of the man's dog sitting in front of a spot of beach grass was centered on the wall in a dusty wooden frame. A heater whirred from the corner of the office next to a small refrigerator.

"You want something to drink?" the old man asked. "I got beer and Coke."

"I'm okay," Milk said.

The old man looked around the office. "Shit," he said. He shook his head and stood there with his hands on his hips. "I got some bad news. We got this contractor out of Rutland—and he dropped us. Decided to go with some New York outfit. I just found out last night." The man removed his hat and held it by his side. "That's most of our winter work. I didn't expect nothing like this when I saw you the other day. Shit," the old man said again. "I feel awful."

The old man wasn't making eye contact with Milk. He was looking every which way around the office, and Milk could tell that he did feel awful. He thought he should say something. But he was thinking about how he was going to find another job and how he was going to pay the next month's rent and the heating bill.

"It could be that something will open up," the man said. "I can take down your number. Sometimes we get guys leaving in the summer—run off to work on blank sites. You'd be the first one I'd call."

"Sure," Milk said.

"Here," the old man said. He went to the desk and picked up a pen and a scrap of paper. "What's the number?" Milk gave the man his old number, even though he had tossed his phone across the road and into the snow when he pulled the overdue bill he couldn't afford from the mailbox a couple of days back.

THE SUN WAS setting behind the clouds when Milk left the Miller Lumber office, and it glowed in the distance like something nuclear. Milk wasn't quite ready to go back to his boy, so he headed east toward Anvil. He followed the road until it straightened out, and then he shifted and pushed down on the gas. The gray birches and the quaking aspens and the white pines with flecks of snow caught in their needles rushed past his window. He put the truck into fourth gear. The road rushed under his tires like a river.

In the distance a flock of birds appeared like a handful of river stones tossed into the air. The woods broke, and he passed a small home with a flagpole in the front yard surrounded by a stone ring. He put the truck into fifth gear and followed the winding road through forest. It felt good to be moving. He had come to hate sitting still. Moving felt like purpose. Though he knew it wasn't the same thing.

RUTH FENN

THERE WAS A LITTLE LIGHT STILL LEFT WHEN DANIEL FINALLY LEFT with his father. Ruth tucked her hands in her coat pockets and came up the porch steps and inside the home and found her mother sitting in the chair in the living room.

"Come on, then," Ruth said.

Ruth's mother turned in her chair. "Come on where?"

"You wanted to see Mathew—let's go see him."

"It's almost dark."

"We'll take a flashlight. You said yourself we need to go before the snow comes, and it's already falling. It's already piling up."

Ruth's mother nodded slowly. "All right, then," she said. "Yes. All right."

The two left the home in their winter coats and gloves and boots. The dogs followed, not wanting to be left out of whatever was happening. Ruth's mother walked slowly, and Ruth stayed behind her so that she wouldn't force her into keeping a pace she wasn't comfortable keeping. The dogs ran ahead and then circled back. The light was almost gone and there were flurries that came down through the tangle of tree limbs.

"What's wrong with this one?" Ruth's mother asked.

"What one?"

"The boy. Daniel. What's happened to him?"

"I don't know. I don't know that anything has happened to him."

"Something happened."

"His father was in Iraq. The boy was living with his grandmother."

Ruth's mother turned to the side a little as she made her way down a gentle slope toward the narrow clearing that had at one time been a road. "Where was his mother?"

"I don't know."

"Well, I guess it don't matter. Gone, I guess. Not there."

Ruth kept close to her mother in case she started to fall. The ground was hard, and the forest floor was dark enough that it was difficult to see the tree roots. It would be pitch-black on the walk home. Ruth had brought the flashlight, but with their eyes focused on the ground, they were bound to walk into a tree limb.

"It's good what you're doing," Ruth's mother said. "I just worry about you."

Ruth nodded. Grateful that her mother seemed alert.

It had been a long time since Ruth had been in these woods after dark. There were times her and Elam would walk through the woods and listen to the sounds. There were times Mathew would join them. The three of them shadows cutting through shadows under stars.

"You got something on your mind," Ruth's mother said.

"I'm just worried about Elam is all."

"Have you heard something more?"

"No."

"You'll worry yourself into a circle—won't know which way is which."

"Not much I can do about that."

"No, there's not. We fill our pockets with our worries. That's different than men. They don't let go of theirs exactly, but they keep them hidden somewhere and come back to them now and again. We carry ours with us. Into every room and then into our graves. You got more than your fair share. I won't lie and tell you different." Ruth's mother slowed and then stopped.

"Everything okay?" Ruth asked.

"Everything's fine." Ruth's mother continued forward a few feet, then stopped again and turned to her right and walked a couple of feet and sat down on a partial stone wall. She gripped her knees and struggled to catch her breath.

"What is it?" Ruth asked. "What's wrong?"

"I think this will have to do." Ruth's mother looked north toward the hill and the field of goldenrod—just dark stalks in the near dark. "I'll have to look on from here."

Ruth sat beside her mother on a pocked stone that was cold and damp. "This is far enough. He can see you from here." Ruth felt foolish as soon as the words left her mouth, but her mother didn't seem to notice. She continued to stare at the field of goldenrod.

"I know you miss Mathew," Ruth's mother said.

Ruth was quiet. It was worse than that. She felt that her memories had turned to muscle and been stretched over her bones so that she couldn't move without them. It had gotten so there was nothing in her future. Only a series of reactions born from her past.

"We ought to get back inside where it's warm," Ruth said.

The dogs returned from whatever they had been doing and stood wagging their tails and tilting their heads, confused by Ruth and her mother sitting still in the dark woods.

"We can sit here another moment, though," Ruth's mother said.

"Yes," Ruth said. "We can sit here as long as you like."

MILK RAYMOND

Jessica showed up at the blue duplex on Stub Hollow sometime in the early evening. Milk saw her pull in next to his truck in a gray Jeep Cherokee, and he knew it was her before she even got out of the Jeep and stopped in the drive to fix her hair and rub the bags out from under her eyes.

She came up the concrete steps, and Milk opened the door enough to stick his head out. Her face was blistered and caked with foundation.

"Don't get mad," she said. "I just got to talk to you."

Milk stood there staring at her and not saying anything. He heard Daniel shift in his chair at the kitchen table but didn't turn around.

"How did you find me?"

"Marcy gave me your address. How is he?"

"Like you care."

"I'm sorry," she said. "I'm sorry."

"It's too late for that."

"Can I come in—please?"

Milk shook his head. "That's not a good idea."

"Please—Jesus, Milk. I just want to see him." Jessica craned her neck around Milk. "Daniel," she said. "Daniel, it's Mommy."

Milk stepped outside and shut the door behind him. "You need to go," he said. "He doesn't want to see you."

"He's my boy. I have every right to see him."

"That's not the way I see it."

"I'm his mother."

Milk remembered how Jessica had told him she'd wanted a child since she was a little girl. How she used to cut out pictures of mothers and fathers and children from magazines and hang them on the walls around her room. She had names for all the men and all the children. But the mother never changed. The pretty blonde in the tennis outfit and the brunette in the black pantsuit with shoulder pads were all just incarnations of the woman she thought she would become.

"I'm his mother," Jessica said again.

"A mother doesn't leave her boy for some junkie."

Jessica fingered the cuff of her sleeve. "I made a mistake, Milk."

"You made a big mistake."

"You ain't perfect yourself. You left him too."

Milk raised his finger and struggled to keep his voice level. "That was different. I left for us. We agreed to that."

"I already told you I made a mistake. What do you want me to say?"

"I don't want you to say nothing unless it's that you're leaving and you don't plan on ever coming back."

"I'm not gonna say that."

"Well just say nothing then. I don't care."

Jessica crossed her arms. Tears began to well up in her eyes. "You don't need to forgive me. But that's still my boy, and we gotta figure something out—for Daniel."

Milk motioned toward the Jeep. "Where is he?"

"Who?"

"You know who."

"He's gone."

"That's a fucking surprise, isn't it?"

"I told you it was a mistake."

Jessica wiped her eyes with the back of her hand. "You can't care for him. You don't know nothing about raising a child."

"I know more than you."

"That ain't true. You never knew what to do with him. You hardly knew him before you left." Jessica shook her head. Her foot started tapping on the concrete. "You can't have him."

"Go home," Milk said. "Wherever that is."

"I'll call the cops on you. I'll call them on you for kidnapping."

"Call them. I already been talking to Social Services."

"What are you talking about?"

"I told you. They been out here."

"You called them?"

"I didn't need to. You left our boy alone with a crazy woman. That's the type of thing they take an interest in."

"What did you tell them? Did you lie to them?"

"I didn't tell them nothing but the truth."

Jessica lunged past Milk for the door handle, but Milk caught her around the waist and pulled her back. She swung at Milk and caught him across the chin, and he heard a dull pop. Milk wrapped his arms tighter around her waist and took her down the steps, and when they were standing in the gravel, he pushed her toward her car and she hit the ground. She stayed there a moment with the palms of her hands on the cold snow, and then she stood.

"I'm calling the cops," she said. "I'm telling them you assaulted me in front of my boy and that you've got him in an apartment against his will."

"Go on, then. See if they'll listen to a druggie whore."

Jessica took a step forward. "Ask him. Ask Daniel what he wants. If he wants me to leave, then I'll go. You let him decide."

"He's already decided," Milk said. "We both decided."

Jessica started to cry. She wiped her eyes with the sleeve of her coat and stood there in the driveway watching Milk, and then she turned and headed to her car.

"Don't you tell him no lies about me. Don't you go making up things."

"I don't need to lie, Jessica. He was there—remember?"

A truck drove by on the road with sandbags stacked in the bed. The man watched Milk from the driver's side window. Milk watched the truck until it disappeared, and then he waited for the Jeep to back out of the drive and disappear down the road. When it was gone, he turned back to the duplex and the shriveled shrubs crowded in front of it.

MILK SAT ON the couch after dinner, not paying attention to the highlights of the baseball game that played on the television or his boy, who was sitting on the floor working his way through a book Milk didn't recognize. He nursed a beer and thought about Jessica. He wondered what it meant that she was in town. Wondered where she was staying and whether her boyfriend would come looking for her. He wondered if she would return to the duplex or if she would try to see Daniel at school. It wasn't what he needed—not with everything else going on.

The familiar pain started behind his right eye. He had hoped the headaches would stop when he got back to the States, but if anything they had gotten worse.

There was a small part of him that missed being in Iraq. Even the unexpected was expected in the sense that there was a protocol for handling surprises. You fought fire with fire. When all else went to shit, you doubled down. But in the States there was no such protocol. The surprises kept on coming and you just sort of took it.

He finished his beer and stood from the couch. In the kitchen he swallowed a tablet of Zoloft and pulled a fresh beer from the refrigerator.

"Is she staying?"

Milk looked toward the living room. "What?"

"Is she staying here?"

"Who?"

"Mom."

"No."

"Where is she going to stay?"

"I don't know." The pain on the right side of Milk's head expanded. It felt like his head had been split open.

"Where is she going to sleep?"

"What?"

"Mom. Where is she going to sleep?"

"Daniel—Jesus. I don't know."

Daniel's eyes narrowed and his lip quivered like he was going to cry, but he just turned back to his book.

Milk swallowed another tab of Zoloft and twisted the cap from the beer. He leaned against the kitchen counter and watched the snow fall outside the window. He wondered if the heating company would keep the heat on in the winter even if he didn't pay the bill. It used to be they would leave it on until the spring at least. But Milk didn't know if that was how it still worked. He figured everyone was tightening their belts and he might just be shit out of luck come next month.

He took another sip of his beer, watched the falling snow, and hoped the winter wouldn't be too long. He looked back to his boy reading on the dirty carpet. Milk carried his beer into the living room and set it on the cardboard box and went to the door and put on his boots.

"Wait here," he said. "I want to show you something."

The snow seemed like it was coming down even harder once he was outside. Earlier in the day he had heard the weatherman encouraging people to check their vents and stay off the roads on account of whiteout conditions. Milk opened the passenger door of the truck and grabbed the balsam fir branch he had spotted on his drive home from dropping his boy off at school and forgotten about until this moment.

"What is it?" Daniel asked.

"Go on and get my knife from the counter."

The boy got up from the floor and went to the table and grabbed the six-inch folding knife.

Milk sat down on the couch. "This stick predicts the weather," he said when Daniel got back.

"The stick?"

Milk nodded. "First you have to strip the bark. Then you hang it outside." Milk took a sip of the warming beer and then opened the knife and began to shave the bark from the stick. The boy watched him quietly. "When the stick points toward the ground, that means the weather is bad. When it curls upward, that means good weather is on the way. I had one of these when I was your age, and it worked better than the weatherman."

Milk removed most of the bark and closed the knife and held it out to the boy. "Go on," he said. "Finish it off."

"I don't want to."

"Jesus, Daniel."

The boy looked down at his hands.

"I'm sorry," Milk said. "I'm sorry. Why don't you want to do it?"

"I'll cut myself."

"Is that it? Is that the only thing you're worried about?"

The boy nodded.

"Okay, here. Can I show you something?"

The boy hesitated and then nodded.

"This part here is called the spine of the knife. Do you see that?"

"Yes."

"You always want to hold the spine against your palm. That way the blade will open facing away from your skin. See, watch." Milk opened the blade and then closed it. He held the knife out to the boy again. This time Daniel took it and held it so that the spine was pressed tight against his palm.

"Good. Now take your right finger and thumb and put them on the sides of the blade here and slowly open it."

The boy did as he was told.

"Set the stick down on your leg there and hold it behind the blade."

The boy set the stick on his leg and held it with his left hand.

"Now push the blade edgewise along the stick—away from you, so that if it slips, it will slip away from you. It'll come off easy."

The boy stripped off a line of bark and then another. His tongue hung out of his mouth.

"That's good," Milk said. "You're doing it right."

The boy worked the knife over the stick as slow as molasses moving over a splintered table, but eventually he removed all of the bark, and then he sat there holding the knife three feet from his chest and staring at Milk.

"Good," Milk said. "Now hold the knife the same way you opened it. Grab the spine with one hand. Make sure your fingers are clear of the blade and push the blade down."

A commercial for arthritis medication came on the television. A man in a blue flannel shirt walked along a weathered gray dock with a Boston terrier at his heel.

The boy closed the knife.

"Good," Milk said. "Now let's get her hung."

He went to the kitchen and opened the closet door and removed a hammer and a couple of nails. He put his boots back on, and his boy put on his own boots and tied them slowly and then put on his coat and carefully pulled the zipper all the way up to his chin.

Outside the house, as he helped his boy hang the stick, Milk watched the snow piling on the drive and covering the tracks. He thought of Jessica, and then he thought of a girl he had known in high school. A good student who took her schoolwork seriously and was a member of the track team. She became addicted to pain pills and started driving two hours on the weekends in her parents' minivan to strip at a dive in Palmsville. During her senior year she was shot to death while trying to rob a gas station with a carving knife.

RUTH FENN

Tʜᴇ ᴍᴏᴛɪᴏɴ ʟɪɢʜᴛ ꜱɴᴀᴘᴘᴇᴅ ᴏɴ ᴀɴᴅ ꜱʜᴏɴᴇ ᴅɪᴍʟʏ ᴛʜʀᴏᴜɢʜ ᴛʜᴇ bedroom window. Ruth pulled back the covers and stepped onto the cold floor and put on her slippers and sweater. She listened for her mother and then walked down the hall to the front of the house and opened the door and looked out at the well-lit snow. The cold tightened her skin. She pulled her arms across her chest and eyed the unmarked ground. The snow was coming down hard, but the motion sensor worked on heat, and it wouldn't turn on because of falling snow or even wind if it wasn't carrying with it something warm.

A limb cracked deep in the woods. The wind rose up and bore down on the home, tightening the boards.

Ruth closed the door and went to the kitchen and heated a glass of milk on the stovetop. The clock on the oven read one twenty. She poured the milk into a mug and took a small sip and closed her eyes. The wind whistled as it eddied around the home. The refrigerator hummed.

The house had gotten so quiet after Mathew died. He'd never made much noise, but his death brought a quiet same as a snowstorm. Hushed and still and allowing for unfamiliar sounds a long ways off.

With Elam gone it was even worse. Ruth was suddenly aware of her own sounds. The way her bones creaked when she moved, same as the trees when the sap froze. And the way she breathed hard through her nose even when she was standing still. She took another sip of milk. The motion light turned off. She fiddled with the towel that hung from the lip of the sink, straightening it out some, and then she finished her milk and set the mug in the sink and filled it with tap water and turned toward the bedroom.

The motion light snapped on again.

At the closet she put on her snow boots and coat. There were deer and other animals that came out at night, but she hadn't seen any tracks. She buttoned her coat and turned up the collar and grabbed the flashlight from the drawer.

The wind lifted the snow from the ground. The moon was full. Ruth buried her chin in her coat and listened to the sound of her footsteps and turned back every now and then to make sure she was only being followed by one set of tracks. When she reached the end of the motion light's reach, she flipped on her flashlight and held it tightly beside her hip.

The shed looked smaller covered in snow—like a rabbit den. Ruth went to the window and pressed her hands and forehead against the glass and felt the cold and damp. She could see the long table and the chairs and the wheel. She studied the inside of the shed and then went to the door and turned the knob. The door creaked open. The flashlight uncovered pieces of hardened clay and windblown pieces of paper. She stepped inside the shed and ran the light over the walls. She studied the books on the shelves and the statues and the framed photograph of Elam and the drawings with the names of her students written crookedly in the corners.

The door slammed shut.

Ruth spun and shined the light on the door. She held her breath and thought she heard something small scurry across the snow. She kept the light on the door a long while, long enough to notice the rust on the bottom hinge and the yellow paint on the doorknob, and then she turned back to the shed. She continued to run the light over the walls, and her heart nearly stopped when the light crossed the window and she saw her own reflection, as though someone were standing on the other side of the glass looking through it with a flashlight.

She drew the light over the far wall and the double-basin sink where a ring-necked pheasant that Elam had shot and stuffed was fastened to the one of the edges. She let the light linger on the pheasant, and then she turned back to the door and hesitated before walking toward it and turning the knob.

The trees cast thin shadows across the snow. Ruth raised the beam toward the woods, but it died before it reached the tree line. If there was something out there in the old growth, she wasn't going to find it.

Inside the house she locked the door and removed her boots and set them on the floor next to the wall. She thought she heard something and stopped and listened. The wind picked up and rattled the panes. She pulled off her coat and hung it on the nail and carried the flashlight to her bedroom, where she set it on the nightstand. She removed her socks and climbed under the covers, and after a long time listening to herself breathe, she fell asleep.

She woke again sometime later. She lay quiet and waiting, and then she heard what must have awoken her. The sound of snow crunching underfoot. The other dogs must have still been asleep in the mudroom, but Woodstock had moved into her bedroom, and he stood on point in the middle of the room staring into the darkened hallway.

Ruth pulled the sheets back and listened. The snow continued to crunch, and then there was silence followed by the sound of the porch boards creaking. The dog let out a low growl. Ruth snapped on the bedroom light and made her way to the closet. She pulled the rifle from the magnets and pressed the slide release and chambered the shell and raised the gun to her shoulder.

The wind rapped against the shutters. She stood in the hallway with her bare feet on the cold ground. She flexed the fingers of her right hand and brought her index finger down lightly on the trigger, her palms damp with sweat. The gun felt heavy.

She heard a scraping sound, and then the bent metal pin rubbed against the hinge and the door opened. She blinked her eyes and waited. She could not see the door from where she stood, but she could see the edge of the braided rug in front of it.

The wind blew through the house, and she felt the sweat dry on her forehead. The boards creaked and a man emerged from the living room.

"It's me," he said, and raised his palms.

"Elam?" Ruth lowered the rifle. "What's happened to you?"

Elam's eyelids were swollen like curled slugs. His face was thin and dark underneath his tattered hat. The dog ran up to Elam with its tail wagging and sniffed his boots.

"Are you hurt?"

"I'm fine."

Ruth set down the rifle and turned on the hallway light. She studied her husband. There was dried blood on his coat and on the front of his pants. "You're covered in blood."

"It's not mine."

"You've got to get changed. You can't stand here like this."

"Ruth."

Ruth went quickly to the bedroom and removed a white shirt from the top drawer of the dresser and a pair of long underwear and set them on the bed. Elam followed her and stood in the doorway of the bedroom, dripping melted snow onto the floorboards.

"You've got to get changed," she said. "Get changed and I'll put on some coffee."

"Ruth. I got to talk to you."

"Not in that. Not in what you're wearing." Ruth left the bedroom and walked past Elam to the kitchen. She got the woodstove lit and poured the remaining coffee into the pot and turned on the burner. She sat down at the table and rubbed her fingers over her temples and then over her eyes.

She could hear her husband in the bedroom. His heavy boots on the rickety floorboards and his shirt being pulled over his head and then his leather belt slipping through his belt loops. When he reached the kitchen, he was wearing clean clothes. His hair still dripped water, and thin red scratches ran up and down his arms.

Ruth stood and went to the stove.

"Ruth."

"Sit down at the table there."

"I got to talk to you, Ruth."

"Sit down. You can do that much."

Elam sat at the table. Ruth poured two cups of coffee and brought them over to the table and set them down. Then she looked her husband in the eyes.

"Okay," she said. "Whose blood is it? You can start with that."

"It don't matter."

"It matters. It matters to me and whoever it is that blood belongs to."

"Ruth. I got to tell you something."

Ruth studied her husband. His eyes were glassed over and he looked almost scared.

"I got to tell you something, but I don't know if I can."

"You can," Ruth said. "That's how this works after thirty-five years."

MILK RAYMOND

It seemed this was how it was going to be. Milk waking in the middle of the night to some dream that had him pinwheeling through the air or burning in a Humvee or, more often than not, not even him pinwheeling or burning but someone else pinwheeling or burning and him watching. Helpless from the end of a mile-long convoy.

He pulled back the covers and sat there a moment and then put on his jeans and coat and grabbed his cigarettes and his keys. He stopped when he reached the door and went back to the kitchen and pulled the plastic six-dollar bottle of Maker's Mark from the cupboard, feeling like every sort of used-up cliché about broken war veterans.

He stepped out into the cold. In the distance he heard coyotes howling like injured dogs. His boots crunched the thin layer of snow. He took a pull of whiskey and looked toward the balsam fir branch pointed downward and got in his truck.

He wondered about the stages of his life. For some time he had felt he was at the beginning. That he was choosing a path out of several that lay before him. But he felt now that he had chosen a path and that he had chosen the wrong path and he didn't know how to turn around. He still thought it was possible. He didn't believe in fate. He had seen enough violence to know that if God was all-good, then he wasn't all-powerful. And he didn't know if that made him more or less comfortable. To see God not as supreme but as another man trying and failing to do right in a world where mistakes never seemed to stay with the person who made them.

He followed the road through the center of town, where the streetlights created halos through which falling snow flickered and disappeared. The lights from the diner shone bright, and he could see bar stools lined up on top of the white counter.

He pulled from the whiskey and thought about Jessica and whether there had ever been something more than Daniel between them. He used to think he loved her, but he wondered now if it was love he had felt or obligation. It wasn't something he wondered about with his boy. He felt the obligation, but he felt something else as well, something faint but warm and consistent like a fire burned down to the coals.

He continued along the road. The only sounds were the engine and the busted heater and his own chapped hands regripping the wheel. He slowed as he approached the gas station. The lights were on, and he recalled late nights after Daniel was born when he would drive there for diapers. Half asleep, swerving along the empty road.

The door to the gas station opened, and the girl stepped out in a big winter coat. He could tell who she was from the color of her hair and her boots, and he slowed the truck and pulled to the side of the road. He looked in the rearview mirror, and then he turned in his seat and watched the girl climb into a station wagon and turn on her headlights and start out of the parking lot. Milk looked straight ahead until the station wagon had passed. He sat there for another moment, and then he put his truck in gear and pulled out onto the road and followed her.

RUTH FENN

THE COFFEE STEAMED IN FRONT OF ELAM, BUT HE DIDN'T TOUCH IT. The light over the table buzzed and the wind continued to whip against the side of the house.

Elam looked down at the table. "I know what happened to him. I know what happened to our boy."

"What are you talking about?"

"I heard it from Fred Easton. He's got kids, Fred, two of them."

"Heard what from Fred?"

Elam wiped at his eyes. "Goddammit," he said. "He was selling him. Horace was. He was selling Mathew down at the motel."

"What the hell are you talking about?"

"You know what I'm talking about."

Ruth shook her head. "That ain't true."

Elam's hands were pressed against the table white as sawdust. "Horace is using again. He showed up at Fred's high as a kite talking about how he had sinned and how there wasn't no God in the world that was going to forgive him. Fred thought he was talking about using again, but then Horace started repeating Mathew's name and talking about the motel and what he made him do. What he made our boy do."

"He's making it up."

"No." Elam shook his head. "No, Ruth. I found out for myself. Horace knew a guy at the motel, and this guy set up everything. He paid Horace and Mathew in drugs. Horace didn't know the other men involved. People from out of town, mostly."

Ruth's head felt light, as though it had been stripped of its muscles and skin.

"Horace got Mathew hooked on that stuff. He got Mathew hooked, and when he needed more, that's when he took him down to the motel." Elam lowered his head. "Mathew was going to tell William the night they went camping. He told Horace as much, and Horace tried to stop him, but Mathew ran. Horace went looking for him. Driving along the roads. But he couldn't find him. He didn't bother looking long. He said part of him wanted it all to end."

Ruth's hands were shaking. "Mathew would have said something. For Christ's sake, we would have known."

"He was just a boy. What Horace turned him into." Elam wiped at his eyes. "What Horace made him do."

The branches of the tall oak scratched at the back window.

"We would have known," Ruth said again.

"We didn't." Elam raised his hands as though he wanted to grab on to something, but he just held them there for a moment and then lowered his palms to the table. "We didn't know."

Ruth held her hands over her eyes. "Where is he? Where is Horace?"

"I got him tied up in the old hunting stand."

"Jesus."

"I wanted to kill him for what he done. But I couldn't do it. I've got him tied up there, and I been sitting there with him and going to my truck at night. I been doing it like that for four days. Just going back between the two. Just sitting there. Him talking some. Apologizing. Telling me he had a problem and he wanted to get it fixed."

"How's he not froze to death?"

"There's a steel heater and a couple Sternos. It ain't much. He's not in good shape. It was the truck that kept me going. But then I saw it was gone—and I knew you must've been there. I knew you must've come looking."

Ruth stood.

"Where are you going?"

"To check on my mother."

"She can't hear."

"She hears more than you think."

Ruth walked to the guest room. Her legs were weak. She held on to the door frame and peered into the dark and listened to her mother's shallow breaths.

She wanted to go somewhere. To leave the house and walk through the snow and the cold and keep on walking until she was far away. But she knew she couldn't outrun the truth any more than she could outrun the past. She had tried that plenty and only wound up old and winded.

She turned back to the kitchen. "What else did he say? What else did that son of a bitch say about our boy?"

"Nothing."

"That ain't true. I want to know."

"He admitted to it. That's enough."

"What about Della?"

"What about her?"

"Did she know?"

Elam shook his head. "No. She didn't know nothing."

Ruth stood in the doorway. Again she put her hands on the frame to steady herself and waited for Elam to make eye contact with her, and then she held his eyes. "Do you still keep that old hog pistol in your dresser?"

MILK RAYMOND

MILK FOLLOWED THE STATION WAGON NORTH ALONG CROSS HILL Road. They were the only two vehicles on the road, and he wondered whether the girl could see into the cab of his truck. He figured his head-lights were too bright, but he kept his distance just the same.

They turned onto a narrow road where the dark of the forest seemed to swell, and when the station wagon's brake lights went solid, Milk eased up on the gas. The station wagon pulled into a driveway, and the headlights moved over a small two-story house. Milk continued past the drive for a while and then turned the truck around and killed the headlights. He crept up the road and pulled in front of the house.

There was a porch chair outside with a microwave on the seat. In the front yard a plastic swimming pool was filled with snow. Two uncur-tained windows were lit upstairs, and a shadow caught his attention. He studied the window and saw the girl. She stood staring directly out at the dark, and Milk held his breath, thinking she must have seen him. But he didn't think a person could see into darkness from a well-lit room.

He watched the girl and was struck with the urge to knock on her front door. He felt for some reason that if he could apologize to her, things might begin to fall into place.

He knew guys in Iraq that were superstitious. Some listened to the same song every night. Other guys carried mementos like their father's watch or a photograph of their girlfriend tucked into a vinyl envelope. Milk didn't have any superstitions, and it felt odd to him that he should need one now. But for some reason, apologizing to the girl felt something like that. He watched the girl remove her jacket and toss it somewhere out of view. She tilted her chin slightly, and the desire to confront her—to make things right and to put himself on track—rose up inside him. He unbuckled his seat belt and got out of the truck. His muscles twitched against the cold.

The plastic pool was cracked on one side. He stopped beside the girl's car in the drive and looked in the driver's side window. There was a pack of empty cigarettes on the dash. In the back were two mismatched car seats and between the car seats a folder from the community college. He continued past the car to the stone path that led to the front door. Beyond the house he could see a maze of interwoven branches, and from somewhere beyond those branches he heard a faint humming sound that made him stop.

He looked toward the house and the dead plant that sat in a tall pot on the steps. He could see a second door around the side, and he wondered if the house was split into several apartments. He turned again toward the woods and listened to the humming and thought he saw something move. He took a step forward. The humming grew louder. He could almost make out some sort of rhythm to it. He took another step and then another until he was in the woods.

Thin branches broke under his boots and scraped against his jacket. Milk stopped and listened and then took a few more steps and stopped and listened again. He could hear it more clearly now. It was music. But he couldn't figure out where it was coming from. He saw no lights and no other homes.

He walked for some time, hardly able to see more than a foot in front of him. The moon hung over his left shoulder. The air was still. He pictured the music coming from a hole somewhere in the middle of the woods. Just a hole playing music.

When he pushed through a tangle of branches, he saw the shed. It was just a makeshift thing. Hardly more than a child's fort. The music thumped. He looked over his shoulder, but there was only darkness. He could no longer see the house or the truck or the moon.

The shed had several windows, but they were curtained and the light was dim behind the curtains. Suddenly the door flew open, and Milk instinctively reached for his service weapon, though it wasn't there.

"Oh fuck." A boy stood in the doorway with a cigarette hanging out of his mouth and his fingers secured to his fly. "Jeremiah," he said. "Jeremiah."

Another boy came out of the shed. He seemed to be the same age as the first boy. Not more than sixteen years old. He wore a white snow hat. "Jesus," he said. "Who the hell are you?"

Milk looked back again to where he had come from. "I heard your music."

"What?"

Milk nodded toward the shed. "Your music."

"Yeah, but who the fuck are you?"

"I was at the house back there."

"Are you Rachel's boyfriend?"

The other boy with the cigarette started to laugh. "One in a million," he said.

The boy with the snow hat motioned toward the other boy. "He lives below her."

"Yeah—but I wish I was on top of her." The boy laughed again.

"Shut up, Russ," the boy with the snow hat said. "What do you want?"

"I just heard your music."

The other boy took several steps from the shed and unzipped his pants and started to piss in the snow. Milk could see into the shed. There were blankets on the wood floor and a small coffee table covered with beer bottles and a glass pipe. The song that had been playing stopped and a slower song started up. The boy taking a piss began to sing.

"You want a hit?" The boy with the snow hat jerked his thumb toward the shed.

"No."

The boy taking a piss started laughing again. "He don't want none of that shit, man. He's got the good stank waiting for him back at the house."

"Don't worry about him," the boy with the snow hat said. "He don't got no women in his life."

The boy taking a piss began to sing louder. *Take me piece by piece till there ain't nothing left worth taking away from me.*

"I'll leave you alone," Milk said. "I was just curious about the music."

"Yeah, well. We'll keep it down."

The boy taking a piss tilted his head back and screamed out the chorus.

"Jesus, Russ. Shut the hell up, man."

Milk looked once more at the shed. He saw some foil on the table next to the bottles. The boy taking a piss was still singing along to the music. *And night's a girl who's gone too far.*

Milk headed back through the woods until he reached the house, and then he crossed the grass and passed the plastic swimming pool and the girl's car and stepped out into the road. He turned back to the house just as the upstairs light switched off, and then he got in his truck and started the engine.

The snow was falling harder. The wind blew wisps like ghost soldiers humping across the road. He took a sip of whiskey and wondered what the hell he would have said to the girl. Rachel. He hadn't even known her name. He took another swig and balanced the bottle between his legs.

His best friend in Iraq was a man named Reggie Brenner. He was a skinny kid from North Carolina, and in a lot of ways he was the dumbest person Milk had ever met, though in other ways he was the smartest. For example, Reggie thought that women shouldn't serve because they were more susceptible to disease and if they were to sweat or bleed they would infect others. But on the other hand, Reggie had a knack for saying something so true it usually took Milk a while lying on his cot away from the noise just to parse it out. Like the time they were casualty collecting and Milk picked up the woman's torso. Milk had felt a sort of paralysis at that moment and he just stood there. And then Reggie walked by with his own body bag full of limbs and turned to Milk and said, "Killing women is like killing babies. We're fighting a war of the future and the casualties are piling up."

Milk drove south toward town. He reached for the Merle Haggard disc and put it in the stereo. He turned up the volume and grabbed the bottle and pulled from it.

I can't stand to see a good man go to waste.

He came flying down the hill toward the center of town. In the distance he saw the streetlights and the diner, and suddenly everything went black. He looked in his rearview mirror and saw that the power was out in all the houses that lined the road.

Cause I've got a heartache to hide.

He thought about Reggie and the bloodied limbs and the woman's stomach torn open like a zipper, and he turned up the music. He thought about Rachel bent over the desk and the kids she had in the apartment somewhere and the two boys in the shed, and he turned off his head-lights the way he and his friends had done as teenagers to show off for each other. As teenagers they had only kept the headlights off for a sec-ond or two, but he kept them off much longer. He kept them off for four or five seconds, and then he reached to turn them back on and brought his hand back down instead.

Everything in front of him was dark and still. He could see no road. It was as though the surface of the earth had turned into a hole. He knew the road he was traveling on turned sharply before the diner. He took a deep breath and let the music settle in his mind.

So I never go around mirrors. Cause I've got a heartache to hide.

He thought of the raid in Hawija just before he was discharged and the family of four and their dog. The dog barking nonstop and the little boy trying to keep it quiet. And he thought about Gomez and how he shot that dog clear through the snout so that it spun wildly and then ran in tight circles with blood pouring out of its face. He thought of the boy trying to catch his dog—trying to help it—but the dog just turning wildly, hurt and scared and not wanting to be caught, not knowing anymore what anyone was capable of.

And suddenly the lights in front of Milk turned on. All the street-lights lit up, and one light shone particularly bright, like a soft moon over the diner that Milk was headed straight for. He turned the wheel quickly and pumped the brake. One of the tires leapt the curb, but he managed to get the truck straightened out and back on the road, where he gathered himself and took her down to fifteen and drove her like that, slow and steady, the rest of the way home to his boy.

RUTH FENN

THERE WAS NO SLEEPING. THE TWO SAT AT THE TABLE AND TRIED TO hold down black coffee. The morning came and the splintered light shone through the trees and they could see how much snow had fallen from where they sat at the kitchen table.

Ruth decided she would take Della to the stand. She would take the hog pistol. Elam hadn't argued with her about that.

"I still think we ought to call Leo," Elam said.

"You'll go to jail."

"I'm prepared for it."

"I'm not. I won't see you locked up for what Horace done."

"Della won't believe you."

"Maybe not."

Elam had drawn Ruth a crude map of the stream and the old stone foundation and the hunting stand beyond it, but Ruth knew the general area. She put on her boots and tucked her pants inside the cuffs and grabbed the keys from the table.

Elam stood in front of the window and watched the snow still falling. "I should go with you."

"No. You need to rest. It won't help anyway. It will only make things worse."

Elam continued to stare out the window. "It looks like three feet. It might be less under tree cover. Still, you've got to be careful. You've got to keep along the stream like I told you."

Ruth secured the pistol in her inner coat pocket.

"I don't know what she'll do," Elam said. "I thought about it some, but I can't figure how she'll react."

"Not good is my guess. I suspect something like a cat that's come to learn its tail is on fire."

Elam turned to Ruth. His cheeks were shallow like a dried riverbed. "Horace won't give you no trouble. He's in bad shape."

"I hope to God he is. I hope to God he don't have nothing left inside of him."

THE TIRES SLIPPED and caught on the road. The truck groaned. A dense winter fog had gathered and it hung in the distance. Ruth leaned over the steering wheel and tried to make out the road through the white flakes that hurtled toward her as though she were passing through some sort of ghostly star system.

Her thoughts didn't leave Mathew. She thought of him as an infant, naked and small in her arms, and she pictured him older but still frail, and then all of the sudden she saw it, like an image from a dream that came to her long after she woke. She was driving her mother to the hospital early one morning before Mathew died. She'd found her on the floor outside the bathroom repeating words that didn't go together.

They were somewhere on Main Street. It was still early and there were hardly any other vehicles on the road. But Ruth remembered one. A white Ford Galaxie with a mud-colored hardtop. There was a man in the driver's seat with white hair and beside him a boy the spitting image of Mathew. It was all out of context, though, and the car passed in a split second, and so she told herself it couldn't have been her son. That her boy was home sleeping in his bedroom.

Ruth struggled now to see the image more clearly. She tried to see the boy's face, and when she did she slowed the truck and came to a stop in the middle of the road. The snow continued to fall. She laid her forehead on the steering wheel and cried. She wondered if Mathew had seen her. She wondered if he had been mad at her for being so blind. For not knowing. For not making it stop.

The heat roared through the vents. She picked her head up and wiped her eyes and pressed her foot to the gas. She blinked as she passed buried fences and snow-covered hills and cragged trees whose branches reached across the road to each other. She slowed the truck at the black mailbox and turned into the drive and came to a stop and shut the engine. The lights were on inside the home. A thin gray smoke rose from the chimney.

It was true what Elam said. Della might not believe her. And for that reason she hoped Horace was still alive. But for every other reason she hoped he was dead. She couldn't help but hope he was dead and that his death had been slow.

She remained in the truck for a moment more and then opened the door and stepped outside. Flakes of snow found their way underneath her collar and melted against her skin. After several steps the front door opened and Della stood in the doorway wearing a black turtleneck and long pants. She held a mug that steamed.

"Della," Ruth said. "I got to talk to you."

"Inside or out?"

"I think we ought to go inside for this."

Della looked past Ruth. "Is that Elam's truck?"

"It is."

"Tell me outside, then."

"I think you ought to sit down."

"Go on, Ruth. Go on and say what you have to say."

Della's eyes were wide, and save for the wrinkles around them, she looked the same as she did when she was much younger. She had always held a beauty that made Ruth jealous. It wasn't a traditional beauty. It was a beauty the way a crow walking across the snow could be beautiful.

"It's about our boys," Ruth said. And then she wiped the snow from her brow and told Della. Not about the hunting stand. But about what Horace had told Fred Easton and what Fred had told Elam.

Della didn't flinch. She just stood there for what seemed like a long time, and then the mug slipped from her hand and shattered on the metal threshold.

The sun had risen to the top of the chimney, but because of the falling snow and the thick fog, it appeared only like a glow and not a solid thing.

Ruth took a small step toward Della. "There's more," she said.

RUTH FENN

A THICK WAIST-HIGH FOG PARTED AND SWIRLED AROUND THE WOMEN as they moved along the unmarked trail through the hardwood forest and into the driving snow.

"How far is it?" Della asked.

"Not much further now."

"It had to be so far?"

Ruth turned and saw the breath plume from Della's mouth. The woods around the women were dense and the branches sagged with the weight of the snow. "I guess it did."

The stream flowed north through thick stands of maple. The wind blew and the snow hissed and the water lapped the stones.

Ruth's thoughts drifted back to the night before Mathew died. She had come home from the factory and found him alone at the kitchen table with a block of clay. It was a warm summer night and the windows were open and the wind pushed and tugged at the curtains. A stack of index cards and torn pieces of paper sat piled in the middle of the table.

For several years Ruth and Mathew had taken the three-word descriptions that Ruth's students had come up with and tried to sculpt the objects themselves. But they hadn't sculpted together in a long time, and that summer the two were hardly talking. Ruth figured it was a stage he was going through, a stage all boys had to go through, and she tried to give him space, but it hurt her just the same. She knew Elam had picked up on it, and Ruth figured he had talked Mathew into pulling the clay out of the cupboard.

Some other day she might have let it go. But she had worked an extra shift inspecting LED boards and she was tired from being up late the previous night tending to her mother, who had begun to wake in the darkness unsure of where she was, and so Ruth was in no mood to be pitied and she told Mathew as much—a little sharper than she should have.

A crow cawed in the distance and branches rustled.

"You could have told me where to go," Della said.

Ruth passed between beanpole poplars and stepped over a section of crisscrossed rabbit prints with spots of blood and clumps of gray fur. "This is a bad place to get lost."

The two women slugged through the woods. The fog had smothered the trunks in the distance, but the tops of the trees were still visible.

"You've been out here before," Della said.

"A long time ago."

They continued north and the fog thickened. Ruth's upper body moved through what seemed like a light drift of snow while her legs worked through the heavier mounds below. The long branches of the trees blurred as though laid beneath wax paper.

"I don't know that he'll come back with me," Della said.

"I can't say what he'll do."

"It might be we should stop now. Go back and call an ambulance."

"It's too late for that." To the east the fog seemed to move. Ruth studied the movement and saw that it was smoke.

"What is it?" Della asked.

"Smoke." Ruth pointed. She studied the smoke but could not locate its source.

"Who else would be out here?"

Ruth headed toward the smoke. The crust broke and sank underfoot. The wind quickened and the snow continued to lash down on them. Ruth followed the smoke through a stand of pines. When she reached the spot where the smoke rose, she still could not tell where it came from. It seemed to rise directly from the snow.

"What is this?" Della asked.

Ruth shook her head. "I don't know. I don't know what causes that."

The smoke was like that of a campfire, but there was no fire. Ruth reached out with her gloved hand and held it in the middle of the smoke, but it only felt cold. "It's like something come up from the ground."

Della turned to the east. "I have to piss," she said.

"What?"

"I have to piss." Della scanned the woods. Her snow hat sat unevenly on her head and her black hair came down over her shoulders and was dusted with flurries. "I'll only be a minute."

Ruth watched Della push through the pine boughs and become enveloped by the fog. She turned back to the smoke. It rose and captured the muted light. She watched the coiling strands of gray and thought of Mathew sculpting figures from clay. She imagined him sculpting the woods from the fog, giving shape to the trees and the bushes. The lost bull wheels and the rusted derricks.

A branch rustled behind her and a gray squirrel emerged. The squirrel studied Ruth with its black-pellet eyes, and Ruth wondered why it wasn't somewhere safe waiting for the storm to pass. She pulled her glasses from her face and wiped her eyes. The snow crunched somewhere close but beyond the fog. The squirrel's eyes darted side to side and it skittered up the tree. Ruth put her glasses back on and turned to the sound.

"Della?" Ruth studied the fog. She thought of wolves and black bears and coyotes. "Della?" She grabbed hold of the zipper of her coat. "Who's there?"

The crunching stopped. The wind came up from the north. Ruth held her breath and listened, and then the crunching started again and Della cut through the fog. Her eyes were wide and unsettled. "The fog is getting worse," she said. "I can't hardly see."

"We don't have far," Ruth said, relaxing some. "We're close now."

MILK RAYMOND

MILK ENTERED THE DUPLEX AND SET HIS CIGARETTES ON THE TABLE and walked down the hall to his boy's room. He stood in the doorway and watched Daniel sleep under the covers. Milk could smell the alcohol on himself and it bothered him. He wondered what Jett would say if she were here and figured she probably had a number for him to call. A support group for the alcohol and probably the reckless driving and the headaches. He wondered if she had a number to call after you fucked a stranger in a gas station and then followed her home in the middle of the night believing she might be the solution to your fucked-up, miserable life.

The light from the hallway was low and soft and Milk felt worn out. The hamper sat beside the wall still full of clothes and toys. Milk picked it up and brought it over to the bed and sat down on it, trying not to put his full weight on the cheap wicker. He watched his boy breathe. Heard the faint whistling sound as the air moved through his lips. Studied his arm pulled to the side of his face with his fingers spread out as though he were pushing something away. Watched his eyes flicker and then still.

The poster of the solar system leaned against the boy's closet door, and Milk stood from the hamper and went to it. He unrolled the poster and examined it and then reached into his pocket and removed the tacks he had kept. He took the poster over to the wall opposite the boy's bed and quietly tacked it there. He stood back from the wall and saw that the poster was crooked, and so he removed the tacks, and when the poster was finally straight he secured it to the wall and turned again to his boy and watched him. The steady rise of his quilt.

In the living room he pulled a cigarette from the pack on the table and removed his shirt and his jeans. He sat down on the pullout couch in the half nude and smoked his cigarette. He wondered what he would do about work and about the bills piling up on the table. He thought back to Rachel and her station wagon with the car seats and the folder from the community college and told himself that he would have to do something. He couldn't just sit around waiting to be saved. He couldn't just get drunk and drive around all night looking for answers. He pictured the rise and fall of his boy's chest and thought back to himself as a boy and saw his father drunk and passed out on the kitchen floor. His mother dead at thirty-seven of a brain aneurysm. His father dead at forty in a car wreck. No one saving either of them. He watched the sun begin to rise, and then he put out his cigarette on the cardboard box and pulled the blanket over his tired body and tried to steal a little sleep.

RUTH FENN

THE HUNTING STAND WAS SURROUNDED BY PILLARED HARDWOODS. It would have been difficult to see in the fall. The timber frame and four spidery legs would have disappeared behind the brown leaves. But in the winter it stood out.

Ruth stopped in front of the stand and looked up at the timber frame that supported tin walls roughly twelve feet in length. The wind carried the scent of damp pine. A ruffed grouse exploded from a cranberry bush in a shower of flakes and wings.

"I can't go up there," Della said.

Ruth turned to where Della stood, partially hidden by the fog. "You can."

Della shook her head and looked down at the ground.

Ruth turned back to the stand. A window had been boarded up with two sheets of plywood. Somebody could have been inside it or not and nobody would have known the difference.

The wind whistled off the tin walls. Ruth pictured Horace inside the stand. Bloodied but alive. She heard a sound and turned and saw Della with her eyes closed praying under her breath.

"That's enough," Ruth said. "That's not helping anyone."

Della wiped her nose. She kept her eyes closed for another moment, and when she opened them it seemed as though something inside her had changed. She nodded her head several times in quick succession and wiped her nose again and headed for the ladder. Her boots kicked up snow. She grabbed the wooden rails and began to climb. Snow came loose from the rungs and fell to the ground with a whisper.

The fog seemed to be getting higher. It enveloped the lower half of the ladder. Ruth swept her hand in front of her face as though she might be able to disperse the fog and felt the pistol shift in her coat pocket. Della reached the top rung and opened the trapdoor. Her arms disappeared into the stand, followed by her legs.

Ruth heard muffled sounds but couldn't distinguish them. She knew most hunting stands were lined with carpet to cut down on the noise. She listened to the sounds and thought of Mathew and the way he used to sing to himself in the woods. She would open the window above the kitchen sink in the summertime while she was making dinner and listen to his far-off voice traveling between tree limbs and around thick trunks; shaped by the woods so that when it reached the window, it sounded like her boy was singing in some language partly born from him and partly born from the forest. Though she knew better, there were days after he died that she opened the window above the sink and listened, as though some of those sounds were still out there nestled under the wolf trees and caught in the thorny bushes.

The trapdoor swung open and snow fell through the fog to the forest floor. Della emerged from the stand and began climbing down the ladder. A moment later, Horace followed after her.

He was in bad shape. He was alive. But that's the best thing Ruth could say of him. He stood in front of the hunting stand in the thin shadows of the branches and blinked his eyes like he had been in the dark all his life and was seeing sunlight for the first time. His face was purpled and blistered. The skin above his right eye had been lacerated.

Ruth felt the weight of the gun against her chest and thought to pull it out. She could shoot him dead and leave him for the animals to pick apart. She stood with her body tense and glanced over at Della, who moved through the snow. She asked herself how Elam had fought against the urge and whether Mathew would have wanted her to pull the trigger.

Della didn't say a word. She continued down the hill toward the tracks. Horace remained behind the stand focused on Ruth. He looked at her for a long time, and then he opened his mouth and closed it and opened it again.

"It wasn't nothing particular about your boy," he said. "I thought you'd want to hear that." He turned to where Della had disappeared and then turned back to Ruth. "I caught him pinching my pain pills." Horace looked down at the ground for a moment. "I told him I had something stronger. It all started like that. If I hadn't known this guy Dwyer, it would have never gone so far."

Ruth felt her stomach turn to fire. She pictured the man in the lawn chair with the red muttonchops and her hand moved toward her gun.

"It takes you," Horace said. "You think there are things you won't do. But there aren't." He wiped something from his mouth and turned from Ruth and began to walk unevenly after Della.

THE FOG BROKE and twisted around their bodies. Ruth remained several feet behind Della and Horace. Horace stumbled every few steps. She could hear his labored breath and his harsh cough. Every now and then he seemed to get stuck in the snow, and then he'd lurch forward like a truck with a busted transmission. She could no longer see Della through the fog, but she knew Della only had to follow the tracks to find her way home.

Pieces of Horace cut through the fog. An arm. The side of his head. But Ruth was losing sight of him, as though he were a set piece in a dream she was waking up from. She listened to the crunching snow and tried to distinguish Della's footsteps from Horace's and both of theirs from hers. She thought again of the gun in her coat pocket, and though she wanted to know everything that had happened to her boy, she wanted Horace dead even more, and so she unzipped her coat.

When she reached the creek, a sound made her stop. The rhythmic crunching of snow had suddenly doubled. Something was moving toward the creek. Ruth stopped and held her hand on the gun and waited. She strained her eyes but couldn't see through the fog.

The footsteps stopped altogether, and for several seconds there was no sound. Only wind slithering around the trees. Then the footsteps started up again—even quicker this time. They were coming toward her. Ruth pulled the gun from her coat and steadied her arms and tried to slow her breathing by counting: one, two, three. She heard a crack and then a thud followed by a footstep and another crack. She kept the gun pointed toward the sounds, her arms shaking.

The wind whistled. A flock of geese flew somewhere overhead. She narrowed her eyes, but all she saw was white and gray, and so after a moment she took a small step forward and then another and then another.

She saw the blood first. Just a small amount splattered on the white snow where her boot came down. Then the ungloved hand and the arm and finally the whole body. The side of Horace's head was caved in and the bone fragments had mixed with the skin and the blood so that there was no order to it anymore.

Della stood at Horace's feet, her snow hat uneven and her shoulders moving up and down as she struggled to catch her breath. Ruth didn't bother trying to hide the gun. She looked again at Horace and thought she might be sick.

"Were you planning on shooting us both?" Della asked.

"No."

"I wouldn't blame you."

The wind blew, and specks of snow landed on Horace and melted into the crevices of his face. Ruth lowered the gun and then put it in her coat pocket. "There's a well," she said. "At the top of the hill on the other side of the creek."

Della shook her head.

"If you leave him here, it's only a matter of time before some animal drags him onto the trail and not much longer after that before someone finds him."

"You don't need to do this," Della said.

"I know it." Ruth studied Horace and then set herself in motion. She grabbed one of his legs just above his boot. She could feel his waxy skin and the prickly hairs underneath his pant leg. "Come on," she said. "I won't do it alone."

HORACE'S HEAD BROKE through the sheet of ice, and Ruth could hear running water. She struggled to keep her balance. Her right foot punched through, and she felt the cold water instantly. She lifted her foot and put it back on solid ground and pulled.

The two women ascended the hill. Horace's arms had rolled back and they extended above his head. He was leaving a small trail of blood behind him.

"I've got to stop a minute," Della said when they reached flat ground. She dropped Horace's foot and fell into the snow.

Ruth set down Horace's other foot.

An old stone foundation one room deep stretched in a half square some twenty yards behind them. In the center of the foundation were the remains of a chimney. Two walls of granite built up and topped horizontally by long stones.

All of the sudden Della began to scream. She sat there in the snow with her fists clenched in front of her and stared at nothing and screamed. A guttural scream that seemed to shake as it left her mouth.

Then she stopped.

The two sat quiet for some time, and then Della stood and Ruth followed. They grabbed Horace's legs and begin pulling him through the deep snow. Ruth kept her eyes on the ground, and when she spotted the stone well, the lip of which was flush with the snow, she turned her body sideways and picked up her pace.

They didn't give much thought to how they would do it. Neither said a word to the other. They didn't count to three and they didn't position themselves differently. They just pulled and tugged and pushed and when Horace was gone, fallen and disappeared to somewhere they couldn't see, they collapsed in the snow like two old stones toppled from a boundary wall that had been standing since before they were ever born.

All at once Della began to talk. She talked about Horace and the time she first met him when she was just ten years old at the ballpark where he was waiting in line to buy a hot dog with a quarter that his mother had given him, and how years later he wanted to name their son William after Ted Williams, and how he had started buying pain pills from some guy after hurting his back logging, and how she had threat-ened to leave him the first time she found him shooting heroin in the school bus and he hit her hard enough to leave a five-inch bruise the color of dishwater over her right kidney.

She told Ruth that William worshiped his father and that she had come to feel like a roommate in her own home. She told Ruth that she had always been jealous of her and Elam and what they appeared to have. At first it was easy to let people treat her like a victim after the boys were found, because it made her feel like she was finally part of her own family—like she was connected to her husband and son in some way that she hadn't been before. She told Ruth that she felt awful about it later and had wanted to speak out and had driven to Ruth's a couple of times but lost confidence and turned around before she got to the drive.

Ruth let Della talk and again took to noticing things in the woods. Fire-cracked rocks. Cairns placed between trees with no discernible pattern. A single withered apple tree in a copse of oaks. She thought that after fifty-two years there might be something she could say to Della or to herself. That she might be able to draw on something to help her see the events of the last couple of days more clearly. But she couldn't see the form the events took—everything was dull at the edges. Everything without shape.

MILK RAYMOND

MILK DREAMT HE WAS LOST IN THE MOUNTAINS AND VALLEYS ALONG the Zagros range. He had been lost for several days but saw no sheep and no goats. There were farms scattered within the valleys, but the farms were abandoned. The winter had come and the nylon uppers of his boots were tipped with ice.

He followed a path down a steep mountainside and reached a square mud hut. He peered inside the hut and found it empty save for several pomegranate rinds laid over a sheet. He looked out over the snow-covered field. In the middle of the field he saw an old man sitting with his back toward Milk, facing the mountains. Milk drew his rifle and started toward him. The wind blew and carried with it the faint scent of dried clover.

The man didn't turn when Milk reached him. He held a shotgun between his legs with the barrel pressed against the underside of his chin. The man began to speak quietly, but Milk couldn't understand the words. He heard something off in the distance and turned. A small boy stood at the edge of the tree line, his face blurred. Again Milk smelled dried clover. The boy stood still, watching Milk, and then he turned and ran into the woods.

THE DUPLEX WAS cold when Milk woke. He gathered his clothes from the pile next to the pullout couch and dressed. He walked over to the heater and held his hands over the plastic casing. No heat came out. He went to the thermostat and cranked it to the right, but there was no sound and no heat.

He pulled back the curtains and saw his truck buried in snow. A bluebird clung to an empty suet cage that hung from a tree in the yard. He watched it for a moment and then walked down the carpeted hall to his boy's room and opened the door. The bed was empty. He checked the bathroom and the kitchen, but no one was there. He paused in the middle of the hall, and then he went quickly to the front door and put on his boots and coat.

He hurried around the side of the house to the storm doors, wondering if his boy might have gone into the basement at night and been trapped when the snow piled up. He fell to his knees and dug out the doors and pulled them open. The basement was dark. He started down the wooden stairs and pulled the string and looked around at the bright-blue floor and the plastic chairs and the workbench. His boy wasn't there.

He came up from the basement and jogged down the drive. He stood at the end of it and looked down the road in both directions, but there was nothing. He turned back to the house. The weather stick extended from the siding, and above it he saw that one of the blinds over Daniel's bedroom window had been flipped horizontal. His eye started to throb.

The snow was still coming down. He watched it collect on the drive on top of the already fallen snow and knew that any tire marks would have quickly disappeared. Same for tiny footprints.

RUTH FENN

THE TWO WOMEN REACHED THE TRUCK OUT OF BREATH. RUTH pulled the keys from her pocket. Her fingers were numb. She opened the door and collapsed onto the bench seat like someone who had been shot in the stomach. Her face burned. She looked in the rearview mirror and saw that her skin had gone white save for her ear, which was a deep purple. She started the engine and turned up the heat and backed the truck away from the red-flocked hobblebush.

The fog had dissipated some, but the snow covered the roads and continued to fall. Her wipers thumped against the windshield. The cold air pushed through the vents.

Della didn't speak. Ruth thought she had worn herself out and probably regretted some of the things she had already said. But Ruth had questions. She wanted to know how it was possible that Della didn't know what was going on. But she also wanted to know about the last time Della had seen Mathew. She wanted to know if he had said anything and how he looked. She wanted to see him one more time, but she wasn't sure what good it would do, and she was afraid of the answers she might get, so she sat there with the silence as heavy as chunkwood.

She followed the road north past steep banks crowded with hemlocks and fields covered with snow, where shorthorn cattle walked slowly along the barbed-wire fences. She turned east and headed in that direction for some time, past houses with their curtains pulled closed and then long stretches of woods broken only by the occasional gravel drive that led to homes settled so deep in the woods that no one could see them.

She continued past an empty field and then a small farmhouse. Lights winked through a stand of oak trees. Ruth slowed the vehicle. She thought at first the lights were from a dump plow. A reinforcement from Bennington. A ten-wheel plow with massive tire chains and wings that tore pavement. But the lights were flashing blue and red.

Della leaned forward. "We need to turn around."

Ruth slowed the car around the bend.

"Turn around," Della said.

The police cruiser sat in the middle of the road with no one behind the wheel. There were no other vehicles. None pulled over to the side of the road and none in the ditches. There was only a ruined deer fence and partially filled tracks cutting into a snowbank. Ruth pulled behind the cruiser and put the truck in park and opened the door and stepped out onto the road.

"Ruth," Della said.

Ruth saw him then. His upturned boot and then his entire leg and then his body and the faint tracks in the snow beside his head.

He was breathing when she reached him. But his breath was labored and his eyes were closed and it looked to her like maybe Leo Strobridge was dead and it was only the wind passing through his mouth causing the sound she mistook for his breath.

Ruth crouched there in the snow beside him. He wore a wool shirt with royal-blue epaulets on the shoulders and a matching tie. The tops of two blue pens were visible in his coat pocket below his badge. His rimless glasses covered with snow still clung crookedly to his small nose, and his mouth was as straight as a piece of paper on a desk. That was one thing that always bothered Ruth. The way his mouth never seemed to turn one way or the other. It was as though it was detached from the rest of him, something he put on in front of the mirror every morning just like his belt and holster.

Leo's hat had fallen from his head and lay upright in the road. His right hand rested by his hip and his left hand laid palm-up next to his ear, as though he were telling someone to stop. She saw that he still had his gun on him—that whatever had happened, he hadn't pulled it from his holster. She looked around the woods and then back to the police cruiser and the flashing lights and then to her own truck, where Della sat watching from the passenger seat. She turned back to Leo and thought she saw his upper lip twitch.

She studied him for a moment, and then she stood and went to the cruiser and peered inside the window. She hesitated and grabbed the handle. The door opened. She sat down in the leather seat. There was a large black screen and a keyboard in front of the dash. She struck the keyboard, but the screen didn't change.

Between the seats was a shotgun rack with a single upright Remington, and behind the rack was a metal cage covered with Plexiglas. The radio chattered but she couldn't make out the words. She looked out the windshield at Leo lying in the snow with flurries gathering on his uniform and thought of Mathew in the tent naked and bruised and of Horace and the snow melting in the sunken parts of his face. She thought again of Mathew sitting at the table with the window open and the wind pushing the curtains inward. She tried to read his face, but it wouldn't take shape, and she felt a sinking in her stomach thinking that she might not have even looked at him—that she might have simply glanced at the block of clay and the index cards on the table and headed upstairs to her bath. She wondered what words she could have spoken to him then and what effect those words might have had.

The police radio chattered again. The wind bore down on the cruiser. Ruth studied the radio and reached for it. With her numb fingers she thumbed it to life and called for help.

MILK RAYMOND

MILK HAD NEVER BELIEVED THAT HIS BOY LOOKED LIKE HIM. WHEN Daniel was five years old—the night before Milk left for basic—Milk was drinking beers and playing cards in his apartment with Jessica and a man he worked with at the Jiffy Lube. The man had brought his wife, who Milk had never met and who worked selling makeup from home. Daniel was in bed, but he woke at some point during the game and made his way to the dining room where everyone was sitting. His brown hair was disheveled and he wore a white T-shirt that hung loose from his chest. The woman stood when she saw him. "My god," she said. "He looks just like you." She had had a couple of beers by then, and she made a big deal of it. Walking over to Daniel and touching his face and looking back at Milk. She wasn't the first person to say it. People he didn't know came up to him all the time. Customers that saw Daniel when Jessica brought him into the Jiffy Lube. Old women behind them in the checkout line at the grocery store. But Milk didn't see it.

The wipers pushed snow from the windshield. Milk resisted the urge to press down on the gas, knowing it wouldn't take much to lose control. The thumping of the wipers kept him calm. Kept him thinking of his boy.

Jessica had probably been right when she told Milk he'd hardly known Daniel before he left for the war. He had gone through the motions of dressing and feeding his boy and putting him to bed. He loved Daniel and would have done anything for him. But he didn't know him. And he wondered now how Jessica had gotten Daniel to go with her. He wondered if she had called him outside and grabbed him and forced him into her car or if she had simply asked.

Rae Brakeman—the sapper in Iraq—told his baby girl over the telephone that he had gone to the moon when he left for his second tour of Iraq. Even though she was too young to understand. Reggie Brenner told his boy that he had gone off to slay dragons. But Milk couldn't recall what he told Daniel. He wasn't sure he told him anything at all.

It wasn't something anyone had told him back then. That you had to get to know your child. That it didn't just happen. That it was work like anything else. But there were lots of things people didn't tell him. Nobody had told him about Iraq. About how the enemy might not really be the enemy. Or how the fear of killing was so much worse than the fear of dying. Nobody had told him how to turn it on and nobody had told him how to shut it all off.

The snow continued to fall and Milk watched the road, but he saw nothing. He struggled to keep the truck steady. Long strands of barbed wire on either side of him. Abandoned farms and abandoned lives. The snow coming down over all of it. He slowed the truck when he spotted the birch trees in the distance and then the woodshed. He whispered *Please, God, be home* and pulled into the drive.

RUTH FENN

Rᴜᴛʜ ꜱᴀᴡ Mɪʟᴋ ꜱᴛᴀɴᴅɪɴɢ ɪɴ ʜᴇʀ ᴅʀɪᴠᴇᴡᴀʏ ʙᴇꜱɪᴅᴇ ʜɪꜱ ᴛʀᴜᴄᴋ wearing the falling snow on his arms and shoulders. She watched him for a moment and then shut the engine and stepped out of the truck.

"He's gone," Milk said.

Ruth looked to the house and the curtained windows and the light behind them. She thought of all the children she had watched over the years and how so many of them had been stretched thin and then broken as a result of being pulled between their mothers and fathers. "I can't do this right now," she said.

"I need to call the police, but I don't have no phone."

Ruth started across the drive.

"Wait," Milk said.

Ruth stopped.

"This is the only place I could think to come."

The snow fell on Ruth's hair and on the side of her face, where it burned. She studied Milk. His eyes looked everywhere but at her. "What happened?"

"His mother. She took him."

"When?"

"This morning. Not long ago, I don't think."

"In this storm?"

Milk nodded.

Ruth thought of Leo Strobridge lying in the snow with breath hardly coming from him, and then she thought of the deer fence and the tire tracks leading into the snowbank. "Do you know where she might have gone?"

Milk shook his head. "She came to see him yesterday, but she's living somewhere out of state. That's the last I heard."

"She's been staying somewhere close, then?"

"She's an addict. I don't know where she's staying. Nowhere good. Nowhere for my boy to be."

Ruth thought of the motel—pictured Dwyer—and felt the gun still heavy against her chest. She wondered if the woman would be stupid enough to stay in town after running over a police officer but figured it wasn't logic driving her.

"Come on, then," Ruth said. She continued toward the house. The snow still falling. The storm somehow seeming like it was just getting started.

MILK RAYMOND

Milk followed Ruth up the snow-covered porch steps and into her home. A man Milk figured for her husband stood in the foyer, but Milk went straight to the telephone on the table in the hallway and called the police. He spoke to a woman who asked whether he had full custody of Daniel and sighed when he said that he didn't and then seemed almost disinterested while she explained that he needed to go to the police station and fill out a report. He hung up the receiver and gripped the side of the table and listened to Ruth and her husband talk in hushed voices in the next room.

When Milk entered the living room, the two stopped talking. The man didn't look well. He sat on the edge of a burlap chair in blue jeans and a white shirt with the skin around his patchy beard blistered and his body thin. Ruth didn't look well either. Her eyes were bloodshot, and in the light Milk could see that the side of her face was frostbitten.

"There was an accident just now," Ruth said. "Out on Higgins Road. The trooper was hit by a car, it looked like."

"Jessica."

"Maybe. Maybe not. The roads are bad. It could have been someone else. Someone who got scared and ran."

"It's Jessica."

Ruth held her left hand in her right and rubbed her bare knuckles. "If it was her, there's only two places I can think she'd go. One of them is that she's left town. Maybe she stopped at the gas station to fill up first. But the police will put out an alert. The police will be looking for her vehicle on the highway."

"What's the other place?"

"There's a place she could be staying. But it's a long shot."

"Tell me where."

"I'll show you."

Ruth's husband stood quickly and walked into the other room. Ruth watched him for a moment and then turned back to Milk. "If anything goes wrong, you'll need someone with you who can call for help. And there's a devil's chance of things going wrong. I need you to understand that."

MILK DROVE CAREFULLY against the storm, resisting again the urge to press down on the gas. Ruth kept fidgeting in her seat and pulling at the front of her coat. She told Milk about the motel where the dealers stayed, and she told him she hoped Jessica wouldn't be staying in one of those rooms but that it was as good a place as any to start looking. She told Milk that she would call the police from the pay phone outside the Whistler. She would tell them that she saw Jessica's vehicle leaving the scene of the accident even though she hadn't. If Leo hadn't already called in her vehicle, it would be enough to get the police looking for her.

Milk followed the road over the bridge and then along Main Street, where small homes were nearly hidden in the snow. He drove past an American flag that hung bright and limp from a pole and passed cars parked in narrow drives and on front lawns instead of on the road. He ascended a hill, and in the distance he saw the motel and the Whistler that wouldn't be open for several hours. He continued up the hill, and then he saw a couple of vehicles parked in the lot, covered in snow.

"That's hers," he said quickly. "The Jeep there. It's the same car she was driving yesterday." He pulled into the lot and shut the engine.

"Listen to me," Ruth said. She grabbed Milk's forearm before he removed the key from the ignition. "I know the men in that motel."

"I'm not waiting on the police."

"I'm not asking you to. But I got my own problems with them. It's only right you know that."

Milk looked at Ruth. Whatever she showed on her face was something he hadn't seen before. He thought of her boy and how he had been found in a tent dead of a heroin overdose. Milk had asked around a little after meeting Ruth and was told that some people thought her boy lured the other boy into the tent with promises of alcohol and drugs and then assaulted and murdered him but that Ruth maintained they were friends and maybe something more. Everyone he spoke to told him that her child had been unusual. That he used to sit in class all day with his head on his desk and a book in his lap and that teachers tried to get him to participate but eventually just gave up. He heard about the school plays and how he aced all his tests despite not seeming to pay much attention and how nobody knew about his addiction, but then nobody knew much of anything about him. Milk figured he understood Ruth's problem with the dealers, but he didn't see how it mattered now and he didn't have time to find out.

Milk pushed open the door. He walked up to the Jeep with the wind whipping around him and wiped the snow from the passenger window and cupped his hands over the glass. He couldn't see much. He pulled at the door handle and the door cracked open. There was a piece of crumpled paper on the floor and a can of Coke in the cup holder. He opened the glove box and saw several packs of cigarettes stuffed with small plastic baggies. Some of them unmarked and others marked with brown cow stamps. He left the glove box open and put his knee on the passenger seat and looked in the back and saw some clothes and a soiled pair of underwear on the floor.

Ruth had already started toward the motel. She walked quickly but with a slight limp. Milk closed the door and followed after her but stopped shy of the motel when he spotted something in the snow.

"Ruth," he said. He started jogging toward the object, and when he got within a few feet his stomach went hollow. He bent down in the snow and picked up the bright-yellow goggles. He looked across the lot and thought he could make out small footprints leading to the tree line behind the motel, but he wasn't sure if the footprints were real or if his mind was putting them there.

"Go on," Ruth said.

Milk looked back at Ruth, and then he rose and tightened his grip on the goggles and started for the woods.

RUTH FENN

Ruth watched Milk disappear into the woods under tall pines and then turned back to the motel. The light above the door glowed orange. The blinds were drawn and the metal lawn chair where she had first seen Dwyer sat to the side of the door collecting snow.

She was of the mind that she would shoot first. If he opened the door, she would shoot him, and she would just keep shooting.

The wind picked up and pushed snow across the apron of light. She hesitated only a moment and then slammed her fist against the door. She waited and eyed the peephole, but there was no answer. She tried the doorknob and then pounded the door again. She studied the blinds and slammed the side of her fist against the window. When the door didn't open, she reached for her gun, but hesitated and drew her hand back and walked over to the metal lawn chair. She lifted the chair using the wide arms and shook free the snow and then swung the chair violently against the window. The window shattered instantly, and she stood there staring at the shaking blind and expecting bullets to rain out from the hole. When none came, she used the chair to scrape away the shards of glass, and then she reached through the window and unlocked the door.

The lights were off in the room. Ruth held the gun out in front of her and stepped over the threshold. She smelled cigarette smoke and something rancid. One of the two beds was stripped of its sheets, and there was a large brown stain on the mattress and a black backpack in the middle of the stain. There was trash on the carpeted floor and more trash on the nightstand—empty chip bags and bottles of water and playing cards and a Styrofoam cup filled with cigarette butts atop a Bible where it looked like some of the pages had been torn out and then stuffed back crookedly behind the false-leather front.

Ruth thought of Mathew and the time she had seen him walking along Merino Street on her way home from work the summer before he died. Mathew hadn't seen her, and so she pulled her truck to the side of the road and sat there watching him and wondering what he was doing on the road they used to walk together to look at the roses that grew wild against the stone wall. She saw him place something under a stone, and she waited for him to disappear down the road before getting out of her truck and walking up to the wall and pulling a piece of paper from between the stones.

DEAR MATHEW—YOU MADE IT.

That was all it said. Like some sort of letter to his future self.

Ruth heard a faint noise behind the bathroom door. A hollow thumping. Her breath stopped and she raised the gun and waited. No light came from the bathroom, but she could make out what looked like the tip of a boot darkening the gap beneath the door.

MILK RAYMOND

H<small>IS HANDS STUNG WITH COLD AS HE ASCENDED THE STEEP HILL</small> behind the motel. He pocketed the goggles and pushed away branches. He slipped and fell several times and had to grab onto the raveled undergrowth that barely pushed up through the snow. The footprints had widened like the brushstrokes of an owl's wings and then widened even more so that he couldn't tell if the tracks were from his boy or an animal or something else. His legs ached and he began to question whether the footprints he had seen were real. Could his boy make it up this hill? The trees blurred together and the snow and the sky seemed to merge. The wind picked up and he thought he heard someone moving behind him and then in front of him. He clenched and unclenched his fists to keep the circulation moving through his hands. He grabbed the trunk of a sapling and turned back to where he had come from and then grabbed another sapling and pulled himself up the hill. He looked from tree to tree and spotted an open grove of pines at the top of the hill and then a close grouping of paper birches and then something at the base of one of the birches.

He scrambled up the hill toward the object huddled there, and as he got closer he made out a small figure sitting with his legs pulled to his chest against the trunk. He thought for a moment he was dead, but he was upright, and Milk ran to him, and when he saw his boy's eyes track him, he reached down and grabbed his coat collar and pulled him close.

It was a long time before Milk let go.

"I'm sorry," Daniel said.

"Are you okay?"

The boy nodded. His face was pale and his lips were chapped.

"What happened?"

"I don't know."

"Where's your mother?"

"She was in the motel. She told me to wait in the car, but she didn't come back. I knocked on the door, and a man answered and I saw her on the floor." The boy started to cry.

"Did the man follow you?"

"I don't know. He grabbed my arm and I ran. He told me to stop, but I just ran."

Milk turned back to the woods. He scanned the fallen snow and the deep gray furrows and steep ridges of the white ash trees. Everything was quiet. He saw nothing and heard nothing. The falling snow seemed to slow for just a moment, and then the report of a gun broke the silence and he felt something like a sledgehammer strike his leg. He fell, and the palms of his hands punctured the snow. Cold moved through his body and his heart beat against his chest like a battering ram. He struggled to his feet, and an intense pain moved through his right leg. He fell again and closed his eyes and let the breath move through his lips and told himself that it wouldn't be here and that it wouldn't be now, and then he stood, grabbed his boy, and did his best to run.

RUTH FENN

Ruth studied the dark spot beneath the door and braced herself. She listened to the hollow thumping and watched the dark spot suddenly jerk away.

She kept the gun pointed at the door and quietly approached. Her wet boots caused the floorboards beneath the carpet to whine. She moved slowly past the unmade bed and stepped around a row of plastic bottles. The wind picked up and the blind that covered the broken window trembled. The thumping continued.

When she reached the bathroom door, she stood to the side of it and pressed her back against the wall and waited. Her palms were sweaty and she had to switch the gun from her right hand to her left and then back to her right. She tightened her fingers around the grip and reached for the doorknob.

She turned the doorknob quickly, and all at once she pushed the door inward, but the door caught on something and she struck the wood clumsily with her shoulder and stumbled a little. She regained her balance and held the gun high and forced her way through the opening but stopped when she saw the body.

A woman not more than thirty years old on the floor in the nude. Her back arched and her legs and fingers twitching. A thin line of foam spread from her mouth, and the back of her skull struck the base of the toilet over and over. *Thump. Thump.* Ruth dropped the gun on the floor and bent down beside the woman, unsure of what she could do. She grabbed the woman's shoulders and pulled her away from the toilet. A spot of red blood crisscrossed with black hairs shone on the white porcelain.

Ruth studied the fresh bruises on the woman's neck and the dried blood on her fingertips. She settled on the woman's eyes. Her pinpoint pupils seemed to register Ruth for a brief moment, and then her body came still. Ruth reached out and touched the woman's neck gently but couldn't find a pulse. She studied her damp hair and pale face. Ruth's breath seemed to release from some unknown grip all of the sudden, and she fell back against the wall.

She studied the small bathroom. The moldy shower curtain and the toilet spackled with puke and the torn wallboard over the mirror where someone had written in black marker URINE THE WORST PLACE and beside it I JUST FUCKED AN ALIEN.

The smell of the room grabbed her all at once. The puke, piss, and smoke. She sat there for a long time with the bathroom door open, the motel door open, and the woman lying there dead. She lost track of time and lost track of her thoughts.

She watched the snow swirl in the wind. It seemed to bend around the dark motel room, and she thought back to the book Mathew had left on his desk and the page he had marked with a leaf. She had sat down at his desk holding the leaf between her fingers and studying the illustration of the black hole surrounded by bright matter. She had read the caption about how light became distorted around the hole and how once the light slipped beyond the horizon it could not escape. And she wondered, was she the light being distorted, or had she already been pulled into the hole? Had Mathew known where he was? Did he think he could escape? Could she escape? She studied the snow, turned a cloudy orange by the outdoor light, and pictured the orbits of stars that circled the darkness.

She heard something then. Snow crunching underfoot. She got to her knees and grabbed the pistol from the floor and then stood and pointed the gun at the open door. She stood there exhausted and saw the back of a child in the far distance. Thin shoulders covered in snow and held by someone. Then she saw Milk's face. She watched him walking slowly—dragging his foot across the parking lot like it was stuck to the ground—and she started to tell him to stop, not to enter the motel, but he stopped on his own and then she heard something else. More snow crunching and then a voice that sounded familiar.

MILK RAYMOND

MILK SLOWED AS HE CROSSED THE LOT TOWARD THE TRUCK. HE pulled his boy close to his chest.

A voice cut through the wind. "You ought not run from me."

Milk's foot had gone numb, and it dragged through the snow as though fastened to a track. He felt his boy's thin body against his chest and his chin on his shoulder. He hoped the boy's eyes were closed.

"Stop," the man said. "I won't ask you again."

He stopped thirty yards from the truck, knowing from the sound of the man's voice that he was close enough to shoot and not miss. Milk's only chance was to draw the man even closer where Milk might lunge at him.

He heard the man's boots crunching the snow. Two steps and then three.

"Goddamn," the man said. He coughed, and Milk heard him spit. "I ain't fit to run. You ain't either by the looks of it."

Milk cradled the boy with his right arm and held the top of his damp head with his left. He looked again at the truck.

"I am fit to shoot you, though," the man said. "And I don't like shooting more than I have to. Because so much as I don't like running, I don't like to clean up neither. Hell, there isn't a lot I do like, which is

267

why I prefer to be left alone. Why I prefer children don't come knocking on my door and seeing things they ain't supposed to be seeing."

Milk tried to clear his mind the way he had learned to do in Iraq and focus only on the moment. He heard the wind whip around his coat and heard the man behind him spit again and wipe his mouth. He studied the snow-covered road beyond the truck and the homes on the other side of the road. His eyes focused on a small yellow home with a dim orange light visible through the curtains and faint gray smoke rising from the chimney and mixing with the snow.

"I won't kill your boy," the man said. "I'll take good care of him. But you and me got a bit of a problem. It's my experience that some men don't really give a shit about their wives getting involved with me. Those are the ones looking for someone to blame and not really giving a shit who it is. Others, they take issue. And you running through the snow with your leg half detached from the rest of your body makes me think you're the kind of guy that might take issue. That might not let a sleeping dog lie."

Milk thought to put the boy down and turn and run at the man. He figured if he moved quick enough, the man might get spooked and miss with the first shot, and even if he didn't miss he might not land the shot clean and Milk might not go down.

"Let me put the boy down," Milk said.

"Fine. I ain't no monster."

Milk set his boy in the snow. Daniel's eyes were wet. The snow swirled around him. Milk studied him for a long moment and then lipped the words *Run to the yellow house*, and when the boy turned and started to run, Milk spun around.

The man wore gray sweat pants tucked into his boots and a long-sleeved shirt. Flakes of snow were caught in his red muttonchops and in his thinning hair. He smiled a toothy smile and raised the gun, and before Milk could take his first step he heard a shot and saw blood bubble out of the right side of the man's neck.

The man reached for the opposite side of his neck as though his ability to tell his right from his left had been ruined. He took a small step forward and a second bullet went through his ear.

RUTH FENN

THE SKY WAS BLUE AND THE SUN SHONE BRIGHT OVER THE WHITE hills. Ruth stood behind the shed gripping a broad aluminum shovel. The dogs wrestled in the snow and she watched them for a while, and then she turned back to the shed and continued to dig.

She understood that some of the pots were broken beyond repair. But she believed there were others that were merely cracked and could be fixed with steel wire, and she believed there were still others that weren't broken at all. Elam had asked her why she didn't wait until the snow melted to retrieve the pots and she couldn't explain why any more than she could explain why she had started dumping them outside the shed in the first place. The best she could do was tell him that it felt like something close to a compulsion.

The sun reflected off the snow. It was the sort of day that seemed like it might be warm from inside but proved cold when confronted. Ruth wondered how it could be so cold when the sun shone so bright, and she heard Mathew as though he were standing right behind her say that it was because the sun was farther away from the earth.

She lifted a shovelful of snow and tossed it in the direction of the dogs. Woodstock dove on the pile and then spun in a tight circle and trampled the area where Ruth was shoveling. Ruth jabbed the shovel and shouted

271

until he retreated. She stuck the shovel in the snow again and pulled it back when she felt the end strike something solid. She tossed the shovel aside and bent down and pushed away the snow and pulled three brown speckled pots from the ground. She wiped them clean and started toward the house.

Inside Ruth set the pots on the table. The sun painted a square across the kitchen floor.

"They aren't so bad."

Ruth turned and saw Elam standing in the doorway. He wore a knitted sweater and blue jeans, and his face was still scratched and the hair on his face was coarse. He had his hands in his pockets.

"No," Ruth said, turning back to the pots. "They're not so bad. Of course, these were at the top. I can't say how the rest of 'em will look."

She studied one of the wares. The small handless jar with bands of blue at the shoulder and base.

"I can help," Elam said.

"That's okay. I won't be much longer."

Ruth left Elam standing in the doorway. She was between the house and the shed when Della's truck turned off the road and pulled into the drive. Ruth stood still with the snow up to her knees and watched Della get out of the truck and put her keys in her coat pocket.

"Deeper than a tall Swede," Della said.

"Just about."

Della stopped several feet from Ruth. "I brought bourbon. I couldn't stand being inside any longer. It seems so quiet."

Ruth nodded.

"You're in the middle of something, though."

Ruth scratched at her forehead with her gloved hand. "I got a couple years' worth of pottery buried under the snow behind the shed. Sometime this morning I got the smart idea to unbury it."

"How's it look?"

"So far as I can see, it's held up pretty well."

Waxwings buzzed somewhere in the distance. Ruth removed her glasses from her face. "I could use a break, though. Something to warm my bones sounds nice, too."

THE WORLD LOOKED bleached from the porch. The wind stirred, snow speckled. Della uncapped the bourbon and hesitated a moment and then handed it to Ruth.

"Old Wives' Tale," Ruth said, holding up the bottle.

"I got it a while back from a place just over the New York line. I liked the label."

Ruth studied it. A long shadow of women standing together on top of a hill like a copse of misshapen trees. She took a sip. The bourbon had some kick and it warmed her stomach.

"It's finally let up a little," Della said. "For a while I thought this storm would be like '89."

"It was getting there."

"Eleven days we were without power."

Ruth shook her head. "Part of me hoped I'd give birth early just so I could lay in a warm hospital bed and watch the television. Of course Mathew had other ideas." Ruth took another sip from the bottle and studied the falling snow. Watched it collect on the roof of the shed.

"I drove him to a private school in Burlington just before he died. One of those places where you pick your own grades and grow your lunch in the community garden. I could see he was hurting." Ruth wiped a watery drip from her nose. "I could see he was different. But we had no money to pay for a private school and I had no idea how we would make a move work. I guess I thought it would come to me. I guess I thought I had to try."

She hesitated a moment. "He was quiet the whole way out there. All two and a half hours and then all through the tour with the vice principal. On the way back we pulled into a roadside hamburger stand, and I finally got him to look at me long enough to see how sad his eyes were. He told me he couldn't go to school in Burlington. I asked him how come, and he told me he couldn't leave William. I know they didn't talk none at school. But he felt like he couldn't leave him. Like he needed to be there. I'm guessing they both felt that way."

Ruth handed Della the bottle. Della took a sip and wiped her mouth and sat there a long moment.

"I gave all the group meeting duties to Ethel. Gave her my Sunday reading slot as well."

Ruth was quiet.

"I understand there were things I lost sight of." Della stared straight ahead, her hand tight around the bottle. "It seems an insult to apologize."

The two women were quiet for several minutes. The dogs continued to wrestle in the snow by the shed. Every now and then Woodstock would start to get the best of Emmylou and then back off like he didn't want Emmylou to quit, and he'd spin around excitedly and then go right back at her.

"It's not that I don't believe," Della said finally. "It's that maybe God gave us a brain and an able body for a reason. It's that maybe I been looking for a savior when I should have been the one doing the saving."

Ruth readjusted her hands in her lap. "Sometimes I think we don't give ourselves enough credit. It freezes us. Keeps us from doing things we're capable of doing. Saying things we should be saying. I suppose a lot of people feel that way. I suspect it's worse for women."

Della turned the bottle in her hands. "I guess we got to stick together some."

Ruth nodded. "It's not a bad thing to recognize."

MILK RAYMOND

Spring had come to North Falls. The air was cold but without the bitterness of winter. Milk squinted at the dappled light that hung above the trees that crowned the hills in the far distance. He turned to his boy, who sat in the passenger seat beside the clay sculpture wrapped in thick plastic.

He thought about Daniel sculpting the face with Ruth over the last six weeks. Pushing his thumbs into the wet clay to form Milk's sunken eyes and lifting the thin ridges of his ears till they stood like hollow bird bones. He thought about his boy removing the face carefully from the kiln and checking it for cracks.

"What's wrong?" Daniel asked.

"Nothing's wrong."

Milk passed a barn and a hillside grave and an old yellow house that slumped like it had given up. He thought about Jessica and the void she had left for her son. The state had paid for the funeral from the indigent burial fund, but Milk had managed a couple hundred dollars for the headstone. An ash-colored slab with a name and a date.

Daniel hadn't said much. He watched the casket being lowered into the damp earth through still and narrow eyes that reminded Milk of his own. It made Milk proud, but it worried him, too. The unexpected toughness of his boy.

The forest swelled on both sides of the road and then broke completely. Homes appeared and the light reddened the sides of them.

"We might drive out to see your great-grandmother tomorrow," Milk said. "Show her your sculpture." He looked over at his boy, who nodded.

Milk had been surprised by how much his boy had wanted to see Marcy since they moved her into the assisted-care facility. She didn't recognize either one of them, and she was often so fatigued she couldn't do much more than lie there in the bed. But Daniel liked to sit on the chair next to her and watch television, and it seemed important that Milk do what he could to make sure his boy was able to see her as much as he might want.

He turned onto Pine Street, where an old wheelbarrow with wooden handles lay tipped over in the grass on the side of the road. He glanced at the clock and checked the rearview mirror and then made a quick turn east on Holcomb Hill. "I want to show you something," he said.

He followed the road past canted trees with new leaves and around a bend flanked by a rusted guardrail. He climbed the road until it leveled out, and then he drove for another quarter mile until he reached an old brick building with two ruined chimneys and three white pillars chalky with flaked paint. He pulled the truck in front of the building and cut the engine. "Come on," he said.

Milk got out of the truck and closed the door. He crossed the sidewalk and ascended the concrete steps scarred by decades of rock salt. When he reached the door, he pressed his hands against the split-pane window and peered into the hallway.

"What is it?" Daniel asked.

"Nothing. You can't see much through here. It's too dark."

Milk descended the steps and walked through the overgrown grass alongside the building. "This used to be the library," he said. "It hasn't been nothing for a long time." He approached a large window positioned behind an oak tree in full bloom and looked in through the glass. The old wood floors were dusty. There were holes in the walls. He could see where the radiators had been. Their footprints pressed into the wood like tobacco stains. "I spent just about every day in this place during the summer when I was your age."

Daniel got up on his toes and peered in through the window.

"My father drove trucks. He'd be gone weeks at a time in the summer. My mother worked for the church as a secretary, and so she'd take me to the playground behind the church in the morning, and then when the library opened she'd drive me here and leave me for the day." Milk removed his cap and tightened the brim. "I sat in the room next to this one. In a leather chair with big brass nailheads along the arms and a stack of books on my lap. I doubt that chair's still here. You can't see it from where you're standing anyway."

Daniel continued to peer through the window. The light faltered.

"I met your mother here," Milk said. "This would've been in the first grade. She was here every day same as me. It was just the two of us most times." He put his cap back on and watched his boy. A small boy still not seeming to grow into his shiny spring jacket and faded blue jeans.

A bird sang in the distance.

"It's okay to miss her," Milk said. "It's okay to be mad at her too."

Daniel pulled away from the window. "Are you mad at her?"

"I suppose I am, a little. I'm sad too."

"I didn't like it when she was sick."

"No," Milk said. "I don't suppose she liked it either. She wanted to be better."

"She left me."

"I know it. That was part of it. That was part of her being sick."

Daniel squinted at something past Milk. "Look," he said. He stepped around Milk and started toward the back of the library. Milk turned and followed. The sun reappeared at the tops of the trees, and the light flickered in front of Milk like something he could reach out and touch.

"They're like ours," Daniel said. He stood behind the library in front of two storm doors nearly hidden in the tall grass.

The doors were painted red. A branch no bigger than a grown man's finger had been wedged between them. Daniel bent down and pulled the handle on one of the doors, and the branch slipped free. He continued to pull until the door fell open against the ground with a loud metallic clang. The boy peered into the cellar. He looked back at Milk and then started down the steps. Milk thought to stop him but followed instead.

The only light came from the sun, but it was enough that Milk could make out the wooden stairs on the other side of the cellar along with a cardboard box and a stack of masonry bricks. Daniel crossed the cellar and started up the wooden steps, making use of the crude handrail. At the top of the stairs he turned the doorknob and pushed.

A thick layer of dust had turned the library floors the color of wood smoke. The built-in shelves that lined the walls were cobwebbed but still in good shape. A metal cage held an old fire extinguisher. There was some graffiti on the bare walls, symbols that Milk didn't recognize. Daniel walked to the center of the room and stopped and turned to Milk. "Where was the chair?" he asked.

The question caught Milk off guard. He looked around the library. "Come on," he said.

He crossed the large room where the checkout counter had once been, his boots leaving tracks in the dust. He tried to recall the last time he had been in the library. His mother had taken him through elementary school, and then when he was old enough to stay home alone, he stopped coming.

In the library now, he imagined himself as a child watching his future projected on one of the library walls. His older self moving through the abandoned building, trailed by his own boy who would have been his age. He saw himself leaving for Iraq and tried to imagine seeing Jessica beaten nearly to death on the floor of the motel.

He wondered what he could have done if he had seen it all. Even now it was so much to take on. And he thought of his boy and how the images were real for him, how hard it must have been—how hard it still was.

He moved down the dark hall and stepped into a carpeted room that smelled of damp wood and cigarette smoke and something unfamiliar. "It was right here," he said.

The chair was no longer in the corner. It was just an empty space. An orange sleeping bag lay in the middle of the room. In the corner opposite where the chair had been were three plastic crates surrounding a stack of cardboard boxes like a firepit. There was a dusty shadow on the wall where a bookshelf had once leaned. Milk's eyes returned to the empty space where his boy now stood in place of the chair, looking out across the room.

"I can see it," Daniel said. "I can see you here."

"It was a long time ago."

"I know. But you were right here."

The light reached in through the north-facing window. It spread flawlessly across the ruined library. Milk studied his boy. Seemed to recognize him as though he were a thought that had been dammed up inside of him for all these years and had only now come loose.

RUTH FENN

Ruth studied the band of scar tissue on her ear and buttoned her coat in the half-light among the particles of dust and then walked down the narrow hallway past the empty guest room where the bed that once held her mother had been made neatly and the floor had been swept clean.

In the kitchen she poured a cup of coffee and went outside onto the front porch, where Elam was already sitting wearing slacks and a white button-down shirt.

"You look like you're waiting on someone to snap your picture," Ruth said.

"You think I'd make the catalogs?"

"You haven't seen the catalogs in a long time. The models are all young and buff now. They've got veins crawling up their forearms like hookworms."

"I don't find nothing attractive about hookworms."

"Neither do I. But then we're old."

"Are we?"

"Yup."

"It seemed not long ago we weren't."

"Did it?"

"Maybe. Maybe not." Elam took a sip of his coffee and rested his boot on the rail. "It don't ever seem to work out the way you plan it."

"What's that?"

"Any of it. All of this. Our lives."

"My mother used to say it's a good thing we're not born long for this world. We might come to expect more. It takes me a while sometimes—to dig up some of the things she used to say to me."

Elam took another sip of his coffee.

"We been married thirty-six years this summer," Ruth said. "My mother hadn't even been alive thirty-six years on the day of our wedding."

"That puts things in perspective."

"We didn't know a thing then, did we?"

"I suppose we didn't."

"Do we know much now?"

"A little, maybe. As much as anyone." Elam adjusted his boot on the rail. "Our boy knew some things."

Ruth was quiet. Then she said, "How do you figure that happened?"

"How's that?"

"How do you figure someone as special as him came from people as ordinary as us?"

Elam shook his head. "You ain't ordinary."

"I ain't special either."

"You are."

"You trying to sweet-talk me?"

"I couldn't sweet-talk a bee into a flower shop. I'm just being honest with you."

"Well, I don't know."

The sky was bright, and the long drive had turned a copper color in between shallow pools of water like frameless oval mirrors.

"We don't want to be late," Ruth said.

THE OLD TRUCK rattled and heaved along Main Street. Ruth sat in the passenger seat worried the whole town could hear them every time they left the house. She looked out over the brook where the water was high from the melted snow. The truck slowed as it turned up Wicket Street, and in the distance she saw Leo's house and then his small figure on the big front porch. He was sitting in a ladderback chair with the newspaper opened across his lap and a pipe hanging from his mouth.

"Heard the new trooper got into it with Elroy Biggins the other day," Elam said.

"Well, I don't imagine Elroy Biggins is used to taking direction from a woman."

"You're right about that."

"I suppose he might want to start, though."

Elam nodded. "It's been a hell of a first week for her."

"Has it?"

Elam nodded again. "George told me he had to call her out to the shop on her first night on account of Steve Hayward being laid out across East Hopping Road with vomit running all down his shirt."

"That's a long night."

"Longer than it had to be. George said she got him cleaned up, and then she sat there with him on the curb in front of the shop for damn near two hours." Elam reached for a cigarette from his shirt pocket but stopped himself. "Said she didn't arrest him for the needle in his pocket neither. He found out later she gave Steve a choice—jail or treatment. When he chose the latter, she drove him to Bennington, and when she found out the treatment center there was full, she drove him clear over an hour to Granville."

"How do you figure she's able to give him a choice like that?"

"Don't know if she is or isn't. She seems like the type to have her own mind about things."

Ruth looked out the window at the marbled mountains. Along the roadside, black-and-yellow-striped butterflies fluttered in place. "Well—that's different," she said. "That's something different."

THE BRICK SCHOOLHOUSE looked the same as it had several years ago, though the brick had spalled in places and the swing set that occupied the field behind the school had been replaced with a wooden pirate ship and a metal backstop for the children to play baseball. The brook was still hidden behind a thick wall of willows and dogwoods at the bottom of a steep bank, but Ruth could picture it: the water eddying around the smooth rocks and continuing under the metal bridge and coursing through the center of North Falls.

The parking lot was about half full, and some people—parents and grandparents of children, mostly—were filing into the gymnasium through the red metal doors. Ruth spotted Jett's purple Volkswagen beetle, and Elam pulled into a spot beside it and turned off the engine. The two got out of the pickup and adjusted their coats and walked side by side across the freshly paved lot under the bright sun.

The gymnasium was lined with long plastic folding tables that held the children's art projects, paintings mostly, but some sculptures and pencil drawings too. Along the wall underneath the south-facing window was a clothed table covered with doughnuts and cardboard boxes full of coffee. Ruth and Elam stood off to the side where children had piled their coats and backpacks.

"I don't see 'im yet," Elam said.

Ruth studied the crowded gymnasium. "There," she said. "In the back there."

Daniel stood near a folding table underneath the basketball hoop talking with a group of children—a few girls and some boys. All seeming to be friendly with one another.

"Who's that he's with?"

"I don't know," Ruth said. "Why would I know that?"

Elam scratched at the stubble underneath his chin. "I just thought you might."

Ruth looked around the gymnasium and found Milk standing in the opposite corner wearing a AAA Northern New England cap pulled down tight. Jett stood beside him smiling with a water bottle pulled close to her chest. Some of the other people Ruth recognized. Children of parents she knew or had known—now with children of their own. But most of the people were unfamiliar to her.

Ruth and Elam remained against the wall near the entrance and listened to Principal Hayworth tap a microphone at the front of the room. The parents and grandparents and some of the children turned to face the principal.

"We're going to start," the principal said. "We're going to start in a minute here and announce the prizes. But I wanted first to thank all of the children for all of the work they put into this show."

Some of the adults clapped, and the principal nodded and clasped his hands behind his back. "Everything you see here was the work of these students—even the doughnuts. Though it was my idea to bring the coffee."

Some of the people in the gymnasium laughed, and the principal smiled and unclasped his hands and put them in his pockets. "It's important," he said, "to recognize how talented all of these students are here. All of you have been walking around and looking at the various projects, and I have been, too. They're all good. The committee and I had a heck of a time picking only three. We wanted to pick more. We wanted to pick them all."

The principal looked around the room. A bead of sweat ran down his temple, though it was not warm in the gymnasium. "As a reminder before we announce the winners—the winning projects will be displayed at the library for the entire spring, and the students will be photographed for the *North Falls Citizen*."

The parents clapped, and the students looked at each other like they could picture themselves in the paper and the fame and fortune it would bring them. Daniel remained with the group of children, all of them laughing and gesturing at one another.

RUTH AND ELAM left the schoolhouse before most of the crowd. They stayed long enough to see Daniel win the first-place ribbon and to see him smile and look at the floor the way Ruth had grown accustomed to seeing him look when he did something that impressed her and she told him about it. The clouds had moved over the sun and thinned the light. The wind stirred the leaves of the maples that surrounded the small school.

"It's a nice day," Elam said.

"First one in a long time."

"I don't know—we've had some nice ones already for it only being May."

"You say that every year."

"And every year it's true. They say the earth is warming."

"Let 'em come to Vermont and say it."

Elam laughed. He patted his pocket that held his cigarettes but hesitated and dropped his hand.

"I got this feeling," Ruth said. "It's been going on a couple days now."

"You're coming down with something maybe."

"No. Not like that. A feeling like we might build something. A new shed, maybe."

"A shed?"

"Something bigger than the one we have now."

"You're thinking about taking on more students?"

"I'd like to. There's no reason I couldn't."

They reached the truck. Ruth stood there with her hand on the handle and looked back at the school and the rough hills behind it, and she listened appreciatively to the sound of small voices behind the schoolhouse walls.

"We can go back if you want—congratulate him on his ribbon."

"No," Ruth said. "Let him be."

"You want to go home then?"

"Yes. Let's go home. Let's go home and sit outside a while."

THE ROAD UNFURLED in front of them. The tall trees cast shadows across the road and across the hood of the truck. The radio was off. "I don't know as I can see it exactly," Ruth said.

"What's that?"

"The rest of our lives."

"I don't know that you're supposed to. They got names for people who say they can."

"I suppose you're right."

The clouds drifted west, and Ruth felt the sunlight on her face. She closed her eyes and pictured the town from above like a worn quilt of summer green and pale winter straw. The snow visible only in the deepest parts of the woods. The muddy roads and the winding brook where the surface ice had begun to break and push through even the narrowest sections. From above, the town looked both ancient and new. The stiffness of winter slowly giving way to something softer.

The truck groaned as it moved up the rutted road and then up the gravel drive to the small clapboard home. Elam turned off the engine, and Ruth remained in the truck, looking at the house. She heard Elam unbuckle his seat belt and open the door, but he didn't get out of the truck.

"What are you looking at?" he asked.

"I don't know," Ruth said.

She felt Elam's eyes on her and she heard the door close, and then she heard his body shift over the vinyl bench seat to face her.

"There are things I'd like to do," she said. "Things I'd like for us to do. That's part of the feeling I was trying to describe back at the school."

"Have you got something specific in mind?"

Ruth turned to Elam. The light had fallen below the leaves of the birches that lined the drive, and the copper sunlight and white bark and black fissures combined to give the appearance that she was looking at an old photograph. She studied Elam, wanting to tell him that what she meant was she wasn't finished. That she felt like she had started a conversation a long time ago and had stopped it for some reason she could no longer remember. She wanted to tell him how important it seemed to continue. How it might be the most important thing.

She blinked at the shuttering light and let the words take shape in her mind.

MATHEW FENN

HE HAD COME TO THE CAVE EVERY WEEK SINCE THE FIRST TIME HE was picked up at the motel. A middle-aged man who called himself Maidenhair and only liked to sit in the front seat of his car that smelled like chlorine bleach and watch through the rearview mirror while Mathew sat in the back seat and ate sage honey from a jar with a spoon.

Mathew never took anyone to the cave with him. It was the one thing he kept for himself.

The tall woodland ferns still covered the tract of land. The mushrooms still crowded the shaded spots under the pine trees. The rocks and dirt still blocked the entrance. The only difference from the time his mother showed him the cave three years before was that the rain had cleared enough sediment to expose a second entrance. An entrance just wide enough to allow a ninety-eight-pound boy to push himself through feetfirst.

The first few times he entered the cave, he worried the rocks would collapse and block the entrance. But after a while the idea excited him. He imagined living inside the cave. Eating bugs and drinking rainwater and drawing with charcoal on the walls for people to find thousands of years later.

He never walked to the end of the cave. Just like his mother. He never even made it past the first room. He only liked to sit in the dark and imagine that he lived in the cave or that he had been born there. That he had descended from a long line of hardened, prehistoric creatures born among the pockets of limestone and the hanging stalactites.

The sun shone white through the open canopy despite a steady rain that glittered the leaves. He shielded his eyes. He wore stained carpenter shorts and a shirt with the dark clouds of the Carina Nebula printed on the front and back. When he pushed through the opening, he scratched his hip on the bedrock and wondered whether he was getting bigger but recalled how his mother had only recently remarked on how thin he had become.

Inside the cave the light disappeared. He removed his backpack and set it on the floor and then removed a small flashlight from his pocket.

He had been taught to inject the heroin from behind so there were no marks on his arms or legs. He removed the spoon and the needleless syringe from his backpack. He dissolved the solution using a blue plastic lighter and a small amount of water and filled the syringe. He leaned against the side of the cave and pulled down his shorts. He took a deep breath and pushed the plunger inside himself and injected the solution.

A feeling of warmth and safety and then disconnection. A feeling as though part of him had spread across the woods and mountains while a separate part of him remained inside the cave.

He almost always laid still afterward so that his mind would separate more quickly from his body, but today he felt like moving. He adjusted his shorts and picked up the flashlight and started unevenly down the narrow passageway. The rocks around him groaned. A wet wind swirled, and he saw its shape before it settled. He whispered the sounds of the wind and the rocks until his mouth went dry and he could taste salt.

The rain beat down on the ceiling of the cave. He entered the second room and faltered momentarily. The loose rock flooring had turned to sand, and there were puddles of water in the deepest parts and more water dripped from the flowstones so that he had the feeling of being in the bowels of an old boat. He pushed through a narrow crevice and emerged inside a large chamber decorated with stalagmites and stalactites. At the end of the chamber was a dark tunnel, and somewhere inside the tunnel was a tiny light.

Mathew stopped. His breath rolled out in front of him. He turned off the flashlight. The light in the tunnel moved back and forth like a lantern hung from a wire handle. He watched as it grew larger, and as his eyes adjusted he saw that a body held the light, and then he recognized the body as his own.

He understood that he was losing himself. He had started using to dull a pain that seemed impossible to escape. He believed he could outsmart the drug. That he could use its power to change how he perceived pain, so that time might pass more easily until he and William could leave North Falls together. But he understood now that he had not outsmarted anything. The drug was stronger than him and stronger even than the pain he felt. And now he was caught up in it, like leaping from a burning building to avoid the flames.

The light continued to grow, and Mathew saw his face within the throw of light. He could no longer feel the part of him that remained inside the cave, and he began to wonder which of the two bodies belonged to him and even if there might be a third body somewhere outside the cave that was also his. He closed his eyes and tried to concentrate on himself, and though he could not feel his legs or arms, he could feel his fingers gripping the dimpled flashlight, and he tried to move them, and when they came free of the flashlight he heard the sound it made as it struck the floor.

He opened his eyes. He could see his face more clearly. His eyes pleading and his mouth relaxing and his lips beginning to part. He turned and ran. His body remained numb, and so it seemed like he might be flying or that he might have turned to water and was rushing forward, a great wave lapping the sides of the cave. And like a charcoal drawing, he thought he might be leaving his mark along the walls—washing them smooth. He imagined someone entering the cave in the future and running his hand over the rocks and knowing somehow that Mathew had passed through this place and smoothed what was once rough and jagged. And though he had come to feel that so much had been taken from him, this felt like a gift.

ACKNOWLEDGMENTS

I OWE A TREMENDOUS DEBT OF GRATITUDE TO MY AGENT, ALEC SHANE, for his belief and unwavering encouragement, and to my incomparable editor, Jenny Chen, who pushed me to make this a better book every step of the way—along with the entire team at Crooked Lane Books.

This novel benefited from a couple of early readers. First, the brilliant Genevieve Gagne-Hawes, who pulled me from the slush pile and dusted me off. Also, Rebecca Starks, whose early insights were invaluable.

I want to thank my parents for surrounding me with books and for reading to me every night as a child. These are some of my most important memories. You are kind and wise people, and I owe you so much. To Tania, my formidable sister, thank you for accompanying me on the adventures and misadventures of our youth. There's no one I would rather have done it with.

Sarah, because I can't thank you enough, your grace, intelligence, and beauty leave me awestruck. You are truly a treasure this poor man inexplicably found.

ACKNOWLEDGMENTS

To River, the best damn dog a man could ever have. Thank you for keeping me company in cold basements and dusty writing sheds for every page of this book.

Finally, I'd like to thank all the writers, musicians, and other artists out there who shined a light on my uncertain path and who continue to offer a place for people to be seen and heard and to feel less alone.